Polynesian Mythology

The Myths, Legends, Songs and Ancient Traditional History of the New Zealanders and Pacific Islanders

By Sir George J. Grey

Published by Pantianos Classics

ISBN-13: 978-1-78987-165-4

First published in 1854

Contents

Preface

TOWARDS the close of the year 1845 I was suddenly and unexpectedly required by the British Government to administer the affairs of New Zealand, and shortly afterwards received the appointment of Governor-in-chief of those Islands.

When I arrived in them, I found Her Majesty's native subjects engaged in hostilities with the Queen's troops, against whom they had up to that time contended with considerable success; so much discontent also prevailed generally amongst the native population, that where disturbances had not yet taken place, there was too much reason to apprehend they would soon break out, as they shortly afterwards did, in several parts of the Islands.

I soon perceived that I could neither successfully govern, nor hope to conciliate, a numerous and turbulent people, with whose language, manners, customs, religion, and modes of thought I was quite unacquainted. In order to redress their grievances, and apply remedies which would neither wound their feelings nor militate against their prejudices, it was necessary that I should be able thoroughly to understand their complaints; and to win their confidence and regard it was also requisite that I should be able at all times and in all places patiently to listen to the tales of their wrongs or sufferings, and, even if I could not assist them, to give them a kind reply, couched in such terms as should leave no doubt on their minds that I clearly understood and felt for them, and was really well disposed towards them.

Although furnished with some very able interpreters, who gave me assistance of the most friendly nature, I soon found that even with their aid I could still only very imperfectly perform my duties. I could not at all times and in all places have an interpreter by my side; and thence often when waylaid by some suitor, who had perhaps travelled two or three hundred miles to lay before me the tale of his or her grievances, I was compelled to pass on without listening, and to witness with pain an expression of sorrow and keenly disappointed hope cloud over features which the moment before were bright with gladness, that the opportunity so anxiously looked for had at length been secured.

Again, I found that any tale of sorrow or suffering, passing through the medium of an interpreter, fell much more coldly on my ear than what it would have done had the person interested addressed the tale direct to myself; and in like manner an answer delivered through the intervention of a third person appeared to leave a very different impression upon the suitor from what it would have had coming direct from the lips of the Governor of the country. Moreover, this mode of communication through a third person was so cumbrous and slow that, in order to compensate for the loss of time thus occasioned, it became necessary for the interpreters to compress the substance of the representations made to me, as also of my own replies, into the fewest words possible; and, as this had in each instance to be done hurriedly and at the moment, there was reason to fear that much that was material to enable me fully to understand the question brought before me, or the suitor to comprehend my reply, might be unintentionally omitted. Lastly, I had on several occasions reasons to believe that a native hesitated to state facts or to express feelings and wishes to an interpreter, which he would most gladly have done to the Governor, could he have addressed him direct.

These reasons, and others of equal force, made me feel it to be my duty to make myself acquainted, with the least possible delay, with the language of the New Zealanders, as also with their manners, customs, and prejudices. But I soon found that this was a far more difficult matter than I had at first supposed. The language of the New Zealanders is a very difficult one to understand thoroughly: there was then no dictionary of it published (unless a vocabulary can be so called); there were no books published in the language which would enable me to study its construction; it varied altogether in form from any of the ancient or modern languages which I knew; and my thoughts and time were so occupied with the cares of the government of a country then pressed upon by many difficulties, and with a formidable rebellion raging in it, that I could find but very few hours to devote to the acquisition of an unwritten and difficult language. I, however, did my best, and cheerfully devoted all my spare moments to a task, the accomplishment of which was necessary to enable me to perform properly every duty to my country and to the people I was appointed to govern.

Soon, however, a new and quite unexpected difficulty presented itself. On the side of the rebel party were engaged, either openly or covertly, some of the oldest, least civilized, and most influential chiefs in the Islands. With them I had, either personally or by written communications, to discuss questions which involved peace or war, and on which the whole future of the islands and of the native race depended, so that it was in the highest degree essential that I should fully and entirely comprehend their thoughts and intentions, and that they should not in any way misunderstand the nature of the engagements into which I entered with them.

To my surprise, however, I found that these chiefs, either in their speeches to me or in their letters, frequently quoted, in explanation of their views and intentions, fragments of ancient poems or proverbs, or made allusions which rested on an ancient system of mythology; and, although it was clear that the most important parts of their communications were embodied in these figurative forms, the interpreters were quite at fault, they could then rarely (if ever) translate the poems or explain the allusions, and there was no publication in existence which threw any light upon these subjects, or which gave the meaning of the great mass of the words which the natives upon such occasions made use of; so that I was compelled to content myself with a short general statement of what some other native believed that the writer of the letter intended to convey as his meaning by the fragment of the poem he had quoted or by the allusions he had made. I should add that even the great majority of the young Christian natives were quite as much at fault on these subjects as were the European interpreters.

Clearly, however, I could not, as Governor of the country, permit so close a veil to remain drawn between myself and the aged and influential chiefs whom it was my duty to attach to British interests and to the British race, whose regard and confidence, as also that of their tribes, it was my desire to secure, and with whom it was necessary that I should hold the most unrestricted intercourse. Only one thing could under such circumstances be done, and that was to acquaint myself with the ancient language of the country, to collect its traditional poems and legends, to Induce their priests to impart to me their mythology, and to study their proverbs. For more than eight years I devoted a great part of my available time to these pursuits. indeed, I worked at this duty in my spare moments in every part of the country I traversed and during my many voyages from portion to portion of the islands. I was also always accompanied by natives, and still at every possible interval pursued my inquiries into these subjects. Once, when I had with great pains amassed a large mass of materials to aid me in my studies, the Government House was destroyed by fire, and with it were burnt the materials I had so collected, and thus I was left to commence again my difficult and wearying task.

The ultimate result, however, was, that I acquired a great amount of information on these subjects, and collected a large mass of materials, which was, however, from the manner in which they were acquired, in a very scattered state-for different portions of the same poem or legend were often collected from different natives, in very distant parts of the country; long intervals of time, also, frequently elapsed after I had obtained one part of a poem or legend, before I could find a native accurately acquainted with another portion of it; consequently the fragments thus obtained were scattered through different notebooks, and, before they could be given to the public, required to be carefully arranged and rewritten, and, what was still more difficult (whether viewed in reference to the real difficulty of fairly translating the ancient language in which they were composed, or my many public duties), it was necessary that they should be translated.

Having, however, with much toil acquired information which I found so useful to myself, I felt unwilling that the result of my labours should be lost to those whose duty it may be hereafter to deal with the natives of New Zealand; and I therefore undertook a new task, which I have often, very often, been sorely tempted to abandon; but the same sense of duty which made me originally enter upon the study of the native language has enabled me to persevere up to the present period, when I have already published one large volume in the native language, containing a very extensive collection of the ancient traditional poems, religious chants, and songs, of the Maori race, and

I now present to the European reader a translation of the principal portions of their ancient mythology and of some of their most interesting legends.

Another reason that has made me anxious to impart to the public the most material portions of the information I have thus attained is that, probably, to no other person but myself would many of their ancient rhythmical prayers and traditions have been imparted by their priests; and it is less likely that anyone could now acquire them, as I regret to say that most of their old chiefs and even some of the middle-aged ones who aided me in my researches, have already passed to the tomb.

With regard to the style of the translation a few words are required; I fear in point of care and language it will not satisfy the critical reader; but I can truly say that I have had no leisure carefully to revise it; the translation is also faithful, and it is almost impossible closely and faithfully to translate a very difficult language without almost insensibly falling somewhat into the idiom and form of construction of that language, which, perhaps, from its unusualness may prove unpleasant to the European ear and mind, and this must be essentially the case in a work like the present, no considerable continuous portion of the original whereof was derived from one person, but which is compiled from the written or orally delivered narratives of many, each differing from the others in style, and some even materially from the rest in dialect.

I have said that the translation is close and faithful: it is so to the full extent of my powers and from the little time I have had at my disposal. I have done no more than add in some places such few explanatory words as were necessary to enable a person unacquainted with the productions, customs, or religion of the country, to understand what the narrator meant. For the first time, I believe, a European reader will find it in his power to place himself in the position of one who listens to a heathen and savage high-priest, explaining to him, in his own words and in his own energetic manner, the traditions in which he earnestly believes, and unfolding the religious opinions upon which the faith and hopes of his race rest.

That their traditions are puerile is true; that the religious faith of the races who trust in them is absurd is a melancholy fact; but all my experience leads me to believe that the Saxon, Celtic, and Scandinavian systems of mythology, could we have become intimately acquainted with them, would be found in no respects to surpass that one which the European reader may now thoroughly understand. I believe that the ignorance which has prevailed regarding the mythological systems of barbarous or semi-barbarous races has too generally led to their being considered far grander and more reasonable than they really were.

But the puerility of these traditions and barbarous mythological systems by no means diminishes their importance as regards their influence upon the human race. Those contained in the present volume have, with slight modifications, prevailed perhaps considerably more than two thousand years throughout the great mass of the islands of the Pacific Ocean; and, indeed, the religious system of ancient Mexico was, probably, to some extent connected with them. They have been believed in and obeyed by many millions of the human race; and it is still more melancholy to reflect that they were based upon a system of human sacrifices to the gods; so that, if we allow them to have existed for two thousand years, and that, in accordance with the rites which are based upon them, at least two thousand human victims were annually sacrificed throughout the whole extent of the numerous islands in which they prevailed (both of which suppositions are probably much within the truth), then at least four millions of human beings have been offered in sacrifice to false gods; and to this number we should have to add a frightful list of children murdered under the system of infanticide, which the same traditions encouraged, as also a very large number of persons, destroyed for having been believed guilty of the crime of sorcery or witchcraft.

It must further be borne in mind that the native races who believed in these traditions or superstitions are in no way deficient in intellect, and in no respect incapable of receiving the truths of Christianity; on the contrary, they readily embrace its doctrines and submit to its rules; in our schools they stand a fair comparison with Europeans, and, when instructed in Christian truths, blush at their own former ignorance and superstitions, and look back with shame and loathing upon their previous state of wickedness and credulity; and yet for a great part of their lives have they, and for thousands of years before they were born have their forefathers, implicitly submitted themselves to those very superstitions, and followed those cruel and barbarous rites.

Polynesian Myths and Legends

Children of Heaven and Earth

(KO NGA TAMA A RANGI--Tradition relating to the Origin of the Human Race)

MEN had but one pair of primitive ancestors; they sprang from the vast heaven that exists above us, and from the earth which lies beneath us. according to the traditions of our race, Rangi and Papa, or Heaven and Earth, were the source from which, in the beginning, all things originated. Darkness then rested upon the heaven and upon the earth, and they still both clave together, for they had not yet been rent apart; and the children they had begotten were ever thinking amongst themselves what might be the difference between darkness and light; they knew that beings had multiplied and increased, and yet light never broken upon them, but it ever continued dark. Hence these sayings are found in our ancient religious services: 'There was darkness from the first division of time, unto the tenth, to the hundredth, to the thousandth', that is, for a vast space of time; and these divisions of times were considered as beings, and were each termed 'a Po'; and on their account there was as yet no world with its bright light, but darkness only for the beings which existed.

At last the beings who had been begotten by Heaven and Earth, worn out by the continued darkness, consulted amongst themselves, saying: 'Let us now determine what we should do with Rangi and Papa, whether it would be better to slay them or to rend them apart.' Then spoke Tu-matauenga, the fiercest of the children of Heaven and Earth: 'It is well, let us slay them.'

Then spake Tane-mahuta, the father of forests and of all things that inhabit them, or that are constructed from trees: 'Nay, not so. It is better to rend them apart, and to let the heaven stand far above us, and the earth lie under our feet. Let the sky become as a stranger to us, but the earth remain close to us as our nursing mother.'

The brothers all consented to this proposal, with the exception of Tawhiri-ma-tea, the father of winds and storms, and he, fearing that his kingdom was about to be overthrown, grieved greatly at the thought of his parents being torn apart. Five of the brothers willingly consented to the separation of their parents, but one of them would not agree to it.

Hence, also, these sayings of old are found in our prayers: 'Darkness, darkness, light, light, the seeking, the searching, in chaos, in chaos'; these signified the way in which the offspring of heaven and earth sought for some mode of dealing with their parents, so that human beings might increase and live.

So, also, these sayings of old time. 'The multitude, the length , signified the multitude of the thoughts of the children of Heaven and Earth, and the length of time they considered whether they should slay their parents, that human beings might be called into existence; for it was in this manner that they talked and consulted amongst themselves.

But at length their plans having been agreed on, lo, Rongo-ma-tane, the god and father of the cultivated food of man, rises up, that he may rend apart the heavens and the earth; he struggles, but he tends them not apart. Lo, next, Tangaroa, the god and father of fish and reptiles, rises up, that he may rend apart the heavens and the earth; he also struggles, but he rends them not apart. Lo, next, Haumia-tikitiki, the god and father of the food of man which springs without cultivation, rises up and struggles, but ineffectually. Lo, then, Tu-matauenga, the god and father of fierce human beings, rises up and struggles, but he, too, fails in his efforts. Then, at last, slowly uprises Tane-mahuta, the god and father of forests, of birds, and of insects, and he struggles. With his parents; in vain he strives to rend them apart with his hands and arms. Lo, he pauses; his head is now firmly planted on his mother the earth, his feet he raises up and rests against his father the skies, he strains his back and limbs with mighty effort. Now are rent apart Rangi and Papa, and with cries and groans of woe they shriek aloud: 'Wherefore slay you thus your parents? Why commit you so dreadful a crime as to slay us, as to rend your parents apart? But Tane-mahuta pauses not, he regards not their shrieks and cries; far, far beneath him he presses down the earth; far, far above him he thrusts up the sky.

Hence these sayings of olden time: 'It was the fierce thrusting of Tane which tore the heaven from the earth, so that they were rent apart, and darkness was made manifest, and so was the light.'

No sooner was heaven rent from earth than the multitude of human beings were discovered whom they had begotten, and who had hitherto lain concealed between the bodies of Rangi and Papa.

Then, also, there arose in the breast of Tawhiri-ma-tea, the god and father of winds and storms, a fierce desire to wage war with his brothers, because they had rent apart their common parents. He from the first had refused to consent to his mother being torn from her lord and children; it was his brothers alone that wished for this separation, and desired that Papa-tu-a-nuku, or the Earth alone, should be left as a parent for them.

The god of hurricanes and storms dreads also that the world should become too fair and beautiful, so he rises, follows his father to the realm above, and hurries to the sheltered hollows in the boundless skies; there he hides and clings, and nestling in this place of rest he consults long with his parent, and as the vast Heaven listens to the suggestions of Tawhiri-ma-tea, thoughts and plans are formed in his breast, and Tawhiri-ma-tea also understands what he should do. Then by himself and the vast Heaven were begotten his numerous brood, and they rapidly increased and grew. Tawhiri-ma-tea despatches one of them to the westward, and one to the southward, and one to the eastward, and one to the northward; and he gives corresponding names to himself and to his progeny the mighty winds.

He next sends forth fierce squalls, whirlwinds, dense clouds, massy clouds, dark clouds, gloomy thick clouds, fiery clouds, clouds which precede hurricanes, clouds of fiery black, clouds reflecting glowing red light, clouds wildly drifting from all quarters and wildly bursting, clouds of thunder storms, and clouds hurriedly flying. in the midst of these Tawhiri-ma-tea himself sweeps wildly on. Alas! alas! then rages the fierce hurricane; and whilst Tane-mahuta and his gigantic forests still stand, unconscious and unsuspecting, the blast of the breath of the mouth of Tawhiri-ma-tea smites them, the gigantic trees are snapt off right in the middle; alas! alas! they are rent to atoms, dashed to the earth, with boughs and branches torn and scattered, and lying on the earth, trees and branches all alike left for the insect, for the grub, and for loathsome rottenness.

From the forests and their inhabitants Tawhiri-ma-tea next swoops down upon the seas, and lashes in his wrath the ocean. Ah! ah! waves steep as cliffs arise, whose summits are so lofty that to look from them would make the beholder giddy; these soon eddy in whirlpools, and Tangaroa, the god of ocean, and father of all that dwell therein, flies affrighted through his seas; but before he fled, his children consulted together how they might secure their safety, for Tangaroa had begotten Punga, and he had begotten two children, Ika-tere, the father of fish, and Tu-te-wehiwehi, or Tu-te-wanawana, the father of reptiles.

When Tangaroa fled for safety to the ocean, then Tu-te-wehiwehi and Ika-tere, and their children, disputed together as to what they should do to escape from the storms, and Tu-te-wehiwehi and his party cried aloud: 'Let us fly inland'; but Ika-tere and his party cried aloud: 'Let us fly to the sea.' Some would not obey one order, some would not obey the other, and they escaped in two parties: the party of Tu-te-wehiwehi, or the reptiles, hid themselves ashore; the party of Punga rushed to the sea. This is what, in our ancient religious services, is called the separation of Tawhiri-ma-tea.

Hence these traditions have been handed down: 'Ika-tere, the father of things which inhabit water, cried aloud to Tu-te-wehiwehi: "Ho, ho, let us all escape to the sea."

'But Tu-te-wehiwehi shouted in answer: "Nay, nay, let us rather fly inland."

'Then Ika-tere warned him, saying: "Fly inland, then; and the fate of you and your race will be, that when they catch you, before you are cooked, they will singe off your scales over a lighted wisp of dry fern."

'But Tu-te-wehiwehi answered him, saying: "Seek safety, then, in the sea; and the future fate of your race will be, that when they serve out little baskets of cooked vegetable food to each person, you will be laid upon the top of the food to give a relish to it."

'Then without delay these two races of beings separated. The fish fled in confusion to the sea, the reptiles sought safety in the forests and scrubs.'

Tangaroa, enraged at some of his children deserting him, and, being sheltered by the god of the forests on dry land, has ever since waged war on his brother Tane, who, in return, has waged war against him.

Hence Tane supplies the offspring of his brother Tu-matauenga with canoes, with spears and with fish-hooks made from his trees, and with nets woven from his fibrous plants, that they may destroy the offspring of Tangaroa; whilst Tangaroa, in return, swallows up the offspring of Tane, overwhelming canoes with the surges of his sea, swallowing up the lands, trees, and houses that are swept off by floods, and ever wastes away, with his lapping waves, the shores that confine him, that the giants of the forests may be washed down and swept out into his boundless ocean, that he may then swallow up the insects, the young birds, and the various animals which inhabit them--all which things are recorded in the prayers which were offered to these gods.

Tawhiri-ma-tea next rushed on to attack his brothers Rongo-ma-tane and Haumia-tikitiki, the gods and progenitors of cultivated and uncultivated food; but Papa, to save these for her other children, caught them up, and hid them in a place of safety; and so well were these children of hers concealed by their mother Earth, that Tawhiri-ma-tea sought for them in vain.

Tawhiri-ma-tea having thus vanquished all his other brothers, next rushed against Tu-matauenga, to try his strength against his; he exerted all his force against him, but he could neither shake him nor prevail against him. What did Tu-matauenga care for his brother's wrath? he was the only one of the whole party of brothers who had planned the destruction of their parents, and had shown himself brave and fierce in war; his brothers had yielded at once before the tremendous assaults of Tawhiri-ma-tea and his progeny--Tane-mahuta and his offspring had been broken and torn in pieces-Tangaroa and his children had fled to the depths of the ocean or the recesses of the shore--Rongo-ma-tane and Haumia-tikitiki had been hidden from him in the earth-but Tu-matauenga, or man, still stood erect and unshaken upon the breast of his mother Earth; and now at length the hearts of Heaven and of the god of storms became tranquil, and their passions were assuaged.

Tu-matauenga, or fierce man, having thus successfully resisted his brother, the god of hurricanes and storms, next took thought how he could turn upon his brothers and slay them, because they had not assisted him or fought bravely when Tawhiri-ma-tea had attacked them to avenge the separation of their parents, and because they had left him alone to show his prowess in the fight. As yet death had no power over man. It was not until the birth of the children of Taranga and of Makea-tu-tara, of Maui-taha, of Maui-roto, of Maui-pae, of Maui-waho, and of Maui-tikitiki-o-Taranga, the demi-god who tried to beguile Hine-nui-te-po, that death had power over men. If that goddess had not been deceived by Maui-tikitiki, men would not have died, but would in that case have lived for ever; it was from his deceiving Hine-nui-te-po that death obtained power over mankind, and penetrated to every part of the earth.

Tu-matauenga continued to reflect upon the cowardly manner in which his brothers had acted, in leaving him to show his courage alone, and he first sought some means of injuring Tane-mahuta, because he had not come to aid him in his combat with Tawhiri-ma-tea, and partly because he was aware that Tane had had a numerous progeny, who were rapidly increasing, and might at last prove hostile to him, and injure him, so he began to collect leaves of the whanake tree, and twisted them into nooses, and when his work was ended, he went to the forest to put up his snares, and hung them up--ha! ha! the children of Tane fell before him, none of them could any longer fly or move in safety.

Then he next determined to take revenge on his brother Tangaroa, who had also deserted him in the combat; so he sought for his offspring, and found them leaping or swimming in the water; then he cut many leaves from the flax-plant, and netted nets with the flax, and dragged these, and hauled the children of Tangaroa ashore.

After that, he determined also to be revenged upon his brothers Rongo-ma-tane and Haumia-tikitiki; he soon found them by their peculiar leaves, and he scraped into shape a wooden hoe, and plaited a basket, and dug In the earth and pulled up all kinds of plants with edible roots, and the plants which had been dug up withered in the sun.

Thus Tu-matauenga devoured all his brothers, and consumed the whole of them, in revenge for their having deserted him and left him to fight alone against Tawhiri-ma-tea and Rangi.

When his brothers had all thus been overcome by Tu', he assumed several names, namely, Tu-ka-riri, Tu-ka-nguha, Tu-ka-taua, Tu-whaka-heke-tan-gata, Tu-mata-wha-iti, and Tu-matauenga; he assumed one name for each of his attributes displayed in the victories over his brothers. Four of his brothers were entirely deposed by him, and became his food; but one of them, Tawhiri-ma-tea, he could not vanquish or make common, by eating him for food, so he, the last born child of Heaven and Earth, was left as an enemy for man, and still, with a rage equal to that of Man, this elder brother ever attacks him in storms and hurricanes, endeavouring to destroy him alike by sea and land.

Now, the meanings of these names of the children of the Heaven and Earth are as follows:

Tangaroa signifies fish of every kind; Rongo-ma-tane signifies the sweet potato, and all vegetables cultivated as food; Haumia-tikitiki signifies fern root, and all kinds of food which grow wild; Tane-mahuta signifies forests, the birds and insects which inhabit them, and all things fashioned from wood; Tawhiri-ma-tea signifies winds and storms; and Tu-matauenga signifies man.

Four of his brothers having, as before stated, been made common, or articles of food, by Tu-matauenga, he assigned for each of them fitting incantations, that they might be abundant, and that he might easily obtain them.

Some incantations were proper to Tane-mahuta, they were called Tane.

Some incantations were for Tangaroa, they were called Tangaroa.

Some were for Rongo-ma-tane, they were called Rongo-ma-tane.

Some were for Haumia-tikitiki, they were called Haumia.

The reason that he sought out these incantations was, that his brothers might be made common by him, and serve for his food. There were also incantations for Tawhiri-ma-tea to cause favourable winds, and prayers to the vast Heaven for fair weather, as also for mother Earth that she might produce all things abundantly. But it was the great God that taught these prayers to man.

There were also many prayers and incantations composed for man, suited to the different times and circumstances of his life--prayers at the baptism of an infant; prayers for abundance of food, for wealth; prayers in illness; prayers to spirits, and for many other things. The bursting forth of the wrathful fury of Tawhiri-ma-tea against his brothers, was the cause of the disappearance of a great part of the dry land; during that contest a great part of mother Earth was submerged. The names of those beings of ancient days who submerged so large a portion of the earth were--Terrible-rain, Long-continued rain, Fierce-hailstorms; and their progeny were, Mist, Heavy-dew, and Light-dew, and these together submerged the greater part of the earth, so that only a small portion of dry land projected above the sea.

From that time clear light increased upon the earth, and all the beings which were hidden between Rangi and Papa before they were separated, now multiplied upon the earth. The first beings begotten by Rangi and Papa were not like human beings; but Tu-matauenga bore the likeness of a man, as did all his brothers, as also did a Po, a Ao, a Kore, te Kimihanga and Runuku, and thus it continued until the times of Ngainui and his generation, and of Whiro-te-tupua and his generation, and of Tiki-tawhito-ariki and his generation, and it has so continued to this day.

The children of Tu-matauenga were begotten on this earth, and they increased,, and continued to multiply, until we reach at last the generation of Maui-taha, and of his brothers Maui-roto, Maui-waho, Maui-pae, and Maui-tikitiki-o-Taranga.

Up to this time the vast Heaven has still ever remained separated from his spouse the Earth. Yet their mutual love still continues--the soft warm sighs of her loving bosom still ever rise up to him, ascending from the woody mountains and valleys and men can these mists; and the vast Heaven, as he mourns through the long nights his separation from his beloved, drops frequent tears upon her bosom, and men seeing these, term them dew-drops.

The Legend of Maui

ONE day Maui asked his brothers to tell him the place where their father and mother dwelt; he begged earnestly that they would make this known to him in order that he might go and visit the place where the two old people dwelt; and they replied to him: 'We don't know; how can we tell whether they dwell up above the earth, or down under the earth, or at a distance from up.' Then he answered them: 'Never mind, I think I'll find them out'; and his brothers replied: 'Nonsense, how can you tell where they are--you, the last born of all of us, when we your elders have no knowledge where they are concealed from us; after you first appeared to us, and made yourself known to us and to our mother as our brother, you know that our mother used to come and sleep with us every night, and as soon as the day broke she was gone, and, lo, there was nobody but ourselves sleeping in the house, and this took place night after night, and how can we tell then where she went or where she lives? But he answered: 'Very well, you stop here and listen; by and by you will hear news of me.'

For he had found something out after he was discovered by his mother, by his relations, and by his brothers. They discovered him one night whilst they were all dancing in the great House of Assembly. Whilst his relations were all dancing there, they found out who he was in this manner. For little Maui, the infant, crept into the house, and went and sat behind one of his brothers, and hid himself, so when their mother counted her children that they might stand up ready for the dance, she said: 'One, that's Maui-taha; two, that's Maui-roto; three, that's Maui-pae, four, that's Maui-waho'; and then she saw another, and cried out: 'Hallo, where did this fifth come from? Then little Maui, the infant, answered: 'Ah, I'm your child too.' Then the old woman counted them all over again, and said: 'Oh, no, there ought to be only four of you; now for the first time I've seen you.' Then little Maui and his mother stood for a long time disputing about this in the very middle of the ranks of all the dancers.

At last she got angry, and cried out: 'Come, you be off now, out of the house at once; you are no child of mine, you belong to someone else.' Then little Maui spoke out quite boldly, and said: 'Very well, I'd better be off then, for I suppose, as you say it, I must be the child of some other person; but indeed I did think I was your child when I said so, because I knew I was born at the side of the sea, [1] and was thrown by you into the foam of the surf, after you had wrapped me up in a tuft of your hair, which you cut off for the purpose; then the seaweed formed and fashioned me, as caught in its long tangles the ever-heaving surges of the sea rolled me, folded as I was in them, from side to side; at length the breezes and squalls which blew from the ocean drifted me on shore again, and the soft jelly-fish of the long sandy beaches rolled themselves round me to protect me; then again myriads of flies alighted on me to buzz about me and lay their eggs, that maggots might eat me, and flocks of birds collected round me to peck me to pieces, but at that moment appeared there also my great ancestor, Tama-nui-ki-te-Rangi, and he saw the flies and the birds collected in clusters and flocks above the jelly-fish, and the old man ran, as fast as he could, and stripped off the encircling jelly-fish, and behold within there lay a human being; then he caught me up and carried me to his house, and he hung me up in the roof that I might feel the warm smoke and the heat of the fire, so I was saved alive by the kindness of that old man. At last I grew, and then I heard of the fame of the dancing of this great House of Assembly. It was that which brought me here. But from the time I was in your womb, I have heard the names of these your first born children, as you have been calling them over until this very night, when I again heard you repeating them. in proof of this I will now recite your names to you, my brothers. You are Maui-taha, and you are Maui-roto, and you are Maui-pae, and you are Maui-waho, and as for me, I'm little Maui-the-baby, and here I am sitting before you.'

When his Mother, Taranga, heard all this, she cried out: 'You dear little child, you are indeed my last-born, the son of my old age, therefore I now tell you your name shall be Maui-tikitiki-a-Taranga, or Maui-formed-in-the-top-knot-of-Taranga', and he was called by that name.

After the disputing which took place on that occasion, his mother, Taranga, called to her last-born: 'Come here, my child, and sleep with the mother who bore you, that I may kiss you, and that you may kiss me', and he ran to sleep with his mother. Then his elder brothers were jealous, and began to murmur about this to each other. 'Well, indeed, our mother never asks us to go and sleep with her; yet we are the children she saw actually born, and about whose birth there is no doubt. When we were little things she nursed us, laying us down gently on the large soft mats she had spread out for us--then why does she not ask us now to sleep with her? when we were little things she was fond enough of us, but now we are grown older she never caresses us, or treats us kindly. But as for this little abortion, who can really tell whether he was nursed by the sea-tangles or by whom, or whether he is not some other person's child, and here he is now sleeping with our mother. Who would ever have believed that a little abortion, thrown into the ocean, would have come back to the world again a living human being!--and now this little rogue has the impudence to call himself a relation of ours.'

Then the two elder brothers said to the two younger ones: 'Never mind, let him be our dear brother; in the days of peace remember the proverb--when you are on friendly terms, settle your disputes in a friendly way--when you are at war, you must redress your injuries by violence. It is better for us, oh, brothers, to be kind to other people; these are the ways by which men gain influence in the world--by labouring for abundance of food to feed others--by collecting property to give to others, and by similar means by which you promote the good of others, so that peace spreads through the world. Let us take care that we are not like the children of Rangi-nui and of Papa-tu-a-

17

nuku, who turned over in their minds thoughts for slaying: their parents; four of them consented, but Tawhiri-ma-tea had little desire for this, for he loved his parents; but the rest of his brothers agreed to slay them; afterwards when Tawhiri, saw that the husband was separated far from his wife,

then he thought what it was his duty to do, and he fought against his brothers. Thence sprang the cause which led Tu-matauenga to wage war against his brethren and his parents, and now at last this contest is carried on even between his own kindred, so that man fights against man. Therefore let us be careful not to foster divisions amongst ourselves, lest such wicked thoughts should finally turn us each against the other, and thus we should be like the children of Rangi-nui and of Papa-tu-a-nuku.' Two younger brothers, when they heard this, answered: 'Yes, yes, oh, eldest brothers of ours, you are quite right; let our murmuring end here.'

It was now night; but early in the morning Taranga rose up, and suddenly, In a moment of time, she was gone from the house where her children were. As soon as they woke up they looked all about to no purpose, as they could not see her; the elder brothers knew she had left them, and were accustomed to it; but the little child was exceedingly vexed; yet he thought, I cannot see her, 'tis true, but perhaps she has only gone to prepare some food for us. No-- no--she was off, far, far away.

Now at nightfall when their mother came back to them, her children were dancing and singing as usual. As soon as they had finished, she called to her last born: 'Come here, my child, let us sleep together'; so they slept together; but as soon as day dawned, she disappeared; the little fellow now felt quite suspicious at such strange proceedings on the part of his mother every morning. But at last, upon another night, as he slept again with his mother, the rest of his brothers that night also sleeping with them, the little fellow crept out in the night and stole his mother's apron, her belt, and clothes, and hid them; then he went and stopped up every crevice in the wooden window, and in the doorway, so that the light of the dawn might not shine into the house, and make his mother hurry to get up. But after he had done this, his little heart still felt very anxious and uneasy lest his mother should, in her impatience, rise in the darkness and defeat his plans. But the night dragged its slow length along without his mother moving; at last there came the faint light of early morn, so that at one end of a long house you could see the legs of the people sleeping at the other end of it, but his mother still slept on; then the sun rose up, and mounted far up above the horizon; now at last his mother moved, and began to think to herself, 'What kind of night can this be, to last so long? and having thought thus, she dropped asleep again. Again she woke, and began to think to herself, but could not tell that it was broad daylight outside, as the window and every chink in the house were stopped closely up.

At last up she jumped; and finding herself quite naked, began to look for her clothes, and apron, but could find neither; then she ran and pulled out the things with which the chinks in the windows and doors were stopped up, and whilst doing so, oh , dear! oh, dear! there she saw the sun high up in the heavens; then she snatched up, as she ran off, the old clout of a flax cloak, with which the door of the house had been stopped up, and carried it off as her only covering; getting, at last, outside the house, she hurried away, and ran crying at the thought of having been so badly treated by her own children.

As soon as his mother got outside the house, little Maui jumped up, and kneeling upon his hands and knees peeped after her though the doorway into the bright light. Whilst he was watching her, the old woman reached down to a tuft of rushes, and snatching it up from the ground, dropped into a hole underneath it, and clapping the tuft of rushes in the hole again, as if it were its covering, so disappeared. Then little Maui jumped on his feet, and, as hard as he could go, ran out of the house, pulled up the tuft of rushes, and peeping down, discovered a beautiful open cave running quite deep into the earth.

He covered up the hole again and returned to the house, and waking up his brothers who were still sleeping, said: 'Come, come, my brothers, rouse up, you have slept long enough; come, get up; here we are again cajoled by our mother.' Then his brothers made haste and got up; alas! alas! the sun was quite high up in the heavens.

The little Maui now asked his brothers again: 'Where do you think the place is where our father and mother dwell? and they answered: 'How should we know, we have never seen it; although we are Maui-taha, and Maui-roto, and Maui-pae, and Maui-waho, we have never seen the place; and do you think you can find that place which you are so anxious to see? What does it signify to you? Cannot you stop quietly with us? What do we care about our father, or about our mother? Did she feed us with food till we grew up to be men?--not a bit of it. Why, without doubt, Rangi, or the heaven, is our father, who kindly sent his offspring down to us; Hau-whenua, or gentle breezes, to cool the earth and young plants; and Hau-ma-ringiringi, or mists, to moisten them; and Hau-ma-roto-roto, or fine weather, to make them grow; and Touarangi, or rain, to water them; and Tomairangi, or dews, to nourish them: he gave these his offspring to cause our food to grow, and then Papa-tu-a-nuku, or the earth, made her seeds to spring, and grow forth, and provide sustenance for her children in this long-continuing world.'

Little Maui then answered: 'What you say is truly quite correct; but such thoughts and sayings would better become me than you, for in the foaming bubbles of the sea I was nursed and fed: it would please me better if you would think over and remember the time when you were nursed at your mother's breast; it could not have been until after you had ceased to be nourished by her milk that you could have eaten the kinds of food you have mentioned; as for me, oh! my brothers, I have never partaken either of her milk or of her food; yet I love her, for this single reason alone--that I lay in her womb; and because I love her, I wish to know where is the place where she and my father dwell.'

19

His brothers felt quite surprised and pleased with their little brother when they heard him talk in this way, and when after a little time they had recovered from their amazement, they told him to try and find their father and mother. So he said he would go. It was a long time ago that he had finished his first labour, for when he first appeared to his relatives in their house of singing and dancing, he had on that occasion transformed himself into the likeness of all manner of birds, of every bird in the world, and yet no single form that he then assumed had pleased his brothers; but now when he showed himself to them, transformed into the semblance of a pigeon, his brothers said: 'Ah! now indeed, oh, brother, you do look very well indeed, very beautiful, very beautiful, much more beautiful than you looked in any of the other forms which you assumed, and then changed from, when you first discovered yourself to us.'

What made him now look so well in the shape he had assumed was the belt of his mother, and her apron, which he had stolen from her while she was asleep in the house; for the very thing which looked so white upon the breast of the pigeon was his mother's broad belt, and he also had on her little apron of burnished hair from the tail of a dog, and the fastening of her belt was what formed the beautiful black feathers on his throat. He had once changed himself into this form a long time ago, and now that he was going to look for his father and mother, and had quitted his brothers to transform himself into the likeness of a pigeon, he assumed exactly the same form as on the previous occasion, and when his brothers saw him thus again, they said: 'Oh, brother, oh, brother! you do really look well indeed'; and when he sat upon the bough of a tree, oh, dear! he never moved, or jumped about from spray to spray, but sat quite still, cooing to himself, so that no one who had seen him could have helped thinking of the proverb: 'A stupid pigeon sits on one bough, and jumps not from spray to spray'. Early the next morning, he said to his brothers, as was first stated: 'Now do you remain here, and you will hear something of me after I am gone; it is my great love for my parents that leads me to search for them; now listen to me, and then say whether or not my recent feats were not remarkable. For the feat of transforming oneself into birds can only be accomplished by a man who is skilled in magic, and yet here I, the youngest of you all, have assumed the form of all birds, and now, perhaps, after all, I shall quite lose my art and become old and weakened in the long journey to the place where I am going.' His brothers answered him thus: 'That might be indeed, if you were going upon a warlike expedition, but, in truth, you are only going to look for those parents whom we all so long to see, and if they are found by you, we shall ever after all dwell happily, our present sorrow will be ended, and we shall continually pass backwards and forwards between our dwelling-place and theirs, paying them happy visits.'

He answered them: 'It is certainly a very good cause which leads me to undertake this journey, and if, when reaching the place I am going to, I find everything agreeable and nice, then I shall, perhaps, be pleased with it, but if I find it a bad, disagreeable place, I shall be disgusted with it.' They replied to him: 'What you say is exceedingly true, depart then upon your journey, with your great knowledge and skill in magic.' Then their brother went into the wood, and came back to them again, looking just as if he were a real pigeon. His brothers were quite delighted, and they had no power left to do anything but admire him.

Then off he flew, until he came to the cave which his mother had run down into, and he lifted up the tuft of rushes; then down he went and disappeared in the cave, and shut up its mouth again so as to hide the entrance; away he flew very fast indeed, and twice he dipped his wing, because the cave was narrow; soon he reached nearly to the bottom of the cave, and flew along it; and again, because the cave was so narrow, he dips first one wing and then the other, but the cave now widened, and he dashed straight on.

At last he saw a party of people coming alone under a grove of trees, they were manapau trees, [2] and flying on, he perched upon the top of one of these trees, under which the people had seated themselves; and when he saw his mother lying down on the grass by the side of her husband, he guessed at once who they were, and he thought: 'Ah! there sit my father and mother right under me'; and he soon heard their names, as they were called to by their friends who were sitting with them; then the pigeon hopped down, and perched on another spray a little lower, and it pecked off one of the berries of the tree and dropped it gently down, and bit the father with it on the fore-head; and some of the party said: 'Was it a bird which threw that down? but the father said: 'Oh no, it was only a berry that fell by chance.'

Then the pigeon again pecked off some of the berries from the tree, and threw them down with all its force, and struck both father and mother, so that he really hurt them; then they cried out, and the whole party jumped up and looked into the tree, and as the pigeon began to coo, they soon found out from the noise, where it was sitting amongst the leaves and branches, and the whole of them, the chiefs and common people alike, caught up stones to pelt the pigeon with, but they threw for a very long time, Without hitting it; at last the father tried to throw up at it; ah, he struck it, but Maui had himself contrived that he should be struck by the stone which his father threw; for, but by his own choice, no one could have bit him; he was struck exactly upon his left leg, and down he fell, and as he lay fluttering and struggling upon the ground, they all ran to catch him, but lo, the pigeon had turned into a man.

Then all those who saw him were frightened at his fierce glaring eyes, which were red as if painted with red ochre, and they said: 'Oh, it is now no wonder that he so long sat still up in the tree; had he been a bird he would have flown off long before, but he is a man': and some of them said: 'No, in-deed, rather a god--just look at his form and appearance, the like has never been seen before, since Rangi and Papa-tu-a-nuku were torn apart.' Then Taranga said, 'I used to see one who looked like this person every night when I went to visit my children, but what I saw then excelled what I see now; just listen to me. Once as I was wandering upon the sea-shore, I prematurely gave birth to one of my children, and I cut off the long tresses of my hair, and

21

bound him up in them, and threw him into the foam of the sea, and after that be was found by his ancestor Tama-nui-ki-te-Rangi'; and then she told his history nearly in the same words that Maui-the-infant had told it to herself and his brothers in their house, and having finished his history, Taranga ended her discourse to her husband and his friends.

Then his mother asked Maui, who was sitting near her, 'Where do you come from? from the westward? and he answered: 'No.' 'From the north-east then? 'No.' 'From the south-east then? 'No.' 'From the south then?' 'No.' 'Was it the wind which blows upon me, which brought you here to me then?' when she asked this, he opened his mouth and answered 'Yes.' And she cried out: 'Oh, this then is indeed my child'; and she said: 'Are you Maui-taha?' he answered, 'No.' Then said she: 'Are you Maui-tikitiki-o-Taranga?' and he answered 'Yes.' And she cried aloud: 'This is, indeed, my child. By the winds and storms and wave-uplifting gales he was fashioned and became a human being; welcome, oh my child, welcome; you shall climb the threshold of the house of your great ancestor Hine-nui-te-po, and death shall thenceforth have no power over man.'

Then the lad was taken by his father to the water, to be baptized, and after the ceremony prayers were offered to make him sacred, and clean from all impurities; but when it was completed, his father Makea-tu-tara felt greatly alarmed, because he remembered that he had, from mistake, hurriedly skipped over part of the prayers of the baptismal service, and of the services to purify Maui; he knew that the gods would be certain to punish this fault, by causing Maui to die, and his alarm and anxiety were therefore extreme. At nightfall they all went into his house.

Maui, after these things, returned to his brothers to tell them that he had found his parents, and to explain to them where they dwelt.

Shortly after Maui had thus returned to his brothers, he slew and carried off his first victim, who was the daughter of Maru-te-whare-aitu; afterwards, by enchantments, he destroyed the crops of Maru-te-whare-aitu, so that they all withered.

He then again paid a visit to his parents, and remained for some time with them, and whilst he was there he remarked that some of their people daily carried away a present of food for some person; at length, surprised at this, he one day asked them: 'Who is that you are taking that present of food to? And the people who were going with it answered him: 'It is for your ancestress, for Muri-ranga-whenua.'

He asked again: 'Where does she dwell?' They answered: 'Yonder.'

Thereupon he says: 'That will do; leave here the present of food, I will carry it to her myself.'

From that time the daily presents of food for his ancestress were carried by Maui himself; but he never took and gave them to her that she might eat them, but he quietly laid them by on one side, and this he did for many days. At last, Muri-ranga-whenua suspected that something wrong was going on, and the next time he came along the path carrying the present of food, the

22

old chieftainess sniffed and sniffed until she thought she smelt something coming, and she was very much exasperated, and her stomach began to distend itself, that she might be ready to devour Maui as soon as he came there. Then she turned to the southward, and smelt and sniffed, but not a scent of anything reached her; then she turned round from the south to the north, by the east, with her nose up in the air sniffing and smelling to every point as she turned slowly round, but she could not detect the slightest scent of a human being, and almost thought that she must have been mistaken; but she made one more trial, and sniffed the breeze towards the westward. Ah! then the scent of a man came plainly to her, so she called aloud: 'I know from the smell wafted here to me by the breeze that somebody is close to me', and Maui murmured assent. Thus the old woman knew that be was a descendant of hers, and her stomach, which was quite large and distended immediately began to shrink, and contract itself again. If the smell of Maui had not been carried to her by the western breeze, undoubtedly she would have eaten him up.

When the stomach of Muri-ranga-whenua had quietly sunk down to its usual size, her voice was again heard saying: 'Art thou Maui? and he answered: 'Even so.'

Then she asked him: 'Wherefore has thou served thine old ancestress in this deceitful way? and Maui answered: 'I was anxious that thy jaw-bone, by which the great enchantments can be wrought, should be given to me.'

She answered: 'Take it, it has been reserved for thee.' And Maui took it, and having done so returned to the place where he and his brothers dwelt.

The young hero, Maui, had not been long at home with his brothers when he began to think, that it was too soon after the rising of the sun that it became night again, and that the sun again sank down below the horizon, every day, every day; in the same manner the days appeared too short to him. So at last, one day he said to his brothers: 'Let us now catch the sun in a noose, so that we may compel him to move more slowly, in order that mankind may have long days to labour in to procure subsistence for themselves'; but they answered him: 'Why, no man could approach it on account of its warmth, and the fierceness of its heat'; but the young hero said to them: 'Have you not seen the multitude of things I have already achieved? Did not you see me change myself into the likeness of every bird of the forest; you and I equally had the aspect and appearance of men, yet I by my enchantments changed suddenly from the appearance of a man and became a bird, and then, continuing to change my form, I resembled this bird or that bird, one after the other, until I had by degrees transformed myself into every bird in the world, small or great; and did I not after all this again assume the form of a man? [This he did soon after he was born, and it was after that he snared the sun.] Therefore, as for that feat, oh, my brothers, the changing myself into birds, I accomplished it by enchantments, and I will by the same means accomplish also this other thing which I have in my mind.' When his brothers heard this, they consented on his persuasions to aid him in the conquest of the sun.

Then they began to spin and twist ropes to form a noose to catch the sun in, and in doing this they discovered the mode of plaiting flax into stout square-shaped ropes, (*tuamaka*); and the manner of plaiting flat ropes, (*paharahara*); and of spinning round ropes; at last, they finished making all the ropes which they required. Then Maw took up his enchanted weapon, and he took his brothers with him, and they carried their provisions, ropes, and other things with them, in their hands. They travelled all night, and as soon as day broke, they halted in the desert, and hid themselves that they might not be seen by the sun; and at night they renewed their journey, and before dawn they halted, and hid themselves again; at length they got very far, very far, to the eastward, and came to the very edge of the place out of which the sun rises.

Then they set to work and built on each side of this place a long high wall of clay, with huts of boughs of trees at each end to hide themselves in; when these were finished, they made the loops of the noose, and the brothers of Maui then lay in wait on one side of the place out of which the sun rises, and Maui himself lay in wait upon the other side.

The young hero held in his hand his enchanted weapon, the jaw-bone of his ancestress--of Muri-ranga-whenua, and said to his brothers: 'Mind now, keep yourselves hid, and do not go showing yourselves foolishly to the sun; if you do, you will frighten him; but wait patiently until his head and fore-legs have got well into the snare, then I will shout out; haul away as hard as you can on the ropes on both sides, and then I'll rush out and attack him, but do you keep your ropes tight for a good long time (while I attack him), until he is nearly dead, when we will let him go; but mind, now, my brothers, do not let him move you to pity with his shrieks and screams.'

At last the sun came rising up out of his place, like a fire spreading far and wide over the mountains and forests; he rises up, his head passes through the noose, and it takes in more and more of his body, until his fore-paws pass through; then were pulled tight the ropes, and the monster began to struggle and roll himself about, whilst the snare jerked backwards and forwards as he struggled. Ah! was not he held fast in the ropes of his enemies!

Then forth rushed that bold hero, Mau-tikitiki-o-Taranga, with his enchanted weapon. Alas! the sun screams aloud; he roars; Maui strikes him fiercely with many blows; they hold him for a long time, at last they let him go, and then weak from wounds the sun crept along its course. Then was learnt by men the second name of the sun, for in its agony the sun screamed out: 'Why am I thus smitten by you! oh, man! do you know what you are doing? Why should you wish to kill Tama-nui-te-Ra? Thus was learnt his second name. At last they let him go. Oh, then, Tama-nui-te-Ra went very slowly and feebly on his course.

Maui-taha and his brothers after this feat returned again to their own house, and dwelt there, and dwelt there, and dwelt there; and after a long time his brothers went out fishing, whilst Maui-tikitiki-o-Taranga stopped idly at home doing nothing, although indeed he had to listen to the sulky grumblings of his wives and children, at his laziness in not catching fish for them. Then he called out to the women, 'Never mind, oh, mothers, yourselves and your children need not fear. Have not I accomplished all things, and as for this little feat, this trifling work of getting food for you, do you think I cannot do that? certainly; if I go and get a fish for you, it will be one so large that when I bring it to land you will not be able to eat it all, and the sun will shine on it and make it putrid before it is consumed.' Then Maui snooded his enchanted fish-hook, which was pointed with part of the jaw-bone of Muri-ranga-whenua, and when he had finished this, he twisted a stout fishing-line to his hook.

His brothers in the meantime had arranged amongst themselves to make fast the lashings of the top side of their canoe, in order to go out for a good day's fishing. When all was made ready they launched their canoe, and as soon as it was afloat Maui jumped into it, and his brothers, who were afraid of his enchantments, cried out: 'Come, get out again, we will not let you go with us; your magical arts will get us into some difficulty.' So he was compelled to remain ashore whilst his brothers paddled off, and when they reached the fishing ground they lay upon their paddles and fished, and after a good day's sport returned ashore.

As soon as it was dark night Maui went down to the shore, got into his brothers' canoe, and hid himself under the bottom boards of it. The next forenoon his brothers came down to the shore to go fishing again, and they had their canoe launched, and paddled out to sea without ever seeing Maw, who lay hid in the hollow of the canoe under the bottom boards. When they got well out to sea Maui crept out of his hiding place; as soon as his brothers saw him, they said: 'We had better get back to the shore again as fast as we can, since this fellow is on board'; but Maui, by his enchantments, stretched out the sea so that the shore instantly became very distant from them, and by the time they could turn themselves round to look for it, it was out of view. Maui now said to them: 'You had better let me go on with you, I shall at least be useful to bail the water out of our canoe.' To this they consented, and they paddled on again and speedily arrived at the fishing ground where they used to fish upon former occasions. As soon as they got there his brothers said: 'Let us drop the anchor and fish here'; and he answered: 'Oh no, don't; we had much better paddle a long distance farther out.' Upon this they paddle on, and paddle as far as the farthest fishing ground, a long way out to sea, and then his brothers at last say: 'Come now, we must drop anchor and fish here.' And he replies again: 'Oh, the fish here are very fine I suppose, but we had much better pull right out to sea, and drop anchor there. If we go out to the place where I wish the anchor to be let go, before you can get a hook to the bottom, a fish will come following it back to the top of the water. You won't have to stop there a longer time than you can wink your eye in, and our canoe will come back to shore full of fish.' As soon as they hear this they paddle away--they paddle away until they reach a very long distance off, and his brothers then say: 'We are now far enough.' And he replies: 'No, no, let us go out of sight of land, and when we have quite lost sight of it, then let the anchor be dropped, but let it be very far off, quite out in the open sea.'

At last they reach the open sea, and his brothers begin to fish. Lo, lo, they had hardly let their hooks down to the bottom, when they each pulled up a fish into the canoe. Twice only they let down their lines, when behold the canoe was filled up with the number of fish they had caught. Then his brothers said: 'Oh, brother, let us all return now.' And he answered them: 'Stay a little; let me also throw my hook into the sea.' And his brothers replied: 'Where did you get a hook? And he answered: 'Oh, never mind, I have a hook of my own.' And his brothers replied again: 'Make haste and throw it then.' And as he pulled it out from under his garments, the light flashed from the beautiful mother-of-pearl shell in the hollow of the hook, and his brothers saw that the hook was carved and ornamented with tufts of hair pulled from the tail of a dog, and it looked exceedingly beautiful. Maui then asked his brothers to give him a little bait to bait his hook with; but they replied: 'We will not give you any of our bait.' So he doubled his fist and struck his nose violently, and the blood gushed out, and he smeared his hook with his own blood for bait, and then be cast it into the sea, and it sank down, and sank down, till it reached to the small carved figure on the roof of a house at the bottom of the sea, then passing by the figure, it descended along the outside carved rafters of the roof, and fell in at the doorway of the house, and the hook of Maui-tikitiki-o-Taranga caught first in the sill of the doorway.

Then, feeling something on his hook, he began to haul in his line. Ah, ah!-- there ascended on his hook the house of that old fellow Tonga-nui. It came up, up; and as it rose high, oh, dear! how his hook was strained with its great weight; and then there came gurgling up foam and bubbles from the earth, as of an island emerging from the water, and his brothers opened their mouths and cried aloud.

Maui all this time continued to chant forth his incantations amidst the murmurings and wailings of his brothers, who were weeping and lamenting, and saying: 'See now, how he has brought us out into the open sea, that we may be upset in it, and devoured by the fish.' Then he raised aloud his voice, and repeated the incantation called Hiki which makes heavy weights fight, in order that the fish he had caught might come up easily, and he chanted an incantation beginning thus:

'Wherefore, then, oh! Tonga-nui,
Dost thou hold fast so obstinately below there?'

When he had finished his incantation, there floated up, hanging to his line, the fish of Maui, a portion of the earth, of Papa-tu-a-Nuku. Alas! alas! their canoe lay aground.

Maui then left his brothers with their canoe, and returned to the village; but before he went he said to them: 'After I am gone, be courageous and patient; do not eat food until I return, and do not let our fish be cut up, but rather leave it until I have carried an offering to the gods from this great haul of fish, and until I have found a priest, that fitting prayers and sacrifices may be offered to the god, and the necessary rites be completed in order. We shall thus all be purified. I will then return, and we can cut up this fish in safety, and it shall be fairly portioned out to this one, and to that one, and to that other; and on my arrival you shall each have your due share of it, and return to your homes joyfully; and what we leave behind us will keep good, and that which we take away With us, returning, will be good too.'

Maui had hardly gone, after saying all this to them, than his brothers trampled under their feet the words they had heard him speak. They began at once to eat food, and to cut up the fish. When they did this, Maui had not yet arrived at the sacred place, in the presence of the god; had he previously reached the sacred place, the heart of the deity would have been appeased with the offering of a portion of the fish which had been caught by his disciples, and all the male and female deities would have partaken of their portions of the sacrifice. Alas! alas! those foolish, thoughtless brothers of his cut up the fish, and behold the gods turned with wrath upon them, on account of the fish which they had thus cut up without having made a fitting sacrifice. Then indeed, the fish began to toss about his head from side to side, and to lash his tail, and the fins upon his back, and his lower jaw. Ah! ah! well done Tangaroa, it springs about on shore as briskly as if it was in the water.

That is the reason that this island is now so rough and uneven--that here stands a mountain--and there lies a plain--that here descends a valley--that there rises a cliff. If the brothers of Maui had not acted so deceitfully, the huge fish would have lain flat and smooth, and would have remained as a model for the rest of the earth, for the present generation of men. This, which has just been recounted, is the second evil which took place after the separation of Heaven from Earth.

Thus was dry land fished up by Maui after it had been hidden under the ocean by Rangi and Tawhiri-ma-tea. It was with an enchanted fish-hook that he drew it up, which was pointed with a bit of the jaw-bone of his ancestress Muri-ranga-whenua; and in the district of Heretaunga they still show the fish-hook of Maui, which became a cape stretching far out into the sea, and now forms the southern extremity of Hawke's Bay.

The hero now thought that he would extinguish and destroy the fires of his ancestress of Mahu-ika. So he got up in the night, and put out the fires left in the cooking-houses of each family in the village; then, quite early in the morning, he called aloud to the servants: 'I hunger, I hunger; quick, cook some food for me.' One of the servants thereupon ran as fast as he could to make up the fire to cook some food, but the fire was out; and as he ran round from house to house in the village to get a light, he found every fire quite out-he could nowhere get a light.

When Maui's mother heard this, she called out to the servants, and said: 'Some of you repair to my great ancestress Mahu-ika; tell her that fire has been lost upon earth, and ask her to give some to the world again.' But the slaves were alarmed, and refused to obey the commands which their masters, the sacred old people gave them; and they persisted in refusing to go, notwithstanding the old people repeatedly ordered them to do so.

At last, Maui said to his mother: 'Well, then I will fetch down fire for the world; but which is the path by which I must go? And his parents, who knew the country well, said to him: 'If you will go, follow that broad path that lies just before you there; and you will at last reach the dwelling of an ancestress of yours; and if she asks you who you are, you had better call out your name to her, then she will know you are a descendant of hers; but be cautious, and do not play any tricks with her, because we have heard that your deeds are greater than the deeds of men, and that you are fond of deceiving and injuring others, and perhaps you even now intend in many ways, to deceive this old ancestress of yours, but pray be cautious not to do so.'

But Maui said: 'No, I only want to bring fire away for men, that is all, and I'll return again as soon as I can do that.' Then he went, and reached the abode of the goddess of fire; and he was so filled with wonder at what he saw, that for a long time he could say nothing. At last he said: 'Oh, lady, would you rise up? Where is your fire kept? I have come to beg some from you.'

Then the aged lady rose right up, and said: 'Au-e! who can this mortal be? And he answered: 'It's I.' 'Where do you come from? said she; and he answered: 'I belong to this country.' 'You are not from this country', said she; 'your appearance is not like that of the inhabitants of this country. Do you come from the north-east? He replied: 'No.' 'Do you come from the south-east? He replied: 'No.' 'Are you from the south? He replied: 'No.' 'Are you from the westward? He answered: 'No.' 'Come you, then, from the direction of the wind which blows right upon me? And he said: I do.' 'Oh, then', cried she, 'you are my grand-child; what do you want here? He answered: 'I am come to beg fire from you.' She replied: 'Welcome, welcome; here then is fire for you.'

Then the aged woman pulled out her nail; and as she pulled it out fire flowed from it, and she gave it to him. And when Maui saw she had drawn out her nail to produce fire for him, he thought it a most wonderful thing! Then he went a short distance off, and when not very far from her, he put the fire out, quite out; and returning to her again, said: 'The light you gave me has gone out, give me another.' Then she caught hold of another nail, and pulled it out as a light for him; and he left her, and went a little on one side, and put that light out also; then he went back to her again, and said: 'Oh, lady, give me, I pray you, another light for the last one has also gone out.' And thus he went on and on, until she had pulled out all the nails of the fingers of one of her hands; and then she began with the other hand, until she had pulled all the fingernails out of that hand, too; and then she commenced upon the nails of her feet, and pulled them also out in the same manner, except the nail of one of her big toes. Then the aged woman said to herself at last: 'This fellow is surely playing tricks with me.'

Then out she pulled the one toe-nail that she had left, and it, too, became fire, and as she dashed it down on the ground the whole place caught fire. And she cried out to Maui: 'There, you have it all now!' And Maui ran off, and made a rush to escape, but the fire followed hard after him, close behind him; so he changed himself into a fleet-winged eagle, and flew with rapid flight, but the fire pursued, and almost caught him as he flew. Then the eagle dashed down into a pool of water; but when he got into the water he found that almost boiling too: the forests just then also caught fire, so that it could not alight anywhere, and the earth and the sea both caught fire too, and Maui was very near perishing in the flames.

Then he called on his ancestors Tawhiri-ma-tea and Whatitiri-matakataka, to send down an abundant supply of water, and he cried aloud: 'Oh, let water be given to me to quench this fire which pursues after me'; and lo, then appeared squalls and gales, and Tawhiri-ma-tea sent heavy lasting rain, and the fire was quenched; and before Mahu-ika could reach her place of shelter, she almost perished in the rain, and her shrieks and screams became as loud as those of Maui had been, when he was scorched by the pursuing fire; thus Maui ended this proceeding. In this manner was extinguished the fire of Mahu-ika, the goddess of fire; but before it was all lost, she saved a few sparks which she threw, to protect them, into the Kaiko-mako, and a few other trees, where they are still cherished; hence, men yet use portions of the wood of these trees for fire when they require a light.

Then he returned to the village, and his mother and father said to him: 'You heard when we warned you before you went, nevertheless you played tricks with your ancestress; it served you right that you got into such trouble'; and the young fellow answered his parents: 'Oh, what do I care for that; do you think that my perverse proceedings are put a stop to by this? certainly not; I intend to go on in the same way for ever, ever, ever.' And his father answered him: 'Yes, then, you may just please yourself about living or dying; if you will only attend to me you will save your life; if you do not attend to what I say, it will be worse for you, that is all.' As soon as this conversation was ended, off the young fellow went to find some more companions for his other scrapes.

Maui had a young sister named Hinauri, who was exceedingly beautiful; she married Irawaru. One day Maui and his brother-in-law went down to the sea to fish: Maui caught not a single fish with his hook, which had no barb to it, but as long as they went on fishing Maui observed that Irawaru continued catching plenty of fish; so be thought to himself: 'Well, how is this? how does that fellow catch so many whilst I cannot catch one? just as he thought this, Irawaru had another bite, and up he pulled his line in haste, but it had got entangled with that of Maui, and Maui thinking he felt a fish pulling at his own line, drew it in quite delighted; but when he had hauled up a good deal of it, there were himself and his brother-in-law pulling in their lines in different directions, one drawing the line towards the bow of the canoe, the other towards the stem.

Maui, who was already provoked at his own ill-luck, and the good luck of his brother-in-law, now called out quite angrily: 'Come, let go my line, the fish is on my hook.' But Irawaru answered: 'No, it is not, it is on mine.'

Maui again called out very angrily: 'Come, let go, I tell you it is on mine.'

Irawaru then slacked out his line, and let Maui pull in the fish; and as soon as he had hauled it into the canoe, Maui found that Irawaru was right, and that the fish was on his hook; when Irawaru saw this too, he called out: 'Come now, let go my line and hook.' Maui answered him: 'Cannot you wait a minute, until I take the hook out of the fish.'

As soon as he got the hook out of the fish's mouth, he looked at it, and saw that it was barbed; Maui, who was already exceedingly wrath with his brother-in-law, on observing this, thought he had no chance with his barbless hook of catching as many fish as his brother-in-law, so he said: 'Don't you think we had better go on shore now? Irawaru answered: 'Very well, let us return to the land again.'

So they paddled back towards the land, and when they reached it, and were going to haul the canoe up on to the beach, Maui said to his brother-in-law: 'Do you get under the outrigger of the canoe, and lift it up with your back'; so he got under it, and as soon as he had done so, Maui jumped on it, and pressed the whole weight of the canoe down upon him, and almost killed Irawaru.

When he was on the point of death, Maui trampled on his body, and lengthened his back-bone, and by his enchantments drew it out into the form of a tall, and he transformed Irawaru into a dog, and fed him with dung. [3]

As soon as he had done this, Maui went back to his place of abode, just as if nothing unusual had taken place, and his young sister, who was watching for the return of her husband, as soon as she saw Maui coming, ran to him and asked him, saying: 'Maui, where is your brother-in-law? Maui answered: 'I left him at the canoe.'

But his young sister said: 'Why did not you both come home together', and Maui answered: 'He desired me to tell you that he wanted you to go down to the beach to help him carry up the fish; you had better go therefore, and if you do not see him, just call out, and if he does not answer you, why then call out to him in this way, 'Mo-i, mo-i, mo-i.'

Upon learning this, Hinauri hurried down to the beach as fast as she could, and not seeing her husband she went about calling out his name, but no answer was made to her; she then called out as Maui had told her: 'Mo-i, mo-i, mo-i'; then Irawaru, who was running about in the bushes near there, in the form of a dog, at once recognized the voice of Hinauri, and answered: 'Ao! ao! ao! ao-ao-o!' howling like a dog, and he followed her back to the village, frisking along and wagging his tail with pleasure at seeing her; and from him sprang all dogs, so that he is regarded as their progenitor, and all Maoris still call their dogs to them by the words: 'Mo-i, mo-i, mo-i.'

Hinauri, when she saw that her husband had been changed into a dog, was quite distracted with grief, and wept bitterly the whole way as she went back to the village, and as soon as ever she got into her house, she caught up an enchanted girdle which she had, and ran back to the sea with it, determined to destroy herself, by throwing herself into the ocean, so that the dragons and monsters of the deep might devour her; when she reached the sea-shore, she sat down upon the rocks at the ocean's very edge, and as she sat there she first lamented aloud her cruel fate, and repeated an incantation, and then threw herself into the sea, and the tide swept her off from the shore.

Maui now felt it necessary to leave the village where Irawaru had lived, so he returned to his parents, and when he had been with them for some time, his father said to him one day: 'Oh, my son, I have heard from your mother and others that you are very valiant, and that you have succeeded in all feats that you have undertaken in your own country, whether they were small or great; but now that you have arrived in your father's country, you will, per-haps, at last be overcome.'

Then Maui asked him: 'What do you mean, what things are there that I can be vanquished by?' And his father answered him: 'By your great ancestress, by Hine-nui-te-po, who, if you look, you may see flashing, and as it were, opening and shutting there, where the horizon meets the sky.' And Maui re-plied: 'Lay aside such idle thoughts, and let us both fearlessly seek whether men are to die or live for ever.' And his father said: 'My child, there has been an ill omen for us; when I was baptizing you, I omitted a portion of the fitting prayers, and that I know will be the cause of your perishing.'

Then Maui asked his father: 'What is my ancestress Hine-nui-te-po like?' and he answered: 'What you see yonder shining so brightly red are her eyes, and her teeth are as sharp and hard as pieces of volcanic glass; her body is like that of a man, and as for the pupils of her eyes, they are jasper; and her hair is like tangles of long seaweed, and her mouth is like that of a barracou-ta.' Then his son answered him: 'Do you think her strength is as great as that of Tama-nui-te-Ra, who consumes man, and the earth, and the very waters, by the fierceness of his heat?--was not the world formerly saved alive by the speed with which he travelled?--if he had then, in the days of his full strength and power, gone as slowly as he does now, not a remnant of mankind would have been left living upon the earth, nor, indeed, would anything else have survived. But I laid hold of Tama-nui-te-Ra, and now he goes slowly for I smote him again and again, so that be is now feeble, and long in travelling his course, and he now gives but very little heat, having been weakened by the blows of my enchanted weapon; I then, too, split him open in many places, and from the wounds so made, many rays now issue forth, and spread in all directions. So, also I found the sea much larger than the earth, but by the power of the last born of your children, part of the earth was drawn up again, and dry land came forth.' And his father answered him: 'That is all very true, O, my last born, and the strength of my old age; well, then, be bold, go and visit your great ancestress who flashes so fiercely there, where the edge of the horizon meets the sky.'

Hardly was this conversation concluded with his father, when the young hero went forth to look for companions to accompany him upon this enterprise: and so there came to him for companions, the small robin, and the large robin, and the thrush, and the yellow-hammer, and every kind of little bird, and the fantail, and these all assembled together, and they all started with Maui in the evening, and arrived at the dwelling of Hine-nui-te-po, and found her fast asleep.

Then Maui addressed them all, and said: 'My little friends, now if you see me creep into this old chieftainess, do not laugh at what you see. Nay, nay, do not I pray you, but when I have got altogether inside her, and just as I am coming out of her mouth, then you may shout with laughter if you please.' And his little friends, who were frightened at what they saw, replied: 'Oh, sir, you will certainly be killed.' And he answered them: 'If you burst out laughing at me as soon as I get inside her, you will wake her up, and she will certainly kill me at once, but if you do not laugh until I am quite inside her, and am on the point of coming out of her mouth, I shall live, and Hine-nui-te-po will die.' And his little friends answered: 'Go on then, brave Sir, but pray take good care of yourself.'

Then the young hero started off, and twisted the strings of his weapon tight round his wrist, and went into the house, and stripped off his clothes, and the skin on his hips looked mottled and beautiful as that of a mackerel, from the tattoo marks, cut on it with the chisel of Uetonga, and he entered the old chieftainess.

The little birds now screwed up their tiny cheeks, trying to suppress their laughter; at last, the little Tiwakawaka could no longer keep it in, and laughed out loud, with its merry cheerful note; this woke the old woman up, she opened her eyes, started up, and killed Maui.

Thus died this Maui we have spoken of, but before he died he had children, and sons were born to him; some of his descendants yet live in Hawaiki, some in Aotearoa (or in these islands); the greater part of his descendants remained in. Hawaiki, but a few of them came here to Aotearoa. According to the traditions of the Maori, [4] this was the cause of the introduction of death into the world (Hine-nui-te-po being the goddess of death: if Maui had passed safely through her, then no more human beings would have died, but death itself would have been destroyed), and we express it by saying: 'The water-wagtail laughing at Maui-tikitiki-o-Taranga made Hine-nui-te-po squeeze him to death.' And we have this proverb: 'Men make heirs, but death carries them off.'

Thus end the deeds of the son of Makea-tu-tara, and of Taranga, and the deeds of the sons of Rangi-nui, and of Papa-tu-a-Nuku; this is the narrative about the generations of the ancestors of the Maori, and therefore, we the people of that country, preserve closely these traditions of old times, as a thing to be taught to the generations that come after us, so we repeat them in our prayers, and whenever we relate the deeds of the ancestors from whom each family is descended, and upon other similar occasions.

[1] If a child was born before its time, and thus perished without having known the joys and pleasures of life, it was carefully buried with peculiar incantations and ceremonies; because if cast into the water, or carelessly thrown aside, it became a malicious being or spirit, actuated by a peculiar antipathy to the human race, who it spitefully persecuted, from having been itself deprived of happiness which they enjoyed. All their malicious deities had an origin of this kind.

[2] The manapau was a species of tree peculiar to the country from whence the people came, where the priests say it was known by that name.

[3] This quarrel of Maui with his brother-in-law, Irawaru, is sometimes narrated in this way:

Maui and his brother-in-law had been paying a visit to the people of a village not very distant from where they lived; when they were about to return home again, Maui asked his brother-in-law to carry a little provision for them both upon their short journey, but Irawaru answered surlily: 'What should I carry any provision for, indeed? why I have just had an excellent meal': they then started, and Maui, who was very angry, by his enchantments drew out the earth as they proceeded, so as to lengthen exceedingly the road they had top. 37 traverse; at last, being both overcome by hunger and fatigue, they sat down to rest, and Maui, who knew what his intentions were before they started, and had brought provisions with him, ate a good meal, but gave none to his brother-in-law. He then, to throw Irawaru off his guard, asked him to clean and dress his hair for him, and laid his head on his lap for that purpose; when his own was finished he offered to do the same for Irawaru, who suspecting no harm laid his head on Maui's lap, who threw him into an enchanted sleep, and then by his enchantments changed him into a dog.

[4] Inhabitants of New Zealand.

The Legend of Tawhaki

NOW quitting the deeds of Maui, let those of Tawhaki be recounted. He was the son of Hema and Urutonga, and he had a younger brother named Karihi. Tawhaki, having taken Hinepiri-piri as a wife, went one day with his brothers-in-law to fish from a flat reef of rocks which ran far out into the sea; he had four brothers-in-law, two of these when tired of fishing returned towards their village, and he went with them; when they drew near the village, they attempted to murder him, and thinking they had slain him, buried him; they then went on their way to the village, and when they reached it, their young sister said to them: 'Why, where is your brother-in-law? and they replied: 'Oh, they're all fishing.' So the young wife waited until the other two brothers came back, and when they reached the village they were questioned by their young sister, who asked: 'Where is your brother-in-law?' and the two who had last arrived answered her: 'Why, the others all went home together long since.' So the young wife suspected that they had killed her husband, and ran off at once to search for him; and she found where he had been buried, and on examining him ascertained that he had only been insensible, and was not quite dead; then with great difficulty she got him upon her back, and carried him home to their house, and carefully washed his wounds, and staunched the bleeding.

Tawhaki, when he had a little recovered, said to her: 'Fetch some wood, and light a fire for me'; and as his wife was going to do this, he said to her: 'If you see any tall tree growing near you, fell it, and bring that with you for the fire.' His wife went, and saw a tree growing such as her husband spoke of; so she felled it, and put it upon her shoulder, and brought it along With her; and when she reached the house, she put the whole tree upon the fire without chopping it into pieces; and it was this circumstance that led her to give the name of Wahieroa (long-log-of-wood-for-the-fire) to their first son, for Tawhaki had told her to bring this log of wood home, and to call the child after it, that the duty of avenging his father's wrongs might often be recalled to his mind.

As soon as Tawhaki had recovered from his wounds, he left the place where his faithless brothers-in-law lived, and went away taking all his own warriors and their families with him, and built a fortified village upon the top of a very lofty mountain, where he could easily protect himself; and they dwelt there. Then he called aloud to the Gods, his ancestors, for revenge, and they let the floods of heaven descend, and the earth was overwhelmed by the waters and all human beings perished, and the name given to that event was 'The overwhelming of the Mataaho,' and the whole of the race perished.

When this feat was accomplished, Tawhaki and his younger brother next went to seek revenge for the death of their father. It was a different race who had carried off and slain the father of Tawhaki; the name of that race was the Ponaturi--the country they inhabited was underneath the waters, but they had a large house on the dry land to which they resorted to sleep at night; the name of that large house was 'Manawa-Tane'.

The Ponaturi had slain the father of Tawhaki and carried off his body, but his father's wife they had carried off alive and kept as a captive. Tawhaki and his younger brother went upon their way to seek out that people and to revenge themselves upon them. At length they reached a place from whence they could see the house called Manawa-Tane. At the time they arrived near the house there was no one there but their mother, who was sitting near the door; but the bones of their father were hung up inside the house under its high sloping roof The whole tribe of the Ponaturi were at that time in their country under the waters, but at the approach of night they would return to their house, to Manawa-Tane.

Whilst Tawhaki and his younger brother Karihi were coming along still at a great distance from the house, Tawhaki began to repeat an incantation, and the bones of his father, Hema, felt the influence of this, and rattled loudly together where they hung under the roof of the house, for gladness, when they heard Tawhaki repeating his incantations as he came along, for they knew that the hour of revenge had now come. As the brothers drew nearer, their mother, Urutonga, heard the voice of Tawhaki, and she wept for gladness in front of her children, who came repeating incantations upon their way. And when they reached at length the house, they wept over their mother, over old Urutonga. When they had ended weeping, their mother said to them: 'My children, hasten to return hence, or you will both certainly perish. The people who dwell here are a very fierce and savage race.' Karihi said to her: 'How low will the sun have descended when those you speak of return home? And she replied: 'They will return here when the sun sinks beneath the ocean.' Then Karihi asked her: 'What did they save you alive for? And she answered: 'They saved me alive that I might watch for the rising of the dawn; they make me ever sit watching here at the door of the house, hence this people have named me "Tatau", or "Door"; and they keep on throughout the night calling out to me: "Ho, Tatau, there! is it dawn yet?" And then I call out in answer: "No, no, it is deep night--it is lasting night--it is still night; compose yourselves to sleep, sleep on." '

Karihi then said to his mother: 'Cannot we hide ourselves somewhere here?'

Their mother answered: 'You had better return; you cannot hide yourselves here, the scent of you will be perceived by them.'

'But', said Karihi, 'we will hide ourselves away in the thick thatch of the house.'

Their mother, however, answered: ''Tis of no use, you cannot hide yourselves there.'

All this time Tawhaki sat quite silent; but Karihi said: 'We will hide ourselves here, for we know incantations which will render us invisible to all.'

On hearing this, their mother consented to their remaining, and attempting to avenge their father's death. So they climbed up to the ridge-pole of the house, upon the outside of the roof, and made holes in the thick layers of reeds which formed the thatch of the roof, and crept into them and covered themselves up; and their mother called to them, saying: 'When it draws near dawn, come down again and stop up every chink in the house, so that no single ray of light may shine in.'

At length the day closed, and the sun sank below the horizon, and the whole of that strange tribe left the water in a body, and ascended to the dry land; and, according to their custom from time immemorial, they sent one of their number in front of them, that he might carefully examine the road, and see that there were no hidden foes lying in wait for them either on the way or in their house. As soon as this scout arrived at the threshold of the house, he perceived the scent of Tawhaki and Karihi; so be lifted up his nose and turned sniffing all round the inside of the house. As he turned about, he was on the point of discovering that strangers were hidden there, when the rest of the tribe (whom long security had made careless) came hurrying on, and crowding into the house in thousands, so that from the denseness of the crowd the scent of the strange men was quite lost. The Ponaturi then stowed themselves away in the house until it was entirely filled up with them, and by degrees they arranged themselves In convenient places, and at length all fell fast asleep.

At midnight Tawhaki and Karihi stole down from the roof of the house, and found that their mother had crept out of the door to meet them, so they sat at the doorway whispering together.

Karihi then asked his mother: 'Which is the best way for us to destroy these people who are sleeping here? And their mother answered: 'You had better let the sun kill them, its rays will destroy them.'

Having said this, Tatau crept into the house again; presently an old man of the Ponaturi called out to her: 'Ho, Tatau, Tatau, there; is it dawn yet? And she answered: 'No, no, it is deep night-it is lasting night; `tis still night; sleep soundly, sleep on.'

When it was very near dawn, Tatau whispered to her children, who were still sitting just outside the door of the house: 'See that every chink in the doorway and window is stopped, so that not a ray of light can penetrate here.'

Presently another old man of the Ponaturi called out again: 'Ho, Tatau there, is not it near dawn yet? And she answered: 'No, no, it is night; it is lasting night; `tis still night; sleep Soundly, sleep on.'

This was the second time that Tatau had thus called out to them.

At last dawn had broken-at last the sun had shone brightly upon the earth, and rose high in the heavens; and the old man again called out: 'Ho, Tatau there; is not it dawn yet? And she answered: 'Yes.' And then she called out to her children: 'Be quick, pull out the things with which you have stopped up the window and the door.'

So they pulled them out, and the bright rays of the sun came streaming into the house, and the whole of the Ponaturi perished before the light; they perished not by the hand of man, but withered before the sun's rays. [1]

When the Ponaturi had been all destroyed, Tawhaki and Karihi carefully took down their father's bones from the roof of the house, and burnt them with fire, and together with the bodies of all those who were in the house, who had perished, scorched by the bright rays of the sun; they then returned again to their own country, taking with them their mother, and carefully carrying the bones of their father.

The fame of Tawhaki's courage in thus destroying the race of Ponaturi, and a report also of his manly beauty, chanced to reach the ears of a young maiden of the heavenly race who live above in the skies; so one night she descended from the heavens to visit Tawhaki, and to judge for herself, whether these reports were true. She found him lying sound asleep, and after gazing on him for some time, she stole to his side and laid herself down by him. He, when disturbed by her, thought that it was only some female of this lower world, and slept again; but before dawn the young girl stole away again from his side, and ascended once more to the heavens. In the early morning Tawhaki awoke and felt all over his sleeping place with both his hands, but in vain, he could nowhere find the young girl.

From that time Tango-tango, [2] the girl of the heavenly race, stole every night to the side of Tawhaki, and lo, in the morning she was gone, until she found that she had conceived a child, who was afterwards named Arahuta; then full of love for Tawhaki, she disclosed herself fully to him and lived constantly in this world with him, deserting, for his sake, her friends above; and he discovered that she who had so loved him belonged to the race whose home is in the heavens.

Whilst thus living with him, this girl of the heavenly race, his second wife, said to him: 'Oh, Tawhaki, if our baby so shortly now to be born, should prove a son, I will wash the little thing before it is baptized; but if it should be a little girl then you shall wash it.' When the time came Tango-tango had a little girl, and before it was baptized Tawhaki took it to a spring to wash it, and afterwards held it away from him as if it smelt badly, and said: 'Faugh, how badly the little thing smells.' Then Tango-tango, when she heard this said of her own dear little baby, began to sob and cry bitterly, and at last rose up from her place with her child, and began to take flight towards the sky, but she paused for one minute with one foot resting upon the carved figure at the end of the ridge-pole of the house above the door. Then Tawhaki rushed forward, and springing up tried to catch hold of his young wife, but missing her, he entreatingly besought her: 'Mother of my child, oh, return once more to me!' But she in reply called down to him: 'No, no, I shall now never return to you again.

Tawhaki once more called up to her: 'At least, then, leave me some one remembrance of you.' Then his young wife called down to him: 'These are my parting words of remembrance to you--take care that you lay not hold with your hands of the loose root of the creeper, which dropping from aloft sways to and fro in the air; but rather lay fast hold on that which hanging down from on high has again struck its fibres into the earth.' Then she floated up into the air, and vanished from his sight.

Tawhaki remained plunged in grief, for his heart was torn by regrets for his wife and his little girl. One moon had waned after her departure, when Tawhaki, unable longer to endure such sufferings, called out to his younger brother, to Karihi, saying: 'Oh, brother, shall we go and search for my little girl? And Karihi consented, saying: 'Yes, let us go.' So they departed, taking two slaves with them as companions for their journey.

When they reached the pathway along which they intended to travel, Tawhaki said to the two slaves who were accompanying himself and his brother: 'You being unclean or unconsecrated persons must be careful when we come to the place where the road passes the fortress of Tongameha, not to look up at it for it is enchanted, and some evil will befall you if you do.' They then went along the road, and when they came to the place mentioned by Tawhaki, one of the slaves looked up at the fortress, and his eye was immediately torn out by the magical arts of Tongameha, and he perished. Tawhaki and Karihi then went upon the road accompanied by only one slave. They at last reached the spot where the ends of the vines which hung down from heaven reached the earth, and they there found an old woman who was quite blind. She was appointed to take care of the vines, and she sat at the place where they touched the earth, and held the ends of one of them in her hands.

This old lady was at the moment employed in counting some taro roots, which she was about to have cooked, and as she was blind she was not aware of the strangers who stole quietly and silently up to her. There were ten taro roots lying in a heap before her. She began to count them, one, two, three, four, five, six, seven, eight, nine. Just at this moment Tawhaki quietly slipped away the tenth, the old lady felt everywhere for it, but she could not find it. She thought she must have made some mistake, and so began to count her taro over again very carefully. One, two, three, four, five, six, seven, eight. just then Tawhaki had slipped away the ninth. She was now quite surprised, so she counted them over again quite slowly, One, two, three, four, five, six, seven, eight; and as she could not find the two that were missing, she at last guessed that somebody was playing a trick upon her, so she pulled her weapon out, which she always sat upon to keep it safe, and standing up turned round, feeling about her as she moved, to try if she could find Tawhaki and Karihi; but they very gently stooped down to the ground and lay close there, so that her weapon passed over them, and she could not feel anybody; when she had thus swept her weapon all round her, she sat down and put it under her again. Karihi then struck her a blow upon the face, and she, quite frightened, threw up her bands to her face, pressing them on the place where she had been struck, and crying out: 'Oh! who did that?' Tawhaki then touched both her eyes, and, lo, she was at once restored to sight, and saw quite plainly, and she knew her grandchildren and wept over them.

When the old lady had finished weeping over them, she asked: 'Where are you going to?' And Tawhaki answered: 'I go to seek my little girl.' She replied: 'But where is she? He answered: 'Above there, in the skies.' Then she replied: 'But what made her go to the skies?' And Tawhaki answered: 'Her mother came from heaven. She was the daughter of Whatitiri-mata-ka-taka.' The old lady then pointed to the vines and said to them: 'Up there, then, lies your road; but do not begin the ascent so late in the day, wait until to-morrow, for the morning, and then commence to climb up.' He consented to follow this good advice, and called out to his slave: 'Cook some food for us.' The slave began at once to cook food, and when it was dressed, they all partook of it and slept there that night.

At the first peep of dawn Tawhaki called out to his slave: 'Cook some food for us, that we may have strength to undergo the fatigues of this great journey'; and when their meal was finished, Tawhaki took his slave, and presented him to the old woman, as an acknowledgment for her great kindness to them.

The old woman then called out to him, as he was starting: 'There lies the ascent before you, lay fast hold of the vine with your hands, and climb on; but when you get midway between heaven and earth, take care not to look down upon this lower world again, lest you become charmed and giddy, and fall down. Take care, also, that you do not by mistake lay hold of the vine which swings loose; but rather lay hold of the one which hanging down from above, has again firmly struck root into the earth.'

Just at that moment Karihi made a spring at the vines to catch them, and by mistake caught hold of the loose one, and away he swung to the very edge of the horizon, but a blast of wind blew forth from thence, and drove him back to the other side of the skies; on reaching that point, another strong land wind swept him right up heavenwards, and down he was blown again by the currents of air from above: then just as he reached near the earth again, Tawhaki called out: 'Now, my brother, loose your hands: now is the time!'--and he did so, and, lo, he stood upon the earth once more; and the two brothers wept together over Karihi's narrow escape from destruction. And when they had ceased lamenting, Tawhaki, who was alarmed lest any disaster should overtake his younger brother, said to him: 'It is my desire that you should return home, to take care of our families and our dependants.' Thereupon Karihi at once returned to the village of their tribe, as his eldest brother directed him.

Tawhaki now began to climb the ascent to heaven, and the old blind woman called out to him as he went up: 'Hold fast, my child; let your hands hold tight.' And Tawhaki made use of, and kept on repeating, a powerful incantation as he climbed up to the heavens, to preserve him from the dangers of that difficult and terrible road.

At length he reached the heavens, and pulled himself up into them, and then by enchantments he disguised himself, and changed his handsome and noble appearance, and assumed the likeness of a very ugly old man, and he followed the road he had at first struck upon, and entered a dense forest into which it ran, and still followed it until he came to a place in the forest where his brothers-in-law, with a party of their people, were hewing canoes from the trunks of trees; and they saw him, and little thinking who he was, called out: 'Here's an old fellow will make a nice slave for us': but Tawhaki went quietly on, and when he reached them he sat down with the people who were working at the canoes.

It now drew near evening, and his brothers-in-law finished their work, and called out to him: 'Ho! old fellow, there!--you just carry these heavy axes home for us, will you!' [3] He at once consented to do this, and they gave him the axes. The old man then said to them: 'You go on in front, do not mind, I am old and heavy laden, I cannot travel fast.' So they started off, the old man following slowly behind. When his brothers-in-law and their people were all out of sight, he turned back to the canoe, and taking an axe just adzed the canoe rapidly along from the bow to the stem, and lo, one side of the canoe was finished. Then he took the adze again, and ran it rapidly along the other side of the canoe, from the bow to the stem, and lo, that side also was beautifully finished.

He then walked quietly along the road again, like an old man, carrying the axes with him, and went on for some time without seeing anything; but when be drew near the village, he found two women from the village in the forest gathering firewood, and as soon as they saw him, one of them observed to her companion: 'I say here is a curious-looking old fellow, is he not?'--and her companion exclaimed: 'He shall be our slave'; to which the first answered: 'Make him carry the firewood for us, then.' So they took Tawhaki, and laid a load of firewood upon his back, and made him carry that as well as the axes, so was this mighty chief treated as a slave, even by female slaves.

When they all reached the village, the two women called out: 'We've caught an old man for a slave.' Then Tango-tango exclaimed in reply: 'That's right bring him along with you, then; he'll do for all of us.' Little did his wife Tango-tango think that the slave they were so insulting, and whom she was talking about in such a way, was her own husband Tawhaki.

When Tawhaki saw Tango-tango sitting at a fireplace near the upper end of the house with their little girl, he went straight up to the place, and all the persons present tried to stop him, calling out: 'Ho! ho! take care what you are doing; do not go there; you will become tapued from sitting near Tango-tango.' But the old man, without minding them, went rapidly straight on, and carried his load of firewood right up to the very fire of Tango-tango. Then they all said: 'There, the old fellow is *tapu*; it is his own fault.' But Tango-tango had not the least idea that this was Tawhaki; and yet there were her husband and herself seated, the one upon the one side, the other upon the opposite side of the very same fire.

They all stopped in the house until the sun rose next morning; then at daybreak his brothers-in-law called out to him: 'Holloa! old man, you bring the axes along, do you hear.' So the old man took up the axes, and started with them, and they all went off together to the forest, to work at dubbing out their canoes. When they reached them, and the brothers-in-law saw the canoe which Tawhaki had worked at, they looked at it with astonishment, saying: 'Why, the canoe is not at all as we left it; who can have been working at it? At last, when their wonder was somewhat abated, they all sat down, and set to work again to dub out another canoe, and worked until evening, when they again called out to the old man as on the previous one: 'Holloa! old fellow, come here, and carry the axes back to the village again.' As before, he said: 'Yes', and when they started he remained behind, and after the others were all out of sight he took an axe, and began again to adze away at the canoe they had been working at; and having finished his work he returned again to the village, and once more walked straight up to the fire of Tango-tango, and remained there until the sun rose upon the following morning.

When they were all going at early dawn to work at their canoes as usual, they again called out to Tawhaki: 'Holloa! old man, just bring these axes along with you'; and the old man went patiently and silently along with them, carrying the axes on his shoulder. When they reached the canoe they were about to work at, the brothers-in-law were quite astonished on seeing it, and shouted out: 'Why, here again, this canoe, too, is not at all as it was when we left it; who can have been at work at it?' Having wondered at this for some time, they at length sat down and set to again to dub out another canoe, and laboured away until evening, when a thought came into their minds that they would hide themselves in the forest, and wait to see who it was came every evening to work at their canoe; and Tawhaki overheard them arranging this plan.

They therefore started as if they were going home, and when they had got a little way they turned off the path on one side, and hid themselves in the thick clumps of bushes, in a place from whence they could see the canoes. Then Tawhaki, going a little way back into the forest, stripped off his old cloaks, and threw them on one side, and then repeating the necessary incantations he put off his disguise, and took again his own appearance, and made himself look noble and handsome, and commenced his work at the canoe. Then his brothers-in-law, when they saw him so employed, said one to another: 'Ah, that must be the old man whom we made a slave of who is working away at our canoe'; but again they called to one another and said: 'Come here, come here, just watch, why he is not in the least like that old man.' Then they said amongst themselves: 'This must be a demi-god'; and, without showing themselves to him, they ran off to the village, and as soon as they reached it they asked their sister Tango-tango to describe her husband for them; and she described his appearance as well as she could, representing him just like the man they had seen: and they said to her: 'Yes, that must be he; he is exactly like him you have described to us.' Their sister replied: 'Then that chief must certainly be your brother-in-law.'

Just at this moment Tawhaki reappeared at the village, having again disguised himself, and changed his appearance into that of an ugly old man. But Tango-tango immediately questioned him, saying: 'Now tell me, who are you? Tawhaki made no reply, but walked on straight towards her. She asked him again: 'Tell me, are you Tawhaki? He murmured 'Humph!' in assent, still walking on until he reached the side of his wife, and then he snatched up his little daughter, and, holding her fast in his arms, pressed her to his heart. The persons present all rushed out of the court-yard of the house to the neighbouring court-yards, for the whole place was made *tapu* by Tawhaki, and murmurs of gratification and surprise arose from the people upon every side at the splendour of his appearance, for in the days when he had been amongst them as an old man his figure was very different from the resplendent aspect which he presented on this day.

Then he retired to rest with his wife, and said to her: 'I came here that our little daughter might be made to undergo the ceremonies usual for the children of nobles, to secure them good fortune and happiness in this life'; and Tango-tango consented.

When in the morning the sun arose, they broke out an opening through the end of the house opposite to the door, that the little girl's rank might be seen by her being carried out that way instead of through the usual entrance to the house; and they repeated the prescribed prayers when she was carried through the wall out of the house.

The prayers and incantations being finished, lightnings flashed from the arm-pits of Tawhaki; [4] then they carried the little girl to the water, and plunged her into it, and repeated a baptismal incantation over her.

[1] The Maoris say that the 'Kanae', or salmon, had come on shore with the Ponaturi, and escaped out of the house by its power of leaping, gaining the water again by successive springs.
[2] According to some traditions her name was Hapai.
[3] The European reader cannot at all enter into p. 53 the witty nature of this adventure in the estimation of a Maori; the idea of a sacred chief of high rank being by mistake treated as a common slave, conveys impressions to their minds of which we can form no accurate notion.
[4] Tawhaki is said to still dwell in the skies, and is worshipped as a god, and thunder and lightning are said to be caused by his footsteps when he moves.

Rupe's Ascent into Heaven

WE left Hinauri floating out into the ocean; we now return to her adventures: for many months she floated through the sea, and was at last thrown up by the surf on the beach at a place named Wairarawa; she was there found, lying as if dead, upon the sandy shore, by two brothers named Ihuatamai and Ihuwareware; her body was in many parts overgrown with seaweed and barnacles, from the length of time she had been in the water, but they could still see some traces of her beauty, and pitying the young girl, they lifted her up in their arms, and carried her home to their house, and laid her down carefully by the side of a fire, and scraped off very gently the seaweed and barnacles from her body, and thus by degrees restored her.

When she had quite recovered, Ihuatamai and Ihuwareware looked upon her with pleasure, and took her as a wife between them both; they then asked her to tell them who she was, and what was her name; this she did not disclose to them, but she changed her name, and called herself Ihungaru-paea, or the Stranded-log-of-timber.

After she had lived with these two brothers for a long time, Ihuwareware went to pay a visit to his superior chief, Tinirau, and to relate the adventures which had happened; and when Tinirau heard all that had taken place, he went to bring

away the young stranger as a wife for himself, and she was given up to him; but before she was so given to him, she had conceived a child by Ihuatamai, and when she went to live with Tinirau it was near the time when the child should be born.

Tinirau took her home with him to his residence on an island called Motu-tapu: he had two other wives living there--they were the daughters of Mangamanga-i-atua, and their names were Harataunga and Horotata. Now, when these two women saw the young stranger coming along in their husband's company, as if she was his wife, they could not endure it, and they abused Hinauri on account of her conduct with their husband; at last they proceeded so far as to attempt to strike her, and to kill her, and they cursed her bitterly. When they treated her in this manner the heart of Hinauri became gloomy with grief and mortification, so she began to utter incantations against them, and repeated one so powerful that hardly had she finished it when the two women fell flat on the ground with the soles of their feet projecting upwards, and lay quite dead upon the earth, and her husband was thus left free for her alone.

All this time Hinauri was lost to her friends and home, and her young brother Mauimua, afterwards called Rupe, could do nothing but think of her; and excessive love for his sister, and sorrow at her departure, so harassed him, that he said he could no longer remain at rest, but that he must go and seek for his sister.

So he departed upon this undertaking, and visited every place he could think of without missing one of them, yet could he nowhere find his sister; at last, Rupe thought that be would ascend to the heavens to consult his great ancestor Rehua, who dwelt there at a place named Te Putahi-nui-o-Rehua, and in fulfilment of this design he began his ascent to the heavenly regions.

Rupe continued his ascent, seeking everywhere hastily for Rehua; at last, he reached a place where people were dwelling, and when he saw them, he spoke to them, saying: 'Are the heavens above this inhabited?'--and the people dwelling there answered him: 'They are inhabited.' And he again asked them: 'Can I reach those heavens? and they replied: 'You cannot reach them, the heavens above these are those the boundaries of which were fixed by Tane.'

But Rupe forced a way up through those heavens, and got above them, and found an inhabited place; and he asked the inhabitants of it, saying: 'Are the heavens above these inhabited?'--and the people answered him: 'They are inhabited.' And he again asked: 'Do you think I can reach them?'--and they replied: 'No, you will not be able to reach them, those heavens were fixed there by Tane.'

Rupe, however, forced a way through those heavens too, and thus he continued to do until he reached the tenth heaven, and there he found the abode of Rehua. When Rehua saw a stranger approaching, he went forward and gave him the usual welcome, lamenting over him; Rehua made his lamentation without knowing who the stranger was, but Rupe in his lament made use of prayers by which he enabled Rehua to guess who he was.

When they had each ended their lamentation, Rehua called to his servants: 'Light a fire, and get everything ready for cooking food.' The slaves soon made the fire burn up brightly, and brought hollow calabashes, all ready to have food placed in them, and laid them down before Rehua. All this time Rupe was wondering whence the food was to come from with which the calabashes, which the slaves had brought, were to be filled; but presently he observed that Rehua was slowly loosening the thick bands which enveloped his locks around and upon the top of his head; and when his long locks all floated loosely, he shook the dense masses of his hair, and forth from them came flying flocks of the Tui birds, which had been nestling there, feeding upon lice; and as they flew forth, the slaves caught and killed them, and filled the calabashes with them, and took them to the fire, and put them on to cook, and when they were done, they carried them and laid them before Rupe as a present, and then placed them beside him that he might eat, and Rehua requested him to eat food, but Rupe answered him: 'Nay, but I cannot eat this food; I saw these birds loosened and take wing from thy locks; who would dare to eat birds that had fed upon lice in thy sacred head? For the reasons he thus stated, Rupe feared that man of ancient days, and the calabashes still stood near him untouched.

At last, Rupe ventured to ask Rehua, saying: 'O Rehua, has a confused murmur of voices from the world below reached you upon any subject regarding which I am interested? And Rehua answered him: 'Yes, such a murmuring of distant voices has reached me from the island of Motu-tapu in the world below these.'

When Rupe heard this, he immediately by his enchantments changed himself into a pigeon, and took flight downwards towards the island of Motu-tapu; on, on he flew, until he reached the island, and the dwelling of Tinirau, and then he alighted right upon the window-sill of his house. Some of Tinirau's people saw him, and exclaimed: 'Ha! ha!--there's a bird, there's a bird'; whilst some called out: 'Make haste, spear him, spear him'; and one threw a spear at him, but he turned it aside with his bill, and it passed on one side of him, and struck the piece of wood on which he was sitting, and the spear was broken; then they saw that it was no use to try to spear the bird, so they made a noose, and endeavoured to slip it gently over his head, but he turned his head on one side, and they found that they could not snare him. His young sister now suspected something, so she said to the people who were trying to kill or snare the bird: 'Leave the bird quiet for a minute until I look at it'; and when she had looked well at it, she knew that it was her brother, so she asked him, saying: 'What is the cause which has made you thus come here?'- and the pigeon immediately began to open and shut its little bill, as if it was trying to speak. His young sister now called out to Tinirau: 'Oh, husband, here is your brother-in-law'; and her husband said in reply: 'What is his name?'--and she answered: 'It is my brother Rupe.' It happened that upon this very day, Hinauri's little child was born, then Rupe repeated this form of greeting to his sister, the name of which is Toetoetu:

'Hinauri,
Hinauri is the sister,

And Rupe is her brother,
But how came he here?
Came he by travelling on the earth,
Or came he through the air?
Let your path be through the air.'

As soon as Rupe had ceased his lamentation of welcome to his sister, she commenced hers, and answered him, saying:

'Rupe is the brother,
And Hina is his young sister,
But how came he here?
Came he by travelling on the earth,
Or came he through the air?
Let your path be now upwards through the air
To Rehua.'

Hardly had his young sister finished repeating this poem, before Rupe had caught her up with her new-born baby: in a moment they were gone. Thus the brother and sister departed together, with the infant, carrying with them the placenta to bury it with the usual rites; and they ascended up to Rehua, and as they passed through the air, the placenta was accidentally dropped, and falling into the sea, was devoured by a shark, and this circumstance was what caused the multitude of large eggs which are now found in the inside of the shark.

At length the brother and sister arrived at the dwelling-place of Rehua, which was called Te Putahi-nui-o-Rehua. The old man was unable to keep his court-yard clean for himself, and his people neglected to do so from idleness; thus it was left in a very filthy state. Rupe, who was displeased at seeing this, one day said to Rehua: 'Oh, Rehua, they leave this court-yard of yours in a very filthy state'; and then he added: 'Your people are such a set of lazy rogues, that if every mess of dirt was a lizard, I doubt if they could even take the trouble to touch its tail to make it run away'; and this saying passed into a proverb.

At last, Rupe thought that he could clean and beautify, in some respects, Rehua's dwelling for him, so he made two wooden shovels for his work, one of which he called Tahitahia, and the other Rake-rakea, and with them he quite cleansed and purified Rehua's court-yard. He then added a building to Rehua's dwelling, but fixing one of the beams of it badly, Rehua's son Kai-tangata, was one day killed from hanging on to this beam, which giving way and springing back, he was thrown down and died, and his blood running about over part of the heavens stained them, and formed what we now call a ruddiness in the sky; when, therefore, a red and ruddy tinge is seen in the heavens, men say: 'Ah! Kaitangata stained the heavens with his blood.'

Rupe's first name was Maui-mua; it was after he was transformed into a bird that he took the name of Rupe. [1]

[1] The part of the tradition which relates to the death of Kaitangata is considerably shortened in the translation, as not being likely to interest the European reader.

Kae's Theft of the Whale

SOON after Tuhuruhuru was born, Tinirau endeavoured to find a skilful magician, who might perform the necessary enchantments and incantations to render the child a fortunate and successful warrior, and Kae was the name of the old magician, whom some of his friends brought to him for this purpose. In due time Kae arrived at the village where Tinirau lived, and he performed the proper enchantments with fitting ceremonies over the infant.

When all these things had been rightly concluded, Tinirau gave a signal to a pet whale that he had tamed, to come on shore; this whale's name was Tutunui. When it knew that its master wanted it, it left the ocean in which it was sporting about, and came to the shore, and its master laid hold of it, and cut a slice of its flesh off to make a feast for the old magician, and he cooked it, and gave a portion of it to Kae, who found it very savoury, and praised the dish very much.

Shortly afterwards, Kae said it was necessary for him to return to his own village, which was named Te Tihi-o-Manono; so Tinirau ordered a canoe to be got ready for him to take him back, but Kae made excuses, and said he did not like to go back in the canoe, and remained where he was. This, however, was a mere trick upon his part, his real object being to get Tinirau to permit him to go back upon the whale, upon Tutunui, for he now knew how savoury the flesh of that fish was.

At last Tinirau lent Tutunui to the old magician to carry him home, but he gave him very particular directions, telling him: 'When you get so near the shore, that the fish touches the bottom, it will shake itself to let you know, and you must then, without any delay, jump off it upon the right side.'

He then wished Kae farewell, and the old magician started, and away went the whale through the water with him.

When they came close to the shore at Kae's village, and the whale felt the bottom, it shook itself as a sign to Kae to jump off and wade ashore, but it was of no use; the old magician stuck fast to the whale, and pressed it down against the bottom as hard as he could; in vain the fish continued to shake itself; Kae held on to it, and would not jump off, and in its struggles the blow-holes of Tutunui got stopped up with sand, and it died.

Kae and his people then managed to drag up the body of Tutunui on shore, intending to feast upon it; and this circumstance became afterwards the cause of a war against that tribe, who were called 'The descendants of Popohorokewa'. When they had dragged Tutunui on shore, they cut its body up and cooked it in ovens, covering the flesh up with the fragrant leaves of the Koromiko before they heaped earth upon the ovens, and the fat of Tutunui adhered to the leaves of the Koromiko, and they continue greasy to this day, so that if Koromiko boughs are put upon the fire and become greasy, the proverb says: 'There's some of the savouriness of Tutunui'.

Tinirau continued anxiously to look for the return of Tutunui and when a long time had elapsed without its coming back again, he began to say to himself: 'Well, I wonder where my whale can be stopping!' But when Kae and his people had cooked the flesh of the whale, and the ovens were opened, a savoury scent was wafted across the sea to Tinirau, and both he and his wife smelt it quite plainly, and then they knew very well that Kae had killed the pet which they had tamed for their little darling Tuhuruhuru, and that he had eaten it.

Without any delay, Tinirau's people dragged down to the sea a large canoe which belonged to one of his wives, and forty women forthwith embarked in it; none but women went, as this would be less likely to excite any suspicion in Kae that they had come with a hostile object; amongst them were Hine-i-te-iwaiwa, Raukatauri, Raukatamea, Itiiti, Rekareka, and Rua-hau-a-Tangaroa, and other females of note, whose names have not been preserved; just before the canoe started Tinirau's youngest sister asked him: 'What are the marks by which we shall know Kae?'--and he answered her: 'Oh, you cannot mistake him, his teeth are uneven and all overlap one another.'

Well, away they paddled, and in due time they arrived at the village of the old magician Kae, and his tribe all collected to see the strangers; towards night, when it grew dark, a fire was lighted in the house of Kae, and a crowd collected inside it, until it was filled; one side was quite occupied with the crowd of visitors, and the other side of the house with the people of Kae's tribe. The old magician himself sat at the foot of the main pillar which supported the roof of the house, and mats were laid down there for him to sleep on (but the strangers did not yet know which was Kae, for it did not accord with the Maori's rules of politeness to ask the names of the chiefs, it being supposed from their fame and greatness that they are known by everybody).

In order to find out which was Kae, Tinirau's people had arranged, that they would try by wit and fun to make everybody laugh, and when the people opened their mouths, to watch which of them had uneven teeth that lapped across one another, and thus discover which was Kae.

In order, therefore, to make them laugh, Raukatauri exhibited all her amusing tricks and games; she made them sing and play upon the flute, and upon the putorino, and beat time with castanets of bone and wood whilst they sang; and they played at *mora*, and the kind of *ti* in which many motions are made with the fingers and hands, and the kind of *ti* in which, whilst the players sing, they rapidly throw short sticks to one another, keeping time to the tune which they are singing; and she played upon an instrument like a jew'sharp for them, and made puppets dance, and made them all sing whilst they played with large whizgigs; and after they had done all these things, the man they thought was Kae had never even once laughed.

Then the party who had come from Tinirau's, all began to consult together, and to say what can we do to make that fellow laugh, and for a long time they thought of some plan by which they might take Kae in, and make him laugh; at last they thought of one, which was, that they should all sing a droll comic song; so suddenly they all began to sing together, at the same time making curious faces, and shaking their hands and arms in time to the tune.

When they had ended their song, the old magician could not help laughing out quite heartily, and those who were watching him closely at once recognized him, for there they saw pieces of the flesh of Tutunui still sticking between his teeth, and his teeth were uneven and all overlapped one another. From this circumstance a proverb has been preserved among the Maoris to the present day--for if any one on listening to a story told by another is amused at it and laughs, one of the bystanders says: 'Ah, there's Kae laughing.'

No sooner did the women who had come from Tinirau's see the flesh of Tutunui sticking in Kae's teeth than they made an excuse for letting the fire burn dimly in the house, saying, that they wanted to go to sleep--their real object, however, being to be able to perform their enchantments without being seen; but the old magician who suspected something, took two round pieces of mother-of-pearl shell, and stuck one in the socket of each eye, so that the strangers, observing the faint rays of light reflected from the surface of the mother-of-pearl, might think they saw the white of his eyes, and that he was still awake.

The women from Tinirau's went on, however, with their enchantments, and by their magical arts threw every one in the house into an enchanted sleep, with the intention, when they had done this, of carrying off Kae by stealth. So soon as Kae and the people in the house were all deep in this enchanted sleep, the women ranged themselves in a long row, the whole way from the place where Kae was sleeping down to their canoe; they all stood in a straight line, with a little interval between each of them; and then two of them went to fetch Kae, and lifted the old magician gently up, rolled up in his cloaks, just as be had laid himself down to sleep, and placed him gently in the arms of those who stood near the door, who passed him on to two others, and thus they handed him on from one to another, until he at last reached the arms of the two women who were standing in the canoe ready to receive him; and they laid him down very gently in the canoe, fast asleep as he was; and thus the old magician Kae was carried off by Hine-i-te-iwaiwa and Raukatauri.

When the women reached the village of Tinirau in their canoe, they again took up Kae, and carried him very gently up to the house of Tinirau, and laid him down fast asleep close to the central pillar, which supported the ridgepole of the house, so that the place where he slept in the house of Tinirau was exactly like his sleeping-place in his own house. The house of Kae was, however, a large circular house, without a ridge-pole, but with rafters springing from the central pillar, running down like rays to low side posts in the circular wall; whilst the house of Tinirau was a long house, with a ridge-pole running the entire length of the roof, and resting upon the pillar in its centre.

When Tinirau heard that the old magician had been brought to his village, he caused orders to be given to his tribe that when be made his appearance in the morning, going to the house where Kae was, they should all call out loud: 'Here comes Tinirau, here comes Tinirau', as if he was coming as a visitor into the village of Kae, so that the old magician on hearing them might think that he was still at home.

At broad daylight next morning, when Tinirau's people saw him passing along through the village towards his house, they all shouted aloud: 'Here come Tinirau, here comes Tinirau'; and Kae, who heard the cries, started up from his enchanted sleep quite drowsy and confused, whilst Tinirau passed straight on, and sat down just outside the door of his house, so that he could look into it, and, looking in, he saw Kae, and saluted him, saying: 'Salutations to you, O Kae!'--and then he asked him, saying: 'How came you here?'--and the old magician replied: 'Nay, but rather how came you here?'

Tinirau replied: 'Just look, then, at the house, and see if you recognize it?'

But Kae, who was still stupefied by his sleep, looking round, saw he was lying in his own place at the foot of the pillar, and said: 'This is my house.'

Tinirau asked him: 'Where was the window placed in your house?'

Kae started and looked; the whole appearance of his house appeared to be changed; he at once guessed the truth, that the house he was in belonged to Tinirau; and the old magician, who saw that his hour had come, bowed down his head in silence to the earth, and they seized him, and dragged him out, and slew him: thus perished Kae.

The news of his death at last reached his tribe--the descendants of Popohorokewa; and they eventually attacked the fortress of Tinirau with a large army, and avenged the death of Kae by slaying Tinirau's son.

The Murder of Tuwhakararo

How he was Murdered and Avenged

NOW about this time Tuhuruhuru, the son of Rupe's sister, grew up to man's estate, and he married Apakura, and she gave birth to a son whom they named Tuwhakararo, and afterwards to a daughter named Mairatea; she had then several other children; then she gave birth to Whakatau-potiki; afterwards her last child was born, and its name was Reimatua.

When Mairatea grew up, she was married to the son of a chief named Popohorokewa, the chief of the Ati-Hapai tribe, and she accompanied her husband to his home; but Tuwhakararo remained at his own village, and after a time he longed to see his sister, and thought he would go and pay her a visit; so he went, and arrived at a very large house belonging to the tribe Popohorokewa, the name of which was Te Uru-o-Manono; all the family and dependants of Popohorokewa lived in that house, and Tuwhakararo remained there with them. It happened that a young sister of his brother-in-law, whose name was Maurea, took a great fancy to him, and showed that she liked him, although, at the very time, she was carrying on a courtship with another young man of the Ati-Hapai tribe.

Whilst Tuwhakararo was on this visit to his brother-in-law, some of the young men of the Ati-Hapai tribe asked him one day to wrestle with them, and he, agreeing to this, stood up to wrestle, and the one who came forward as his competitor was the sweetheart of his brother-in-law's young sister. Tuwhakararo laid hold of the young man, and soon gave him a severe fall. That match being over they both stood up again, and Tuwhakararo, lifting him in his arms, gave him another severe fall; and all the young people of the Ati-Hapai tribe burst out laughing at the youth, for having had two such heavy falls from Tuwhakararo, and he sat down upon the ground, looking very foolish, and feeling exceedingly sulky and provoked at being laughed at by everybody.

Tuwhakararo, having also finished wrestling, sat down too, and began to put on his clothes again, and whilst he was in the act of putting his head through his cloak, the young man he had thrown in wrestling ran up, and just as his head appeared through the cloak threw a handful of sand in his eyes. Tuwhakararo, wild with pain, could see nothing, and began to rub his eyes, to get the dust out and to ease the anguish; the young man then struck him on the head, and killed him. The people of the Ati-Hapai tribe then ran in upon him and cut his body up, and afterwards devoured it; and they took his bones, and hung them up in the roof, under the ridge-pole of their house, Te Uru-o-Manono.

Whilst they were hung up there the bones rattled together, and his sister heard them, and it seemed to her as if they made a sound like 'Tauparoro, Tauparoro'; and she listened again to the rattling of the bones, and again she heard the words 'Tauparoro, Tauparoro'. And the sister of Tuwhakararo looking up to the bones, said: 'You rattle in vain, O bones of him who was devoured by the Ati-Hapai tribe, for who is there to lament over him or to avenge his death?'

At last the news of the sad event which had taken place reached the ears of his brother, Whakatau-potiki, and of his other brothers, and when they beard it they were grieved and pained at the fate of their brother, and at last Whakatau-potiki adopted a firm resolution to go and avenge Tuwhakararo's death, and as the rest of his tribe agreed in this purpose, they began without delay to build canoes for its execution.

They named some of their canoes the Whiritoa, the Tapatapahukarere, the Toroa-i-taipakihi, the Hakirere, and the Mahunu-awatea, and to all the other canoes which they prepared for this purpose they also gave names; and when they had finished lashing on the top-boards of their canoes, their mother Apakura, with all her female attendants, began to beat and prepare fern root for the warriors to carry with them as provisions for their voyage, and whilst the females were thus engaged in beating and preparing fern root for the war party who were about to start to revenge the death of Tuwha-kararo, they kept on repeating a lament for the young man which might rouse the feelings of the warriors.

Lo, the army of Whakatau-potiki now embarked; they started in a thousand canoes, and floated out into the open sea, and proceeding upon their course, they landed at a certain place which lay in their route, and there the army of Whakatau had a review, to show how well they could go through their manoeuvres. They were formed into columns, and one column, with fierce shouts and yells, after a war dance, sprang upon the supposed enemy, and whilst they were thus engaged with their imaginary foe, a second column, with wild cries, advanced to their support; then the first column of warriors retired to re-form and thus column after column feigned to charge their foes.

Then one body of the warriors rushed to an adjoining creek and tried to jump across it, but they could not. A band of men under Whakatau's immediate command were sitting upon the ground watching the others, and when the first body gave up in despair all thoughts of overleaping the creek, this chosen band of Whakatau rose from the ground, started forward, reached in good order the edge of the creek, and sprang easily across it the whole body of them to the other side.

When the review was ended, Whakatau made a speech to the warriors, saying: 'Warriors, all of you listen to me. We will not finish our voyage until the dark night, lest we should be seen by the people we are about to attack, and thus fail in surprising them.'

Just as it was dark, Whakatau ordered his own chosen band of warriors to go and pull the plugs out of all the canoes but their own, and they, in obedience to his orders, went round and pulled all the plugs out of the canoes, and thus they did to the whole of them without missing a single canoe of the whole thousand.

This having been done, Whakatau called aloud to the whole force: 'Now my men, let us embark at once this very night.' Then the warriors hurriedly arose in the darkness, and all was confusion and noise, and one canoe was launched, and then another, and another, until all were afloat on the sea. Then they all embarked, and the several crews sprang cheerfully into their own canoes; but lo, presently the canoes all began to sink, one after the other, and the crews were compelled again to seek the shore, and to busy themselves there in repairing them. In the meantime the chosen band of warriors of Whakatau urged on their canoes, leaving the others behind, and when they drew near the place where the house called Te Uru-o-Manono was situated, they landed. Then the warriors silently surrounded the house in ranks throughout its whole circumference, and each of the eight doors of the house they guarded by a band of men, and Whakatau laid hold of a man named Hioi, whom they caught outside of the house, and he questioned him, saying: 'Where is my sister now?' And Hioi answered him: 'She is in the house.' And he asked him again: 'In what part of the house does Popohorokewa sleep? Hioi replied: 'At the foot of the large pillar which supports the ridge-pole of the house.' Whakatau next asked: 'Has he any distinguishing mark by which we may know him? Hioi answered: 'You may know him by one of his teeth being broken.' Whakatau asked him one question more, saying: 'In what part of the house does my sister sleep?' And Hioi answered him: 'She sleeps close to that door.'

Whakatau-potiki asked him no further question, but took the fellow and cut out his tongue, and when he had done so he made him talk, and he still spoke quite distinctly, although a great part of his tongue was cut out. Whakatau then took him again, and cut his tongue off quite close to the root, and he made him try to talk again, and nothing but an indistinct mumbling could be heard, so he then ordered the man into the house to send his sister out to him.

Hioi went as he was told to send Whakatau's sister to him, for she was then in Te Uru-o-Manono, the house of her father-in-law, Popohorokewa. When he got inside, the whole mass of the Ati-Hapai tribe who were sitting saw him come in, and some of them asked him where he had been to, and what he had gone for; but what was the use of their talking to him, since be could do nothing but mumble out indistinct words in reply, and those who were sitting near him wondered what could be the matter.

But the sister of Whakatau guessed in a moment that this was some device of her brother's, and at once went out of the house, and found Whakatau, and she and her brother wept together, partly from joy at their meeting, partly from sorrow in thinking of the melancholy death of their brother since they had last met.

When they had done weeping, Whakatau asked her: 'In what part of the house does Popohorokewa sleep? And she answered him: 'He sleeps at the foot of the large pillar which supports the ridge-pole of the house.' And then she added: 'But oh, my brother, a great part of the Ati-Hapai tribe have seen you before, and they will know you.' Her brother then asked her: 'What then do you think I had better do? His sister answered: 'You had better cut your hair quite short to disguise yourself.'

He consented to this being done, so his sister cut his hair quite close for him, and when she had done this she rubbed his face all over with charcoal, and then he and his sister went together into the house. The fire in the house had got quite low some time before, and when they entered, the people near where they went in, cried out: 'Make up the fire, make up the fire; here's a stranger, here's a stranger.' So they blew up the fire and made it bum brightly, and many of them came to see Whakatau-potiki, and when they had looked well at him, they broke out laughing, and said: 'What a black-looking fellow he is!' Even Popohorokewa burst out laughing at his appearance, and Whakatau, when he saw him laugh, at once recognized him by his broken tooth.

Whakatau-potiki had taken a stout rope with him when he went into the house, and he held this ready coiled in his hand, with a noose at one end of it; and as soon as he recognized Popohorokewa, he slily dropped the noose over his head, and suddenly hauling it tight, it got fast round his neck: then, still holding the rope in his hand, and lengthening it by degrees as he went, Whakatau and his sister rushed out of the house; and he still hauling with all his strength on the rope, climbed up on the roof, repeating a powerful incantation.

Then each warrior sprang up into his place from the ground, on which they had been lying down to conceal themselves, and they set fire to the house in several places at once, and slaughtered all those who tried to escape. Thus they burnt Te Uru-o-Manono, and all those who were in it, and then the warriors returned, and carried with them joyful news to Apakura, the mother of Tuwhakararo.

The Legend of Rata

His Adventures with the Enchanted Tree and Revenge of his Father's Murder

BEFORE Tawhaki ascended up into the heavens, a son named Wahieroa had been born to him by his first wife. As soon as Wahieroa grew to man's estate, he took Kura for a wife, and she bore him a son whom they called Rata. Wahieroa was slain treacherously by a chief named Matukutakotako, but his son Rata was born some time before his death. It therefore became his duty to revenge the death of his father Wahieroa, and Rata having grown up, at last devised a plan for doing this: he therefore gave the necessary orders to his dependants, at the same time saying to them: 'I am about to go in search of the man who slew my father.'

He then started upon a journey for this purpose, and at length arrived at the entrance to the place of Matukutakotako; be found there a man who was left in charge of it, sitting at the entrance to the court-yard, and he asked him, saying: 'Where is the man who killed my father? The man who was left in charge of the place answered him: 'He lives beneath in the earth there, and I am left here by him, to call to him and warn him when the new moon appears; at that season he rises and comes forth upon the earth, and devours men as his food.'

Rata then said to him: 'All that you say is true, but how can he know when the proper time comes for him to rise up from the earth? The man replied: 'I call aloud to him.'

Then said Rata: 'When will there be a new moon? And the man who was left to take care of the place answered him: 'In two nights hence. Do you now return to your own village, but on the morning of the second day from this time come here again to me.'

Rata, in compliance with these directions, returned to his own dwelling, and waited there until the time that had been appointed him, and on the morning of that day he again journeyed along the road he had previously travelled, and found the man sitting in the same place, and he asked him, saying: 'Do you know any spot where I can conceal myself, and he hid from the enemy with whom I am about to fight, from Matukutakotako?' The man replied: 'Come with me until I show you the two fountains of clear water.'

They then went together until they came to the two fountains.

The man then said to Rata: 'The spot that we stand on is the place where Matuku rises up from the earth, and yonder fountain is the one in which he combs and washes his dishevelled hair, but this fountain is the one he uses to reflect his face in whilst he dresses it; you cannot kill him whilst he is at the fountain he uses to reflect his face in, because your shadow would be also reflected in it, and he would see it; but at the fountain in which he washes his hair, you may smite and slay him.'

Rata then asked the man: 'Will be make his appearance from the earth this evening?' And the man answered: 'Yes.'

They had not waited long there, when evening arrived, and the moon became visible, and the man said to Rata: 'Do you now go and hide yourself near the brink of the fountain in which he washes his hair'; and Rata went and hid himself near the edge of the fountain, and the man who had been left to watch for the purpose shouted aloud: 'Ho, Ho, the new moon is visible--a moon two days old.' And Matukutakotako heard him, and seizing his two-handed wooden sword, he rose up from the earth there, and went straight to his two fountains; then he laid down his two-handed wooden sword on the ground, at the edge of the fountain where he dressed his hair, and kneeling down on both knees beside it, he loosened the strings which bound up his long locks, and shook out his dishevelled hair, and plunged down his head into the cool clear waters of the fountain. So Rata creeping out from where he lay hid, rapidly moved up, and stood behind him, and as Matukutakotako raised his head from the water, Rata, with one hand seized him by the hair, while with the other he smote and slew him; thus he avenged the death of his father Wahieroa.

Rata then asked the man whom he had found in charge of the place: 'Where shall I find the bones of Wahieroa my father? And the keeper of the place answered him: 'They are not here; a strange people who live at a distance came and carried them off.'

Upon bearing this Rata returned to his own village, and there reflected over many designs by which be might recover the bones of his father.

At length he thought of an excellent plan for this purpose, so he went into the forest and having found a very tall tree, quite straight throughout its entire length, he felled it, and cut off its noble branching top, intending to fashion the trunk into a canoe; and all the insects which inhabit trees, and the spirits of the forests, were very angry at this, and as soon as Rata had returned to the village at evening, when his day's work was ended, they all came and took the tree, and raised it up again, and the innumerable multitude of insects, birds, and spirits, who are called 'The offspring of Hakuturi', worked away at replacing each little chip and shaving in its proper place, and sang aloud their incantations as they worked; this was what they sang with a confused noise of various voices:

> Fly together, chips and shavings,
> Stick ye fast together,
> Hold ye fast together;
> Stand upright again, O tree!

Early the next morning back came Rata, intending to work at hewing the trunk of his tree into a canoe. When he got to the place where he had left the trunk lying on the ground, at first he could not find it, and if that fine tall straight tree, which he saw standing whole and sound in the forest, was the same he thought he had cut down, there it was now erect again; however he stepped up to it, and manfully hewing away at it again, he felled it to the ground once more, and off he cut its fine branching top again, and began to hollow out the hold of the canoe, and to slope off its prow and the stem into their proper gracefully curved forms; and in the evening, when it became too dark to work, he returned to his village.

As soon as he was gone, back came the innumerable multitudes of insects, birds, and spirits, who are called the offspring of Hakuturi, and they raised up the tree upon its stump once more, and with a confused noise of various voices, they sang incantations as they worked, and when they had ended these, the tree again stood sound as ever in its former place in the forest.

The morning dawned, and Rata returned once more to work at his canoe. When he reached the place, was not he amazed to see the tree standing up in the forest, untouched, just as he had at first found it? But he, nothing daunted, hews away at it again, and down it topples crashing to the earth; as soon as he saw the tree upon the ground, Rata went off as if going home, and then turned back and hid himself in the underwood, in a spot whence he could peep out and see what took place; he had not been hidden long, when he heard the innumerable multitude of the children of Tane approaching die spot, singing their incantations as they came along; at last they arrived close to the place where the tree was lying upon the ground. Lo, a rush upon them is made by Rata. Ha, he has seized some of them; he shouts out to them, saying: 'Ha, ha, it is you, is it, then, who have been exercising your magical arts upon my tree?' Then the children of Tane all cried aloud in reply: 'Who gave you authority to fell the forest god to the ground? You had no right to do so.'

When Rata heard them say this, he was quite overcome with shame at what be had done.

The offspring of Tane again all called out aloud to him: 'Return, O Rata, to thy village, we will make a canoe for you.'

Rata, without delay, obeyed their orders, and as soon as he had gone they all fell to work; they were so numerous, and understood each what to do so well, that they no sooner began to adze out a canoe than it was completed. When they had done this, Rata and his tribe lost no time in hauling it from the forest to the water, and the name they gave to that canoe was Riwaru.

When the canoe was afloat upon the sea, 140 warriors embarked on board it, and without delay they paddled off to seek their foes; one night, just at nightfall, they reached the fortress of their enemies who were named Pona-turi. When they arrived there, Rata alone landed, leaving the canoe afloat and all his warriors on board; as be stole along the shore, he saw that a fire was burning on the sacred place, where the Ponaturi consulted their gods and offered sacrifices to them. Rata, without stopping, crept directly towards the fire, and bid himself behind some thick bushes of the Harakeke; [1] he then saw that there were some priests upon the other side of the same bushes, serving at the sacred place, and, to assist themselves in their magical arts, they were making use of the bones of Wahieroa, knocking them together to beat time while they were repeating a powerful incantation, known only to themselves, the name of which was Titikura. Rata listened attentively to this incantation, until he learnt it by heart, and when he was quite sure that he knew it, he rushed suddenly upon the priests; they, surprised and ignorant of the numbers of their enemy, or whence they came, made little resistance, and were in a moment smitten and slain. The bones of his father Wahieroa were then eagerly snatched up by him; he hastened with them back to the canoe, embarked on board it, and his warriors at once paddled away, striving to reach his fortified village.

In the morning some of the Ponaturi repaired to their sacred place, and found their priests lying dead there, just as they were slain by Rata. So, with-out delay, they pursued him. A thousand warriors of their tribe followed af-ter Rata. At length this army reached the fortress of Rata, and an engagement at once took place, in which the tribe of Rata was worsted, and sixty of its warriors slam; at this moment Rata bethought him of the spell he had learnt from the priests, and, immediately repeating the potent incantation, Titikura, his slain warriors were by its power once more restored to life; then they rushed again to the combat, and the Ponaturi were slaughtered by Rata and his tribe, a thousand of them--the whole thousand were slam.

Te Rata's task of avenging his father's death being thus ended, his tribe hauled up his large canoe on the shore, and roofed it over with thatch to pro-tect it from the sun and weather. Rata now took Tongarautawhiri as one of his wives, and she bore him a son whom he named Tuwhakararo; when this son came to man's estate, he took Apakura as one of his wives, and from her sprang a son named Whakatau. He was not born in the manner that mortals are, but came into being in this way: one day Apakura went down upon the sea-coast, and took off a little apron which she wore in front as a covering, and threw it into the ocean, and a god named Rongotakawiu took it and shaped it, and gave it form and being, and Whakatau sprang into life, and his ancestor Rongotakawiu taught him magic and the use of enchantments of every kind.

When Whakatau was a little lad, his favourite amusement was flying kites. Mortals then often observed kites flying in the air, and could see nothing else, for Whakatau was running about at the bottom of the waters, still holding the end of the string of the kite in his bands. One day he stole up out of the water by degrees, and at length came upon the shore, when the whole of his body was quite plainly seen by some people who were near, and they ran as fast as they could to catch him. When Whakatau observed them all running to seize him, he slipped back again into the water, and continued flying his kite as before; but the people who had seen him were surprised at this strange sight, and being determined to catch him the next time he came out, they sat down upon the bank to wait for him. At last Whakatau came up out of the water again, and stepped on shore once more; then the people who were watching for him, all ran at full speed to catch him. When Whakatau saw them coming after him again, he cried out: 'You had better go and bring Apakura here, she is the only person who can catch me and hold me fast.'

When they heard this, one of them ran to fetch Apakura, and she came with him at once, and as soon as she saw little Whakatau, she called out to him: 'Here I am, I am Apakura.' Whakatau then stopped running, and Apakura caught hold of him with her hands, and she questioned him, saying: 'Whom do you belong to? And Whakatau. answered her: 'I am your child; you one day threw the little apron which covered you on the sands of the sea, and the god Rongotakawiu, my ancestor, formed me from it, and I grew up a human being, and he named me Whakatau.'

From that time Whakatau left the water and continued to live on shore. His principal amusement, as long as he was a lad, was still flying kites; but he understood magic well, and nothing was concealed from him, and when he grew up to be a man he became a renowned hero.

This second legend of the destruction by Whakatau-potiki of the house called Te Tihi-o-Manono, or Te Uru-o-Manono, is added because it differs consistently from the other, and is often alluded to in ancient poems.

Tinirau determined to attempt to avenge the death of his descendant Tuhuruhuru, and he thought that the best person to do this was Whakatau, whom he knew to be very skilful in war, and in enchantments, so he directed his wife Hine-i-te-iwaiwa to find Whakatau, and she went in search; when she reached a village near where she expected to find him, she asked some people whom she saw, where Whakatau was, and they answered her: 'He is on the top of yonder hill flying a kite.' She at once proceeded on her way until she came to the hill, and seeing a man there, she asked him: 'Can you tell me where I can find Whakatau?'--and he replied: 'You must have passed him as you came here.' Then she returned to the village where she had seen the people, and said to them: 'Why, the man upon the hill says that Whakatau is here'; but they told her that the man who had spoken to her must have been Whakatau himself, and that she had better return to him, and told her marks by which she might know him; she therefore returned, and he, after some time, when she showed him that she knew certain marks about his person, admitted that he was Whakatau; and he then asked her what had made her come to him, and she replied: 'Tinirau sent me to you to ask you to come and assist in revenging the death of my son; the warriors are all collecting at the village of Tinirau, but they fear to go to attack this enemy, for it is the bravest of all the enemies of Tinirau.' Whakatau then asked her: 'Have you yet given a feast to the warriors?'--and she said, 'Not yet.' He then spoke to her, saying: 'Return at once and when you reach your village, give a great feast to the warriors; give them abundance of potted birds from the forest, but let all the oil in which the birds were preserved be kept for me; as for yourself, do not go to the feast, but, decking your head with a mourning dress of feathers, remain seated close in the house of mourning.' Then Hine-i-te-iwaiwa at once returned to Tinirau, to do as she had been directed.

Shortly after his visitor had left him, Whakatau called aloud to his people, saying: 'Let the side-boards be at once fresh lashed on to our canoe, to the canoe of our ancestor of Rata.' His men were so anxious to fulfil their chief's orders, that almost as soon as he had spoken they were at work, and had finished the canoe that very day, and dragged it down to the sea; when night fell, six of his warriors embarked in it, and Whakatau made the seventh; they then paddled off, following a direct course, until they reached the village of Tinirau where they found Hine-i-te-iwaiwa seated in her house of mourning. Whakatau then asked her: 'Have the warriors all left yet?'--and she replied: 'They will not do it, they are afraid.' Whakatau then said to her: 'Farewell, then; do you remain here until you hear further from me.'

Whakatau and his men having re-embarked in their canoe, made a straight course for the place where was situated the great house called Te Tihi-o-Manono, and they let their anchor drop, and floated there.

When the next morning broke, and some of the people of the village coming out of the house, and beyond their defences, saw the canoe floating at the anchorage, they gave the alarm, crying out: 'A war party! a war party!' Then the warriors came rushing forth to the fray in crowds, and arranged themselves in bands. Then stood forth one of their champions whose name was Mango-huritapena, and he defied Whakatau, who was standing up in his canoe, calling out: 'Were you fool enough, then, to come here of your own accord?'--and Whakatau answered him, by shouting out: 'Which of the arts of war do you consider yourself famous for?'--and Mango-huritapena shouted out in answer: 'I am a most skilful diver.' 'Dive here, then, if you dare', shouted out Whakatau in reply. Then the champion of the enemy gave a plunge into the water, and dived under it. just as he got right under the canoe, one of

58

Whakatau's men poured the oil which Hine-i-te-iwaiwa had given them into the sea, and its waters immediately became quite transparent, so that they saw the warrior come floating up under the canoe, and Whakatau transfixed him with a wooden spade; so that champion perished.

Then forward stepped another champion named Pitakataka, and he defied Whakatau, shouting out: 'Ah! You only killed Mango-huritapena because he chanced to put himself in a wrong position.' Whakatau shouted out in reply: 'Which of the arts of war are you skilled in, then?'--and he answered:

[paragraph continues] 'Oh! I leap so skilfully that I seem to fly in the air.' 'Then leap here, if you dare', answered Whakatau; and the champion of his enemies took a run and made a spring high into the air; but Whakatau laid a noose on the canoe, and as the warrior alighted in it, he drew it tight, and caught him as a bird in a springe, and thus slew that warrior also.

And thus, one after the other, he slew ten of the most famous warriors of his enemies; one whom he had seized, he saved alive, but he cut out his tongue, and then said to him: 'Now, off with you to the shore again, and tell them there bow I have overcome you all'; having done this, Whakatau retired a little distance back from the place, so that his canoe could not be seen by his enemies.

In the afternoon Whakatau landed on the coast, and before eating anything, offered the prescribed sacrifice of the hair and a part of the skin of the head of one of his victims to the gods; and when the religious rites were finished, he ate food; and having done this, he directed the people he had with him to return, saying: 'Return at once, and when you reach the residence of Hine-i-te-iwaiwa, speak to her, saying: "Whakatau told us to come, and tell you, that he could not return with us"';--and he further said: 'If heavy rain falls in large drops, it is a sign that I have been killed; but if a light, misty rain falls, and the whole horizon is lighted up with flames, then you may know that I have conquered, and that I have burnt Te Tihi-o-Manono'; he also said that 'he wished you to sit upon the roof of your house watching until you saw Te Tihi-o-Manono burnt.' Whakatau's people at once returned to Hine-i-te-iwaiwa to deliver the message he had given them.

Just before nightfall, Whakatau drew near the great house, called Te Tihi-o-Manono, and as the people of Whitinakonako, a great chief, were collecting firewood at the edge of a forest, he stealthily dropped in amongst them, pretending to be collecting firewood too; and as they were going home with their loads of firewood upon their backs, he managed to push on in front of them, and got into the house first with a long rope in his hand: one end of this he pushed between one of the side posts which supported the roof, and the plank walls of the house, and did the same with every post of the house, until the rope had gone quite round it, and then he made one end of it fast to the last post, and held the other end in his band.

By this time the people who lived in the house all came crowding in to pass the night in it, and soon filled it up: the house was so large, and there were so many of them, that they had to light ten fires in it.

59

When their fires had burnt up brightly, some of them called out to Mango-Pare, the man whom Whakatau bad saved alive, and whose tongue he had cut out: 'Well, now, tell us what kind of looking fellow that was who cut your tongue out'; and Mango-Pare answered: 'There is no one I can compare him to, he was not like a man in the proportion of his frame.' One of them then called out: 'Was he at all like me? But Mango-Pare answered: 'There is nobody I can compare him to.' Then another called out: 'Was he at all like me?'-and another: 'Was he like me?'--until, at length, Mango-Pare cried out: 'Have I not already told you, that there is not one of you whom I can compare to him?

Whakatau himself then exclaimed: 'Was he at all like me? And Mango-Pare, who had not before seen him in the crowd, looked attentively at him for a minute, and then cried out: 'I say, look here all of you at this fellow, he is not unlike the man, he looks very like him, perhaps it is he himself.' But Whakatau coolly asked him again: 'Was the man really something like me? And Mango-Pare replied: 'Yes, he was like you; I really think it was you'; and Whakatau shouted aloud: 'You are right, it was I.' As soon as they heard this, all of them in a moment sprang to their feet. But, at the same instant, Whakatau laid hold of the end of the rope which he had passed round the posts of the house, and, rushing out, pulled it with all his strength, and straightway the house fell down, crushing all within it, so that the whole tribe perished, and Whakatau, who had escaped to the outside of the house, set it on fire, and Hine-i-te-iwaiwa, who was sitting upon the roof of her own house watching for the event, saw the whole of one part of the heavens red with its flames, and she knew that her enemies were destroyed. Whakatau, having thus avenged the death of Tuhuruhuru the son of Tinirau, returned to his own village.

[1] New Zealand flax.

The Legend of Toi-te-huatahi and Tama-te-kapua

The Dissensions which led to the migrations from Hawaiki

OUR ancestors formerly separated--some of them were left in Hawaiki, and some came here in canoes. Tuamatau and Uenuku paddled in their canoes here to Aotea; again, at that time some of them were separated from each other, that is to say, Uenuku and Houmai-tawhiti.

For in the time of Houmai-tawhiti there had been a great war, and thence there were many battles fought in Hawaiki; but this war had commenced long before that time, in the days of Whakatauihu, of Tawhaki, and of Tuhuruhuru, when they carried off Kae alive from his place as a payment for Tutunui; and the war continued until the time of the disputes that arose on ac-

60

count of the body of warriors of Manaia. Again after that came the troubles that arose from the act of desecration that was committed by the dog of Houmai-tawhiti and of his sons in eating the matter that had sloughed from an ulcer of Uenuku's. Upon this occasion, when Toi-te-huatahi and Uenuku saw the dog, named Potaka-tawhiti, do this, they killed it, and the sons of Houmai-tawhiti missing the dog, went everywhere searching for it, and could not find it; they went from village to village, until at last they came to the village of Toi-te-huatahi, and as they went they kept calling his dog.

At last the dog howled in the belly of Toi' 'Ow!' Then Tama te-kapua and Whakaturia called their dog again, and again it howled 'Ow!' Then Toi' held his mouth shut as close as ever he could, but the dog still kept on howling in his inside. Thence Toi' said as follows, and his words passed into a proverb: 'O, hush, hush! I thought I had hid you in the big belly of Toi', and there you are, you cursed thing, still howling away.'

When Tama-te-kapua and his brother had thus arrived there, he asked: 'Why did you not kill the dog and bring it back to me, that my heart might have felt satisfied, and that we might have remained good friends? Now, I'll tell you what it is, O my relations, you shall by and by hear more of this.' Then as soon as the two brothers got home, they began immediately to make stilts for Tama-te-kapua, and as soon as these were finished, they started that night and went to the village of Toi' and Uenuku, and arrived at the fine poporo tree of Uenuku, covered with branches and leaves, and they remained eating the fruit of it for a good long time, and then went home again.

This they continued doing every night, until at last Uenuku and his people found that the fruit of his poporo tree was nearly all gone, and they all wondered what had become of the fruit of the poporo tree, and they looked for traces, and there were some--the traces of the stilts of Tama'. At night they kept watch on the tree: whilst one party was coming to steal, the other was lying in wait to catch them; this latter had not waited very long when Tama' and his brother came, and whilst they were busy eating, those who were lying in wait rushed upon them, and caught both of them.

They seized Whakaturia at the very foot of the tree; Tama' made his escape, but they gave chase, and caught him on the sea-shore. As soon as they had him firmly, those who were holding on cried out: 'Some of you chop down his stilts with an axe, so that the fellow may fall into the water'; and all those who had hold of him cried out: 'Yes, yes, let him fall into the sea.' Then Tama' called down to them: 'If you fell me in the water, I shall not be hurt, but if you cut me down on shore, the fall will kill me.' And when those who were behind, and were just running up, heard this, they thought well of it, so they chopped him down on shore, and down he came with a heavy fall, but in a moment he was on his feet, and off he went, like a bird escaped from a snare, and so got safe away.

Then all the village began to assemble to see Whakaturia put to death; and when they were collected, some of them said: 'Let him be put to death at once'; and others said: 'Oh, don't do that; you had much better hang him up

61

in the roof of Uenuku's house, that he may be stifled by the smoke, and die in that way.' And the thought pleased them all, so they hung him up in the roof of the house, and kindled a fire, and commenced dancing, and when that ceased they began singing, but their dancing and singing was not at all good, but indeed shockingly bad; and this they did every night, until at last a report of their proceedings reached the ears of his brother Tama' and of their father.

And Tama' heard: 'There's your brother hanging up in the roof of Uenuku's great house, and he is almost stifled by the smoke.' So he thought he would go and see him, and ascertain whether he still lived in spite of the smoke. He went in the night, and arrived at the house, and gently climbed right upon the top of the roof, and making a little hole in the thatch, immediately over the spot where his brother hung, asked him in a whisper: 'Are you dead?'--but he whispered up to him: 'No, I'm still alive.' And his brother asked again in a whisper: 'How do these people dance and sing, do they do it well?' And the other replied: 'No, nothing can be worse; the very bystanders do nothing but find fault with the way in which they dance and sing.'

Then Tama' said to him: 'Would not it be a good thing for you to say to them: "I never knew anything so bad as the dancing and singing of those people"; and if they reply: "Oh, perhaps you can dance and sing better than we do", do you answer: "That I can". Then if they take you down, and say: "Now, let us see your dancing", you can answer: "Oh I am quite filthy from the soot; you had better in the first place give me a little oil, and let me dress my hair, and give me some feathers to ornament my head with"; and, if they agree to all this, when your hair is dressed, perhaps they will say: "There, that will do, now dance and sing for us". Then do you answer them: "Oh, I am still looking quite dirty, first lend me the red apron of Uenuku, that I may wear it as my own, and his carved two-handed sword as my weapon, and then I shall really look fit to dance"; and if they give you all these things, then dance and sing for them. Then I your brother will go and seat myself just outside the doorway of the house, and when you rush out, I'll bolt the house-door and window, and when they try to pursue and catch you, the door and window will be bolted fast, and we two can escape without danger.' Then he finished talking to him.

Then Whakaturia called down to Uenuku, and to all his people, who were assembled in the house: 'Oh, all you people who are dancing and singing there, listen to me.' Then they all said: 'Silence, silence, make no more noise there, and listen to what the fellow is saying who is hanging up there; we thought he had been stifled by the smoke, but no such thing; there he is, alive still.' So they all kept quiet.

Then those who were in the house called up to him: 'Holloa, you fellow hanging up in the roof there, what are you saying; let's hear you.' And he answered: 'I mean to say that you don't know any good dances or songs, at least that I have heard.' Then the people in the house answered: 'Are you and your tribe famous for your dancing and singing then?'--and he answered: 'Their songs and dances are beautiful'; and they asked: 'Do you yourself know how to dance and sing?' Then Uenuku said: 'Let him down then'; and he was let down, and the people all called out to him: 'Now dance away.' And he did everything exactly as Tama-te-kapua had recommended him.

Then Whakaturia called out to them: 'Make a very bright fire, so that there may be no smoke, and you may see well'; and they made a bright clear fire. Then he stood up to dance, and as he rose from his seat on the ground, he looked bright and beautiful as the morning star appearing in the horizon, and as he flourished his sword his eyes flashed and glittered like the mother-of-pearl eyes in the head carved on the handle of his two-handed sword, and he danced down one side of the house, and reached the door, then he turned and danced up the other side of the house, and reached the end opposite the door, and there he stood.

Then he said quietly to them: 'I am dying with heat, just slide back the door, and let it stand open a little, that I may feel the cool air'; and they slid the door back and left it open. Then the lookers-on said: 'Come, you've rested enough; the fresh air from outside must have made you cool enough; stand up, and dance.' Then Whakaturia rose up again to dance, and as he rose up, Tama-te-kapua stepped up to the door of the house, and sat down there, with two sticks in his hand, all ready to bolt up the sliding door and window.

Then Whakaturia, as is the custom in the dance, turned round to his right hand, stuck out his tongue, and made hideous faces on that side; again he turned round to the left hand, and made hideous faces on that side; his eyes glared, and his sword and red apron looked splendid; then he sprung about, and appeared hardly to stand for a moment at the end of the house near the door, before he had sprung back to the other end, and standing just a moment there, he made a spring from the inside of the house, and immediately he was beyond the door. Up sprang Tama-te-kapua, and instantly bolted the door; back ran Whakaturia; he helped his brother to bolt up the window, and there they heard those inside cursing and swearing, and chattering like a hole full of young parrots, whilst away ran Tama' and his brother. A stranger who was presently passing by the house, pulled the bolts out of the door and window for them, and the crowd who had been shut into the house came pouring out of it.

The next morning Toi' and Uenuku felt vexed indeed, for the escape of those they had taken as a payment for the fruit of their luxuriant poporo tree, and said: 'If we had had the sense to kill them at once, they would never have escaped in this way. In the days which are coming, that fellow will return, seeking revenge for our having hung him up in the roof of the house.' And before long Uenuku and Toi-te-huatahi went to make war on Tama-te-kapua and his people, and some fell on both sides; and at length a breach in the fortifications of the town of Houmai-tawhiti and of his sons was entered by a storming party of Uenuku's force, and some of the fences and obstructions were carried; and the people of Houmai-tawhiti cried out: 'Oh, Hou', oh, here are the enemy pressing their way in'; and Houmai-tawhiti shouted in reply:

'That's right; let them in, let them in, till they reach the very threshold of the house of Houmai-tawhiti.' Thrice his men called out this to Hou', and thrice did he answer them in the same manner. At last up rose Hou' with his sons; then the struggle took place; those of the enemy that were not slain were allowed to escape back out of the town, but many of the slain were left there, and their bodies were cut up, baked, and devoured.

Then, indeed, a great crime was committed by Hou' and his family, and his warriors, in eating the bodies of those men, for they were their near relations, being descended from Tamatea-kai-ariki. Thence cowardice and fear seized upon the tribe of Hou': formerly they were all very brave indeed, but at last Hou' and all his tribe became cowardly, and fit for nothing, and Hou' and Whakaturia both died, but Tama-te-kapua and his children, and some of his relations, still lived, and he determined to make peace, that some remnant of his tribe might be saved; and the peace was long preserved.

The Legend of Poutini and Whaiapu

The Discovery of New Zealand

NOW pay attention to the cause of the contention which arose between Poutini and Whaiapu, which led them to emigrate to New Zealand. For a long time they both rested in the same place, and Hine-tu-a-hoanga, to whom the stone Whaiapu [1] belonged, became excessively enraged with Ngahue, and with his prized stone Poutini. [2] At last she drove Ngahue out and forced him to leave the place, and Ngahue departed and went to a strange land, taking his jasper. When Hine-tu-a-hoanga saw that he was departing with his precious stone, she followed after them, and Ngahue arrived at Tuhua with his stone, and Hine-tu-a-hoanga arrived and landed there at the same time with him, and began to drive him away again. Then Ngahue went to seek a place where his jasper might remain in peace, and be found in the sea this island Aotearoa (the northern island of New Zealand), and he thought he would land there.

Then he thought again, lest he and his enemy should be too close to one another, and should quarrel again, that it would be better for him to go farther off with his jasper, a very long way off. So he carried it off with him, and they coasted along, and at length arrived at Arahura (on the west coast of the middle island), and he made that an everlasting resting-place for his jasper; then he broke off a portion of his jasper, and took it with him and returned, and as be coasted along lie at length reached Wairere (believed to be upon the east coast of the northern island), and he visited Whangaparaoa and Tauranga, and from thence he returned direct to Hawaiki, and reported that he had discovered a new country which produced the moa and jasper in abundance. He now manufactured sharp axes from his jasper; two axes were made from it, Tutauru and Hau-hau-te-rangi. He manufactured some portions of one piece of it into images for neck ornaments, and some portions into ear ornaments; the name of one of these ear ornaments was Kaukaumatua, which was recently in the possession of Te Heuheu, and was only lost in 1846, when he was killed with so many of his tribe by a landslip. The axe Tutauru was only lately lost by Purahokura and his brother Reretai, who were descended from Tama-ihu-toroa. When Ngahue, returning, arrived again in Hawaiki, he found them all engaged in war, and when they heard his description of the beauty of this country of Aotea, some of them determined to come here.

Construction of Canoes to Emigrate to New Zealand

They then felled a totara tree in Rarotonga, which lies on the other side of Hawaiki, that they might build the Arawa from it. The tree was felled, and thus the canoe was hewn out from it and finished. The names of the men who built this canoe were, Rata, Wahie-roa, Ngahue, Parata, and some other skilful men, who helped to hew out the Arawa and to finish it.

A chief of the name of Hotu-roa, hearing that the Arawa was built, and wishing to accompany them, came to Tama-te-kapua and asked him to lend him his workmen to hew out some canoes for him too, and they went and built and finished Tainui and some other canoes.

The workmen above mentioned are those who built the canoes in which our forefathers crossed the ocean to this island, to Aotea-roa. The names of the canoes were as follows: the Arawa was first completed, then Tainui, then Matatua, and Taki-tumu, and Kura-hau-po, and Tokomaru, and Matawhao-rua. These are the names of the canoes in which our forefathers departed from Hawaiki, and crossed to this island. When they had lashed the topsides on to the Tainui, Rata slew the son of Manaia, and bid his body in the chips and shavings of the canoes. The names of the axes with which they hewed out these canoes were Hauhau-te-Rangi, and Tutauru. Tutauru was the axe with which they cut off the head of Uenuku.

All these axes were made from the block of jasper brought back by Ngahue to Hawaiki, which was called 'The fish of Ngahue'. He had previously come to these islands from Hawaiki, when he was driven out from thence by Hine-tu-a-hoanga, whose fish or stone was obsidian. From that cause Ngahue came to these islands; the canoes which afterwards arrived here came in consequence of his discovery.

[1] Green jasper.
[2] Obsidian, with which the natives grind down the jasper.

The Voyage to New Zealand

WHEN the canoes were built and ready for sea, they ere dragged afloat, the separate lading of each canoe as collected and put on board, with all the crews. Tama-te-kapua then remembered that he had no skilful priest on board his canoe, and he thought the best thing he could do was to outwit Ngatoro-i-rangi, the chief who had command of the Tainui. So just as his canoe shoved off, he called out to Ngatoro: 'I say, Ngatoro, just come on board my canoe, and perform the necessary religious rites for me.' Then the priest Ngatoro came on board, and Tama-te-kapua said to him: 'You had better also call your wife, Kearoa on board, that she may make the canoe clean or common, with an offering of sea-weed to be laid in the canoe instead of an offering of fish, for you know the second fish caught in a canoe, or seaweed, or some substitute, ought to be offered for the females, the first for the males; then my canoe will be quite common, for all the ceremonies will have been observed, which should be followed with canoes made by priests.' Ngatoro assented to all this, and called his wife, and they both go into Tama's canoe. The very moment they were on board, Tama' called out to the men on board his canoe: 'Heave up the anchors and make sail'; and he carried off with him Ngatoro and his wife, that he might have a priest and wise man on board his canoe. Then they up with the fore-sail, the main-sail, and the mizen, and away shot the canoe.

Up then came Ngatoro from below, and said: 'Shorten sail, that we may go more slowly, lest I miss my own canoe.' And Tama' replied: 'Oh, no, no; wait a little, and your canoe will follow after us.' For a short time it kept near them, but soon dropped more and more astern, and when darkness overtook them, on they sailed, each canoe proceeding on its own course.

Two thefts were upon this occasion perpetrated by Tama-te-kapua; he carried off the wife of Ruaeo, and Ngatoro and his wife, on board the Arawa. He made a fool of Ruaeo too, for he said to him: 'Oh, Rua', you, like a good fellow, just run back to the village and fetch me my axe Tutauru, I pushed it in under the sill of the window of my house.' And Rua' was foolish enough to run back to the house. Then off went Tama' with the canoe, and when Rua' came back again, the canoe was so far off that its sails did not look much bigger than little flies. So he fell to weeping for all his goods on board the canoe, and for his wife Whakaoti-rangi, whom Tama-te-kapua had carried off as a wife for himself. Tama-te-kapua committed these two great thefts when he sailed for these islands. Hence this proverb: 'A descendant of Tama-te-kapua will steal anything he can.'

When evening came on, Rua' threw himself into the water, as a preparation for his incantations to recover his wife, and he then changed the stars of evening into the stars of morning, and those of the morning into the stars of the evening, and this was accomplished. In the meantime the Arawa scudded away far out on the ocean, and Ngatoro thought to himself. 'What a rate this canoe goes at--what a vast space we have already traversed. I know what I'll do, I'll climb up upon the roof of the house which is built on the platform joining the two canoes, and try to get a glimpse of the land in the horizon, and ascertain whether we are near it, or very far off.' But in the first place he felt some suspicions about his wife, lest Tama-te-kapua should steal her too, for he had found out what a treacherous person he was. So he took a string and tied one end of it to his wife's hair, and kept the other end of the string in his hand, and then he climbed up on the roof. He had hardly got on the top of the roof when Tama' laid hold of his wife, and he cunningly untied the end of the string which Ngatoro had fastened to her hair, and made it fast to one of the beams of the canoe, and Ngatoro feeling it tight thought his wife had not moved, and that it was still fast to her. At last Ngatoro came down again, and Tama-te-kapua heard the noise of his steps as he was coming, but he had not time to get the string tied fast to the hair of Kearoa's head again, but he jumped as fast as he could into his own berth, which was next to that of Nga-toro, and Ngatoro, to his surprise, found one end of the string tied fast to the beam of the canoe.

Then he knew that his wife had been disturbed by Tama', and he asked her, saying: 'Oh, wife, has not some one disturbed you? Then his wife replied to him: 'Cannot you tell that from the string being fastened to the beam of the canoe? And then he asked her: 'Who was it? And she said: 'Who was it, indeed? Could it be anyone else but Tama-te-kapua?' Then her husband said to her: 'You are a noble woman indeed thus to confess this; you have gladdened my heart by this confession; I thought after Tama' had carried us both off in this way, that he would have acted generously, and not loosely in this manner; but, since he has dealt in this way, I will now have my revenge on him.'

Then that priest again went forth upon the roof of the house and stood there, and he called aloud to the heavens, in the same way that Rua' did, and he changed the stars of the evening into those of morning, and he raised the winds that they should blow upon the prow of the canoe, and drive it astern, and the crew of the canoe were at their wits' end, and quite forgot their skill as seamen, and the canoe drew straight into the whirlpool, called 'The throat of Te Parata', [1] and dashed right into that whirlpool.

The canoe became engulfed by the whirlpool, and its prow disappeared in it. In a moment the waters reached the first bailing place in the bows, in another second they reached the second bailing place in the centre, and the canoe now appeared to be going down into the whirlpool head foremost; then up started Hei, but before he could rise they had already sunk far into the whirlpool. Next the rush of waters was heard by Ihenga, who slept forward, and he shouted out: 'Oh, Ngatoro, oh, we are settling down head first. The pillow of your wife Kearoa has already fallen from under her head!' Ngatoro sat astern listening; the same cries of distress reached him a second time. Then up sprang Tama-te-kapua, and he in despair shouted out: 'Oh, Ngatoro, Ngatoro, aloft there! Do you hear? The canoe is gone down so much by the bow, that Kearoa's pillow has rolled from under her head.' The priest heard them, but neither moved nor answered until he heard the goods rolling from the decks and splashing into the water; the crew meanwhile held on to the canoe with their hands with great difficulty, some of them having already fallen into the sea.

When these things all took place, the heart of Ngatoro was moved with pity, for he heard, too, the shrieks and cries of the men, and the weeping of the women and children. Then up stood that mighty man again, and by his incantations changed the aspect of the heavens, so that the storm ceased,

and he repeated another incantation to draw the canoe back out of the whirlpool, that is, to lift it up again.

Lo, the canoe rose up from the whirlpool, floating rightly; but, although the canoe itself thus floated out of the whirlpool, a great part of its lading had been thrown out into the water, a few things only were saved, and remained in the canoe. A great part of their provisions were lost as the canoe was sinking into the whirlpool. Thence comes the native proverb, if they can give a stranger but little food, or only make a present of a small basket of food: 'Oh, it is the half-filled basket of Whakaoti-rangi, for she only managed to save a very small part of her provisions.' Then they sailed on, and landed at Whanga-Paraoa, In Aotea here. As they drew near to land, they saw with surprise some pohutukawa trees of the sea-coast, covered with beautiful red flowers, and the still water reflected back the redness of the trees.

Then one of the chiefs of the canoe cried out to his messmates: 'See there, red ornaments for the head are much more plentiful in this country than in Hawaiki, so I'll throw my red head ornaments into the water'; and, so saying, he threw them into the sea. The name of that man was Tauninihi; the name of the red head ornament he threw into the sea was Taiwhakaea. The moment they got on shore they ran to gather the pohutukawa flowers, but no sooner did they touch them than the flowers fell to pieces; then they found out that these red head ornaments were nothing but flowers. All the chiefs on board the Arawa were then troubled that they should have been so foolish as to throw away their red ornaments into the sea. Very shortly afterwards the ornaments of Tauninihi were found by Mahina on the beach of Mahiti. As soon as Tauninihi heard they had been picked up, he ran to Mahina to get them again, but Mahina would not give them up to him; thence this proverb for anything which has been lost and is found by another person: 'I will not give it up, 'tis the red head ornament which Mahina found.'

As soon as the party landed at Whanga-Paraoa, they planted sweet potatoes, that they might grow there; and they are still to be found growing on the cliffs at that place.

Then the crew, wearied from the voyage, wandered idly along the shore, and there they found the fresh carcase of a sperm whale stranded upon the beach. The Tainui had already arrived in the same neighbourhood, although they did not at first see that canoe nor the people who had come in it; when, however, they met, they began to dispute as to who had landed first and first found the dead whale, and as to which canoe it consequently belonged; so, to settle the question, they agreed to examine the sacred place which each party had set up to return thanks in to the gods for their safe arrival, that they might see which had been longest built; and, doing so, they found that the posts of the sacred place put up by the Arawa were quite green, whilst the posts of the sacred place set up by the Tainui had evidently been carefully dried over the fire before they had been fixed in the ground. The people who had come in the Tainui also showed part of a rope which they had made fast to its jaw-bone. When these things were seen, it was admitted that the whale belonged to the people who came in the Tainui, and it was surrendered to them. And the people in the Arawa, determining to separate from those in the Tainui, selected some of their crew to explore the country in a north-west direction, following the coast line. The canoe then coasted along, the land party following it along the shore; this was made up of 140 men, whose chief was Taikehu, and these gave to a place the name of Te Ranga of Taikehu.

The Tainui left Whanga-Paraoa [2] shortly after the Arawa, and, proceeding nearly in the same direction as the Arawa, made the Gulf of Hauraki, and then coasted along to Rakau-mangamanga, or Cape Brett, and to the island with an arched passage through it, called Motukokako, which lies off the cape; thence they ran along the coast to Whiwhia, and to Te Aukanapanapa, and to Muri-whenua, or the country near the North Cape. Finding that the land ended there, they returned again along the coast until they reached the Tamaki, and landed there, and afterwards proceeded up the creek to Tau-oma, or the portage, where they were surprised to see flocks of sea-gulls and oyster-catchers passing over from the westward; so they went off to explore the country in that direction, and to their great surprise found a large sheet of water lying immediately behind them, so they determined to drag their canoes over the portage at a place they named Otahuhu, and to launch them again on the vast sheet of salt-water which they had found.

The first canoe which they hauled across was the Tokomaru--that they got across without difficulty. They next began to drag the Tainui over the isthmus; they hauled away at it in vain, they could not stir it; for one of the wives of Hotu-roa, named Marama-kiko-hura, who was unwilling that the tired crews should proceed further on this new expedition, had by her enchantments fixed it so firmly to the earth that no human strength could stir it; so they hauled, they hauled, they excited themselves with cries and cheers, but they hauled in vain, they cried aloud in vain, they could not move it. When their strength was quite exhausted by these efforts, then another of the wives of Hotu-roa, more learned in magic and incantations than Marama-kiko-hura, grieved at seeing the exhaustion and distress of her people, rose up, and chanted forth an incantation far more powerful than that of Marama-kiko-hura; then at once the canoe glided easily over the carefully-laid skids, and it soon floated securely upon the harbour of Manuka. The willing crews urged on the canoes with their paddles; they soon discovered the mouth of the harbour upon the west coast, and passed out through it into the open sea;

they coasted along the western coast to the southwards, and discovering the small port of Kawhia, they entered it, and, hauling up their canoe, fixed themselves there for the time, whilst the Arawa was left at Maketu.

We now return to the Arawa. We left the people of it at Tauranga. That canoe next floated at Motiti; [3] they named that place after a spot in Hawaiki (because there was no firewood there). Next Tia, to commemorate his name, called the place now known by the name of Rangiuru, Takapu-o-tapui-ika-nui-a-Tia. Then Hei stood up and called out: 'I name that place Takapu-o-wai-tahanui-a-Hei'; the name of that place is now Otawa. Then stood up Tama-te-kapua, and pointing to the place now called the Heads of Maketu, he called out: 'I name that place Te Kuraetanga-o-te-ihu-o-Tama-te-kapua.' Next Kahn called a place after his name, Motiti-nui-a-Kahu.

Ruaeo, who had already arrived at Maketu, started up. He was the first to arrive there in his canoe--Pukeatea-wai-nui--for he had been left behind by the Arawa, and his wife Whakaoti-rangi had been carried off by Tama-te-kapua, and after the Arawa had left he had sailed in his own canoe for these islands, and landed at Maketu, and his canoe reached land the first; well, he started up, cast his line into the sea, with the hooks attached to it, and they got fast in one of the beams of the Arawa, and it was pulled ashore by him (whilst the crew were asleep), and the hundred and forty men who had accompanied him stood upon the beach of Maketu, with skids all ready laid, and the Arawa was by them dragged upon the shore in the night, and left there; and Ruaeo seated himself under the side of the Arawa, and played upon his flute, and the music woke his wife, and she said: 'Dear me, that's Rua'!'--and when she looked, there he was sitting under the side of the canoe; and they passed the night together.

At last Rua' said: 'O mother of my children, go back now to your new husband, and presently I'll play upon the flute and putorino, so that both you and Tama-te-kapua may hear. Then do you say to Tama-te-kapua "O! la, I had a dream in the night that I heard Rua' playing a tune upon his flute", and that will make him so jealous that be will give you a blow, and then you can run away from him again, as if you were in a rage and hurt, and you can come to me.'

Then Whakaoti-rangi returned, and lay down by Tama-te-kapua, and she did everything exactly as Rua' had told her, and Tama' began to beat her (and she ran away from him). Early in the morning Rua' performed incantations, by which he kept all the people in the canoe in a profound sleep, and whilst they still slept from his enchantments, the sun rose, and mounted high up in the heavens. In the forenoon, Rua' gave the canoe a heavy blow with his club; they all started up; it was almost noon, and when they looked down over the edge of their canoe, there were the hundred and forty men of Rua' sitting under them, all beautifully dressed with feathers, as if they had been living on the Gannet Island, in the channel of Karewa, where feathers are so abundant; and when the crew of the Arawa heard this, they all rushed upon deck, and saw Rua' standing in the midst of his one hundred and forty warriors.

Then Rua' shouted out as he stood: 'Come here, Tama-te-kapua; let us two fight the battle, you and I alone. If you are stronger than I am, well and good, let it be so; if I am stronger than you are, I'll dash you to the earth.'

Up sprang then the hero Tama-te-kapua; he held a carved two-handed sword, a sword the handle of which was decked with red feathers. Rua' held a similar weapon. Tama' first struck a fierce blow at Rua'. Rua' parried it, and it glanced harmlessly off; then Rua' threw away his sword, and seized both the arms of Tama-te-kapua; he held his arms and his sword, and dashed him to the earth. Tama' half rose, and was again dashed down; once more he almost rose, and was thrown again. Still Tama' fiercely struggled to rise and renew the fight. For the fourth time he almost rose up, then Rua', overcome with rage, took a heap of vermin (this he had prepared for the purpose, to cover Tama' with insult and shame), and rubbed them on Tama-te-kapua's head and ear, and they adhered so fast that Tama' tried in vain to get them out.

Then Rua' said: 'There, I've beaten you; now keep the woman, as a payment for the insults I've heaped upon you, and for having been beaten by me.' But Tama' did not hear a word he said; he was almost driven mad with pain and itching, and could do nothing but stand scratching and rubbing his head; whilst Rua' departed with his hundred and forty men to seek some other dwelling-place for themselves; if they had turned against Tama' and his people to fight against them, they would have slain them all.

These men were giants--Tama-te-kapua was nine feet high, Rua' was eleven feet high: there have been no men since that time so tall as those heroes. The only man of these later times who was as tall as these was Tu-hou-rangi: he was nine feet high; he was six feet up to the arm-pits. This generation have seen his bones, they used to be always set up by the priests in the sacred places when they were made high places for the sacred sacrifices of the natives, at the times the potatoes and sweet potatoes were dug up, and when the fishing season commenced, and when they attacked an enemy; then might be seen the people collecting, in their best garments, and with their ornaments, on the days when the priests exposed Tu-hou-rangi's bones to their view. At the time that the island Mokoia, in the lake of Roto-rua, was stormed and taken by the Nga-Puhi, they probably carried those bones off, for they have not since been seen.

After the dispute between Tama-te-kapua and Rua' took place, Tama' and his party dwelt at Maketu, and their descendants after a little time spread to other places. Ngatoro-i-rangi went, however, about the country, and where be found dry valleys, stamped on the earth, and brought forth springs of water; be also visited the mountains, and placed Patupaiarehe, or fairies, there, and then returned to Maketu and dwelt there.

After this a dispute arose between Tama-te-kapua and Kahu-mata-momoe, and in consequence of that disturbance, Tama' and Ngatoro removed to Tauranga, and found Taikehu living there, and collecting food for them (by fishing), and that place was called by them *Te Ranga-a-Taikehu*; [4] it lies beyond

71

Motu-hoa; then they departed from Tauranga, and stopped at Kati-kati, where they ate food. Tama's men devoured the food very fast, whilst he kept on only nibbling his, therefore they applied this circumstance as a name for the place, and called it: 'Kati-kati-o-Tama-te-kapua', the nibbling of Tama-te-kapua; they then halted at Whakahau, so called because they here ordered food to be cooked, which they did not stop to eat, but went right on with Ngatoro, and this circumstance gave its name to the place; and they went on from place to place till they arrived at Whitianga, which they so called from their crossing the river there, and they continued going from one place to another till they came to Tangiaro, and Ngatoro, stuck up a stone and left it there, and they dwelt in Moehau and Hauraki.

They occupied those places as a permanent residence, and Tama-te-kapua died, and was buried there. When he was dying, he ordered his children to return to Maketu, to visit his relations; and they assented, and went back. If the children of Tama-te-kapua had remained at Hauraki, that place would not have been left to them as a possession.

Tama-te-kapua, when dying, told his children where the precious ear-drop Kaukau-matua was, which he had hidden under the window of his house; and his children returned with Ngatoro to Maketu, and dwelt there; and as soon as Ngatoro arrived, he went to the waters to bathe himself, as he had come there in a state of *tapu*, upon account of his having buried Tama-te-kapua, and having bathed, he then became free from the *tapu* and clean.

Ngatoro then took the daughter of Ihenga to wife, and he went and searched for the precious ear-drop Kaukau-matua, and found it, as Tama-te-kapua had told him. After this the Wife of Kahu-mata-momoe conceived a child.

At this time Ihenga, taking some dogs with him to catch kiwi [5] with, went to Paritangi by way of Hakomiti, and a kiwi was chased by one of his dogs, and caught in a lake, and the dog ate some of the fish and shell-fish in the lake, after diving in the water to get them, and returned to its master carrying the captured kiwi in its mouth, and on reaching its master, it dropped the kiwi, and vomited up the raw fish and shell-fish which it had eaten.

When Ihenga saw his dog wet all over, and the fish it had vomited up, he knew there was a lake there, and was extremely glad, and returned joyfully to Maketu, and there he had the usual religious ceremonies which follow the birth of a child performed over his wife and the child she had given birth to; and when this had been done, he went to explore the country which he bad previously visited with his dog.

To his great surprise he discovered a lake; it was Lake Roto-iti; he left a mark there to show that he claimed it as his own. He went farther and discovered Lake Roto-rua; he saw that its waters were running; he left there also a mark to show that he claimed the lake as his own. As he went along the side of the lake, he found a man occupying the ground; then he thought to himself that he would endeavour to gain possession of it by craft, so he looked out for a spot fit for a sacred place, where men could offer up their prayers, and for another spot fit for a sacred place, where nets could be hung up, and he found fit spots; then he took suitable stones to surround the sacred place with, and old pieces of seaweed, looking as if they had years ago been employed as offerings, and he went into the middle of the shrubbery, thick with boughs of the taha shrub, of the koromuka, and of the karamu; there he struck up the posts of the sacred place in the midst of the shrubs, and tied bunches of flax-leaves on the posts, and having done this he went to visit the village of the people who lived there.

They saw someone approaching and cried out: 'A stranger, a stranger, is coming here!' As soon as Ihenga heard these cries, he sat down upon the ground, and then, without waiting for the people of the place to begin the speeches, he jumped up, and commenced to speak thus: 'What theft is this, what theft is this of the people here, that they are taking away my land?'--for he saw that they had their store-houses full of prepared fern-roots and of dried fish, and shell-fish, and their heaps of fishing-nets, so as he spoke, he appeared to swell with rage, and his throat appeared to grow large from passion as he talked: 'Who authorized you to come here, and take possession of my place? Be off, be off, be off! Leave alone the place of the man who speaks to you, to whom it has belonged for a very long time, for a very long time indeed.'

Then Maru-punga-nui, the son of Tu-a-roto-rua, the man to whom the place really belonged, said to Ihenga: 'It is not your place, it belongs to me; if it belongs to you, where is your village, where is your sacred place, where is your net, where are your cultivations and gardens?

Ihenga answered him: 'Come here and see them.' So they went together, and ascended a hill, and Ihenga said: 'See there, there is my net hanging up against the rocks.' But it was no such thing, it was only a mark like a net hanging up, caused by part of a cliff having slipped away; 'and there are the posts of the pine round my village'; but there was really nothing but some old stumps of trees; 'look there too at my sacred place a little beyond yours; and now come with me, and see my sacred place, if you are quite sure you see my village, and my fishing-net--come along.' So they went together, and there he saw the sacred place standing in the shrubbery, until at last he believed Ihenga, and the place was all given up to Ihenga, and he took possession of it and lived there, and the descendants of Tu-a-roto-rua departed from that place, and a portion of them, under the chiefs Kawa-arero and Mata-aho, occupied the island of Mokoia, in Lake Roto-rua.

At this time Ngatoro again went to stamp on the earth, and to bring forth springs in places where there was no water, and came out on the great central plains which surround Lake Taupo, where a piece of large cloak made of kiekie-leaves was stripped off by the bushes, and the strips took root, and became large trees, nearly as large as the Kahikatea (they are called Painanga, and many of them are growing there still).

Whenever he ascended a hill, he left marks there, to show that he claimed it; the marks he left were fairies. Some of the generation now living have

73

seen these spirits; they are malicious spirits. If you take embers from an oven in which food has been cooked, and use them for a fire in a house, these spirits become offended; although there be many people sleeping in that house, not one of them could escape (the fairies would, whilst they slept, press the whole of them to death).

Ngatoro went straight on and rested at Taupo, and he beheld that the summit of Mount Tongariro was covered with snow, and he was seized with a longing to ascend it, and he climbed up, saying to his companions who remained below at their encampment: 'Remember now, do not you, who I am going to leave behind, taste food from the time I leave you until I return, when we will all feast together.' Then he began to ascend the mountain, but he had not quite got to the summit when those he had left behind began to eat food, and he therefore found the greatest difficulty in reaching the summit of the mountain, and the hero nearly perished in the attempt.

At last he gathered strength, and thought he could save himself, if he prayed aloud to the gods of Hawaiki to send fire to him, and to produce a volcano upon the mountain; (and his prayer was answered,) and fire was given to him, and the mountain became a volcano, and it came by the way of Whakaari, or White Island, of Mau-tohora, of Okakaru, of Roto-ehu, of Roto-iti, of Roto-rua, of Tara-wera, of Pae-roa, of Orakeikorako, and of Taupo; it came right underneath the earth, spouting up at all the above-mentioned places, and ascended right up Tongariro, to him who was sitting upon the top of the mountain, and thence the hero was revived again, and descended, and returned to Maketu, and dwelt there.

The Arawa had been laid up by its crew at Maketu, where they landed, and the people who had arrived with the party in the Arawa spread themselves over the country, examining it, some penetrating to Roto-rua, some to Taupo, some to Whanganui, some to Ruatahuna, and no one was left at Maketu but Hei and his son, and Tia and his son, and the usual place of residence of Ngatoro-i-rangi was on the island of Motiti. The people who came with the Tainui were still in Kawhia, where they had landed.

One of their chiefs, named Raumati, heard that the Arawa was laid up at Maketu, so he started with all his own immediate dependants, and reaching Tauranga, halted there, and in the evening again pressed on towards Maketu, and reached the bank of the river, opposite that on which the Arawa was lying, thatched over with reeds and dried branches and leaves; then he slung a dart, the point of which was bound round with combustible materials, over to the other side of the river; the point of the dart was lighted, and it stuck right in the dry thatch of the roof over the Arawa, and the shed of dry stuff taking fire, the canoe was entirely destroyed.

On the night that the Arawa was burnt by Raumati, there was not a person left at Maketu; they were all scattered in the forests, at Tapu-ika, and at Waitaha, and Ngatoro-i-rangi was at that moment at his residence on the island of Motiti. The *pa*, or fortified village at Maketu, was left quite empty, without a soul in it. The canoe was lying alone, with none to watch it; they had all gone to collect food of different kinds--it happened to be a season in which food was very abundant, and from that cause the people were all scattered in small parties about the country, fishing, fowling, and collecting food.

As soon as the next morning dawned, Raumati could see that the fortified village of Maketu was empty, and not a person left in it, so he and his armed followers at once passed over the river and entered the village, which they found entirely deserted.

At night, as the Arawa burnt, the people, who were scattered about in the various parts of the country, saw the fire, for the bright glare of the gleaming flames was reflected in the sky, lighting up the heavens, and they all thought that it was the village at Maketu that had been burnt; but those persons who were near Waitaha and close to the sea-shore near where the Arawa was, at once said: 'That must be the Arawa which is burning; it must have been accidentally set on fire by some of our friends who have come to visit us.' The next day they went to see what had taken place, and when they reached the place where the Arawa had been lying, they found it had been burnt by an enemy, and that nothing but the ashes of it were left them. Then a messenger started to all the places where the people were scattered about, to warn them of what had taken place, and they then first heard the bad news.

The children of Hou, as they discussed in their house of assembly the burning of the Arawa, remembered the proverb of their father, which he spake to them as they were on the point of leaving Hawaiki, and when be bid them farewell.

He then said to them: 'O my children, O Mako, O Tia, O Hei, hearken to these my words: there was but one great chief in Hawaiki, and that was Whakatauihu. Now do you, my dear children, depart in peace, and when you reach the place you are going to, do not follow after the deeds of Tu', the god of war; if you do you will perish, as if swept off by the winds, but rather follow quiet and useful occupations, then you will die tranquilly a natural death. Depart, and dwell in peace with all, leave war and strife behind you here. Depart, and dwell in peace. It is war and its evils which are driving you from hence; dwell in peace where you are going, conduct yourselves like men, let there be no quarrelling amongst you, but build up a great people.'

These were the last words which Houmai-tawhiti addressed to his children, and they ever kept these sayings of their father firmly fixed in their hearts. 'Depart in peace to explore new homes for yourselves.'

Uenuku perhaps gave no such parting words of advice to his children, when they left him for this country, because they brought war and its evils with them from the other side of the ocean to New Zealand. But, of course, when Raumati burnt the Arawa, the descendants of Houmai-tawhiti could not help continually considering what they ought to do, whether they should declare war upon account of the destruction of their canoe, or whether they should let this act pass by without notice. They kept these thoughts always close in mind, and impatient feelings kept ever rising up in their hearts. They could not help saying to one another: 'It was upon account of war and its consequences, that we deserted our own country, that we left our fathers, our homes, and our people, and war and evil are following after us here. Yet we cannot remain patient under such an injury, every feeling urges us to revenge this wrong.'

At last they made an end of deliberation, and unanimously agreed that they would declare war, to obtain compensation for the evil act of Raumati in burning the Arawa; and then commenced the great war which was waged between those who arrived in the Arawa and those who arrived in the Tainui.

[1] The Maoris have another name for this whirlpool; they call it 'the steep descent where the world ends.'
[2] Whanga-Paraoa, the bay of the sperm whale, so called from the whale found there.
[3] Kai Motiti koe e noho ana, 'I suppose you are at Motiti, as you can find no firewood.'
[4] The fishing bank of Taikehu.
[5] Apterix australis.

The Curse of Manaia

(Ko Manaia, ko Kuiwai)

WHEN the Tainui and the Arawa sailed away from Hawaiki with Ngatoro-i-rangi on board, he left behind him his younger sister, Kuiwai, who was married to a powerful chief named Manaia. Some time after the canoes had left, a great meeting of all the people of his tribe was held by Manaia, to remove a *tapu*, and when the religious part of the ceremony was ended, the women cooked food for the strangers.

When their ovens were opened, the food in the oven of Kuiwai, the wife of Manaia, and sister of Ngatoro-i-rangi, was found to be much under done, and Manaia was very angry with his wife, and gave her a severe beating, and cursed, saying: 'Accursed be your head; are the logs of firewood as sacred as the bones of your brother, that you were so sparing of them as not to put into the fire in which the stones were heated enough to make them red hot? Will you dare to do the like again? If you do I'll serve the flesh of your brother in the same way, it shall frizzle on the red-hot stones of Waikorora.'

And his poor wife was quite overcome with shame, and burst out crying, and went on sobbing and weeping all the time she was taking the under-done food out of the oven, and when she had put it in baskets, and earned them up to her husband, and laid them before him, she ate nothing herself, but went on one side and cried bitterly, and then retired and hid herself in the house.

76

And just before night closed in on them, she cast her garments on one side, and girded herself with a new sash made from the young shoots of the toe-toe, and stood on the threshold, and spread out her gods, Kahukura, Itupawa, and Rongomai, and she and her daughter, and her sister Haungaroa, stood before them, and the appearance of the gods was most propitious; and when her incantations were ended, she said to her daughter: 'My child, your journey will be a most fortunate one.' The gods were then by her bound up in cloths, and she hung them up again, and returned into the house.

She then said to her daughter: 'Now depart, and when you reach your uncle Ngatoro, and your other relations, tell them that they have been cursed by Manaia, because the food in my oven was not cooked upon the occasion of a great assembly for taking off a *tapu*, and that he then said: "Are the logs in the forest as sacred as the bones of your brother, that you are afraid to use them in cooking; or are the stones of the desert the kidneys of Ngatoro-i-rangi, that you don't heat them; by and by I'll frizzle the flesh of your brother on red-hot stones taken from Waikorora." Now, my child, depart to your uncle and relations; be quick, this is the season of the wind of Pungawere, which will soon waft them here.'

The women then took by stealth the gods of the people, that is to say, Maru, and Te Iho-o-te-rangi, and Rongomai, and Itupawa, and Haungaroa, and they had no canoe for their journey, but these gods served them as a canoe to cross the sea. For the first canoes which had left Hawaiki for New Zealand carried no gods for human beings with them; they only carried the gods of the sweet potatoes and of fish, they left behind them the gods for mortals, but they brought away with them prayers, incantations, and a knowledge of enchantments, for these things were kept secret in their minds, being learnt by heart, one from another.

Then the girl and her companions took with them Kahukura, and Itupawa, and Rongomai, and Marti, and the other gods, and started on their journey; altogether there were five women, and they journeyed and journeyed towards New Zealand, and, borne up by the gods, they traversed the vast ocean till at last they landed on the burning island of Whakaari, and when daylight appeared, they floated again on the waters, and finally landed on the northern island of New Zealand, at Tawhiuwhiu, and went by an inland route, and stopped to eat food at a place whence they had a good view over the plains, and after the rest of the party had done eating, Haungaroa still went on, and two of her companions teased her, saying: 'Holloa! Haungaroa, what a long time you continue eating'; and those plains have ever since been called Kaingaroa, or Kaingaroa-o-Haungaroa (the long meal of Haungaroa). Haungaroa, who was much provoked with the two women who thus teased her, smote them on the face, whereupon they fled from her, and Haungaroa pursued them a long way, but she pursued in vain, they would not come back to her, so by her enchantments she changed them into Ti trees, which stand on the plains whilst travellers approach them, but which move from place to place when they attempt to get close (and the natives believe that the trees are there at the present day).

Then the other three women continued their journey, and they at length reached the summit of a hill, and sat down there to rest themselves, and whilst they were resting, Haungaroa thought of her mother, and love for her overcame her, and she wept aloud--and that place has ever since been called Te Tangihanga, or the place of weeping.

After they had rested for some time, they continued their journey, until they reached the open summit of another high hill, which they named Piopio, and from thence they saw the beautiful lake of Roto-rua lying at their feet, and they descended towards it, and came down upon the geyser, which spouts up its jets of boiling water at the foot of the mountain, and they reached the lake itself, and wound round it along its sandy shores; then leaving the lake behind them, they struck off towards Maketu, and at last reached that place also, coming out of the forests upon the sea-coast, close to the village of Tuhoro, and when they saw the people there, they called out to them: 'Whereabout is the residence of Ngatoro-i-rangi? And the people answered them: 'He lives near the large elevated storehouse which you see erected on the hill there'; and the niece of Ngatoro-i-rangi, saw the fence which surrounded his place, and she walked straight on towards the wicket of the fortification; she would not however pass in through it like a common person, but climbed the posts, and clambered into the fortress over its wooden defences, and having got inside, went straight on to the house of Ngatoro-i-rangi, entered it, and going right up to the spot which was sacred, from his sitting on it, she seated herself down there.

When Ngatoro-i-rangi's people saw this, one of them ran off with all speed to tell his master, who was then at work with some of his servants on his farm, and having found him he said: 'There is a stranger just arrived at your residence, who carries a travelling bag as if she had come from a long journey, and she would not come in at the gate of the fortress, but climbed right over the wooden defences, and has quietly laid her travelling-bag upon the very roof of your sacred house, and has walked up and seated herself in the very seat that your sacred person generally occupies.'

When the servant had ended his story, Ngatoro at once guessed who this stranger from a distance must be, and said: 'It is my niece'; and he then asked: 'Where is Te Kehu?'--and they told him, 'He is at work in his plantation of sweet potatoes.' And he bid them fetch him at once, and to be quick about it; and when he arrived they all went together to the place where his niece was, and when he reached her, he at once led her before the altar, and she gave them the gods which she had brought with her from Hawaiki.

Then she said to them: 'Come now, and let us be cleansed by diving in running water, and let the ceremony of Whangai-horo be performed over us, for you have been cursed by Manahua and his tribe.'

When they heard this they cried aloud, and tore off their clothes, and ran to a running stream and plunged into it, and dashed water over themselves, and the priests chanted the proper incantations, and performed all the pre-scribed ceremonies; and when these were finished they left the stream, and went towards the village again, and the priests chanted incantations for cleansing the court-yard of the fortress from the defilement of the curse of Manaia; but the incantations for this purpose have not been handed down to the present generation.

The priests next dug a long pit, termed the pit of wrath, into which by their enchantments they might bring the spirits of their enemies, and hang them and destroy them there; and when they had dug the pit, muttering the neces-sary incantations, they took large shells in their hands to scrape the spirits of their enemies into the pit with, whilst they muttered enchantments; and when they had done this, they scraped the earth into the pit again to cover them up, and beat down the earth with their hands, and crossed the pit with enchanted cloths, and wove baskets of flax-leaves, to hold the spirits of the foes which they had thus destroyed, and each of these acts they accompanied with proper spells.

The religious ceremonies being all ended, they sat down, and Ngatoro-i-rangi wept over his niece, and then they spread food before the travellers; and when they had finished their meal they all collected in the house of Nga-toro-i-rangi, and the old men began to question the strangers, saying: 'What has brought you here? Then Kuiwai's daughter said: 'A curse which Manaia uttered against you; for when they had finished making his sacred place for him, and the females were cooking food for the strangers who attended the ceremony, the food in Kuiwai's oven was not well cooked, and Manaia cursed her and you, saying: "Is firewood as sacred as the bones of your brethren, that you fear to burn it in an oven? I'll yet make the flesh of your brothers hiss upon red-hot stones brought from Waikorora, and heated to warm the oven in which they shall be cooked." That curse is the curse that brought me here, for my mother told me to hasten to you.'

When Ngatoro-i-rangi heard this, he was very wroth, and he in his turn cursed Manaia, saying: 'Thus shall it be done unto you--your flesh shall be cooked with stones brought from Maketu.' Then he told all his relations and people to search early the next morning for a large totara tree, from which they might build a canoe, as they had no canoe since Raumati had burnt the Arawa.

Then the people all arose very early the next morning, and with them were the chosen band of one hundred and forty warriors, and they went out to search for a large Totara tree, and Kuiwai's daughter went with them, and she found a great Totara tree fallen down, and nearly buried in the earth; so they dug it out, and they framed a large canoe from it, which they named 'The Totara tree, dug from the earth'; and they hauled it down to the shore, and, launching it, embarked, and paddled out to sea, and the favourable wind of Pungawere was blowing strong, and it blew so for seven days and nights, and wafted them across the ocean, and at the end of that time they had again reached the shores of Hawaiki.

The name of the place at which they landed in Hawaiki was Tara-i-whenua; they landed at night-time, and drew their canoe up above high-water mark, and laid it in the thickets, that none might see that strangers had arrived.

Ngatoro-i-rangi then went at once to a fortified village named Whaitiri-ka-papa, and when he arrived there he walked carelessly up to the house of Kuiwai, and peeping in at the door, said that she was wanted outside for a minute; and she, knowing his voice, came out to him immediately; and Nga-toro-i-rangi questioned her saying: 'Have you anything to say to me, that I ought to know? And she replied: 'The whole tribe of Manaia are continually occupied in praying to their gods, at the sacred place; they pray to them to bring you and your tribe here, dead; perhaps their incantations may now have brought you here.' Then Ngatoro asked her: 'In what part of the heav-ens is the sun when they go to the sacred place?'--and she answered: 'They go there early In the morning.' Then Ngatoro-i-rangi asked her again: 'Where are they all in the evening?'--and she replied: 'In the evening they collect in numbers in their villages for the night, in the morning they disperse about.' Then, just as Ngatoro-i-rangi was going, he said to her: 'At the dawn of morn-ing climb up on the roof of your house that you may have a good view, and watch what takes place.' Having thus spoken, he returned to the main body of his party.

Then Ngatoro related to them all that his sister had told him; and when they had heard this, Tangaroa, one of his chiefs, said: 'My counsel is, that we storm their fortress this night'; but then stood up Rangitu, another chief, and said: 'Nay, but rather let us attack it in the morning.' Now arose Ngatoro, and he spake aloud to them and said: 'I agree with neither of you. We must go to the sacred place, and strike our noses until they bleed and we are covered with blood, and then we must he on the ground like dead bodies, every man with his weapon hid under him, and their priests will imagine that their en-chantments have brought us here and slam us; so shall we surprise them.' On hearing these words from their leader they all arose, and following him in a body to the court-yard of the sacred place, they found that the foolish priests had felt so sure of compelling their spirits by enchantments to bring Ngatoro and his tribe there, and to slay them for them, that they bad even prepared ovens to cook their bodies in, and these were all lying open ready for the vic-tims; and by the sides of the ovens they had laid in mounds the green leaves, all prepared to place upon the victims before the earth was heaped in to cov-er them up, and the firewood and the stones were also lying ready to be heated. Then the one hundred and forty men went and laid themselves down in the ovens dug out of the earth, as though they had been dead bodies, and they turned themselves about, and beat themselves upon their noses and their faces until they bled, so that their bodies became all covered with blood, like the corpses of men slain in battle; and then they lay still in the ov-ens: the weapons they had with them were short clubs of various kinds, such as clubs of jasper and of basalt, and of the bones of whales, and the priests whom they had with them having found out the sacred place of the people of that country, entered it, and hid themselves there.

Thus they continued to lie in the ovens until the sun arose next morning, and until the priests of their enemies, according to their custom each day at dawn, came to spread leaves and other offerings to the gods in the sacred place, and there, to their surprise, these priests found the warriors of Ngato-ro-i-rangi all lying heaped up in the ovens. Then the priests raised joyful shouts, crying: 'At last our prayers have been answered by the gods; here, here are the bodies of the host of Ngatoro and of Tama' lying heaped up in the cooking places. This has been done by our god--he carried them off, and brought them here.' The multitude of people in the village hearing these cries, ran out to see the wonder, and when they saw the bodies of the one hundred and forty lying there, with the blood in clots dried on them, they began to cry out--one, 'I'll have this shoulder'; another, 'And I'll have this thigh'; and a third, 'That head is mine'; for the blood shed from striking their noses during the previous night was now quite clotted on their bodies; and the priests of those who were lying in the ovens having hidden themselves in the bushes of the shrubbery round the sacred place, could not be seen by the priests of the town of Manaia when they entered the sacred place, to perform the fitting rites to the gods.

So these latter cried aloud, as they offered thanksgivings to the gods for having granted their prayers, and for having fulfilled their wishes; but just as their ceremonies were finished, the priests of the war party of Ngatoro-i-rangi rushing out of their hiding places upon the other priests, slew them, so that the priests were first slain, as offerings to the gods. Then arose the one hundred and forty men from the ovens, and rushed upon their enemies: all were slain, not one escaped but Manaia, and he fled to the town; but they at once attacked and carried the town by assault, and then the slaughter ceased. And the first battle at the sacred place was called Ihu-motomotokia, or the battle of 'Bruised Noses'; and the name of the town which was taken was Whaitiri-ka-papa, but Manaia again escaped from the assault on the town. They entered the breaches in the town as easily as if they had been walking in at the door of a house left open to receive them, whence this proverb has been handed down to us: 'As soon as ever you have defeated your enemy, storm their town.' The priests now turned over the bodies of the first slain, termed the holy fish, as offerings set apart for the gods, and said suitable prayers, and when these ceremonies were ended the conquerors cooked the bodies of their enemies, and devoured the whole of them; but soon afterwards the warriors of the other towns of Manaia which had not been assaulted, were approaching as a forlorn hope to attack their enemies.

In the meanwhile Ngatoro-i-rangi and his warriors, unaware of this, had retired towards their canoe, whilst the host of warriors whom Manaia had again assembled were following upon their traces. They soon came to a stream which they had to pass, and fording that they left it behind them, and gained their canoe, but by the time they were there their pursuers had reached the stream they had just left.

Ngatoro-i-rangi now felt thirsty, and remembered that they had no water for the crew of the canoe, so he said: 'There is no water here for us'; and Rangitu hearing the voice of his commander, answered cheerfully: 'No, there is none here, but there is plenty in the stream we have just crossed.' So they gave the great calabash of the canoe to Rangitu, and he returned towards the stream, but before he got there the host of Manaia had reached it, and had occupied its banks.

Rangitu, who did not see them, as soon as he got to the edge of the stream, dipped his calabash to fill it, and as it did not sink easily, being empty and very light, he stooped down and put his hand upon it to press it under the water; and whilst he was holding it with one hand to press it down, one of the enemy, stealing on him, made a blow at him with his weapon. Rangitu saw nothing, but merely heard the whizz of the weapon as it was sweeping down through the air upon his head, and quick as thought be jerks the calabash out of the water, and holds it as a shield in the direction in which he heard the blow coming down upon him; the weapon is parried off from one side of his head, but the calabash is shattered to pieces, and nothing but the mouth of the vessel which he was holding is left in his hand.

Then off he darts, fast as he can fly, and reaches before the enemy Ngatoro-i-rangi and his one hundred and forty warriors; as soon as he is thus sure of support, in a moment he turns upon his foes. Ha, ha! he slays the first of the enemy, and carries off his victim. Then lo! Tangaroa has risen up, he is soon amongst the enemy, he slays and carries off the second man. Next, Tama-te-kapua kills and carries off his man; thus is it with each warrior; the enemy then breaks and flees, and a great slaughter is made of the host of Manaia, yet he himself again escapes with his life. The name given to this battle was Tarai-whenua-kura.

Having thus avenged themselves of their enemies, they again returned to these islands and settled at Maketu, and cultivated farms there. Manaia, on his part, was not idle, for shortly after they had left his place of residence, he, with his tribe, set to work at refitting their canoes.

Ngatoro-i-rangi, in the meantime, occupied the island of Motiti, off 'Tauranga, in the Bay of Plenty. There he built a fortified village, which he named Matarehua, and a large house ornamented with carved work, which he named Taimaihi-o-Rongo; and he made a large underground store for his sweet potatoes, which he named Te Marihope; and he and his old wife generally lived nearly alone in their village on Motiti, whilst the great body of their people dwelt on the mainland at Maketu; whilst the old couple were in this way living on Motiti, suddenly one evening Manaia, with a large fleet of canoes and a whole host of warriors, appeared off the coast of the island, and they pulled straight up to the landing-place, opposite to the house of Ngatoro-i-rangi, and lay on their paddles there, whilst Manaia hailed him, calling out: 'Ho! brother-in-law, come out here if you dare, let us fight before the daylight is gone.' Ngatoro-i-rangi no sooner heard the voice of Manaia, than he came boldly out of the house, although he was almost alone, and there be saw the whole host of Manaia lying on their paddles at the anchorage off his landing-place; but he at once hailed them, shouting out: 'Well done, O brother-in-law, just anchor where you are for the night, it is already getting dark, and we shall not be able to see to meet the edge of one weapon with the other; the warriors could not, therefore, parry one another's blows; to-morrow morning we will fight as much as you like.' Manaia no sooner heard this proposal, than he assented to it, saying: 'You are right, it has already grown dark.' And Ngatoro answered him: 'You had better bring-to your canoes in the anchorage outside there.' Manaia therefore told his army to anchor their canoes, and to lose no time in cooking their food on board; and the priest Ngatoro-i-rangi remained in his fortress.

All the early part of the night Ngatoro-i-rangi remained in the sacred place, performing enchantments and repeating incantations, and his wife was with him muttering her incantations; and having finished them, they both returned to their house, and there they continued to perform religious rites, calling to their aid the storms of heaven; whilst the host of Manaia did nothing but amuse themselves, singing Hakas and songs, and diverting themselves thoughtlessly as war parties do: little did they think that they were so soon to perish; no, they flattered themselves that they would destroy Ngatoro-i-rangi, having now caught him almost alone.

So soon as the depth of night fell upon the world, whilst Ngatoro and his aged wife were still in the house, and the old woman was sitting at the window watching for what might take place, she heard the host of Manaia insulting herself and her husband, by singing taunting war-songs. Then the ancient priest Ngatoro, who was sitting at the upper end of the house, rises up, unloosens and throws off his garments, and repeats his incantations, and calls upon the winds, and upon the storms, and upon the thunder and lightning, that they may all arise and destroy the host of Manaia; and the god Tawhiri-ma-tea harkened unto the priest, and he permitted the winds to issue forth, together with hurricanes, and gales, and storms, and thunders and lightnings; and the priest and his wife harkened anxiously that they might hear the first bursting forth of the winds, and thunders and lightnings, and of the rain and hail.

Then, when it was the middle space between the commencement of night and the commencement of the day, burst forth the winds, and the rain, and the lightning, and the thunder, and into the harbour poured all the mountainous waves of the sea, and there lay the host of Manaia overcome with sleep, and snoring loudly; but when the ancient priest and his wife heard the rushing of the winds and the roaring of the waves, they closed their house up securely, and lay composedly down to rest, and as they lay they could hear a confused noise, and cries of terror, and a wild and tumultuous uproar from a mighty host, but before very long, all the loud confusion became hushed, and nothing was to be heard but the heavy rolling of the surges upon the beach; nor did the storm itself last very long--it had soon ceased.

When the next morning broke, the aged wife of Ngatoro went out of her house, and looked to see what had become of the host of Manaia, and as she cast her eyes along the shore, there she saw them lying dead, cast up on the beach. The name Ngatoro-i-rangi gave to this slaughter was Maikukutea; the name given to the storm which slew them all was Te Aputahi-a-Pawa. He gave the name of Maikukutea to the slaughter, because the fish having eaten the bodies of Manaia's warriors, only their bones, and the nails of their hands and feet, but hardly any part of their corpses, could be found.

Of the vast host of Manaia that perished, not one escaped: the body of Manaia himself they recognized by some tattoo marks upon one of his arms. Ngatoro now lighted a signal fire as a sign to his relations and warriors at Maketu that he wanted them to cross over to the island; and when his chosen band of one hundred and forty warriors saw the signal, they launched their canoe and pulled across to join their chief, and on reaching the island, they found that the host of Manaia had all perished.

Thus was avenged the curse of Mutahanga and of Manaia; however, it would have been far better if the canoe Arawa had not been burnt by Raumati, then Ngatoro and his warriors would have had two canoes to return in to Hawaiki, to revenge their wrongs, and the whole race of Manaia would have been utterly destroyed.

It would also have been far better if Ngatoro and his people had remained at Maketu, and had never gone to Moehau; then the Arawa would not have been burnt; for from the burning of that canoe by Raumati sprang the war, the events of which have now been recounted.

The Legend of Hatupatu and His Brothers

WHEN Tama-te-kapua went with his followers to Moe-hau, the hill near Cape Colville, and Ihenga and his followers went to Roto-rua, then Ha-nui, Ha-roa, and Hatupatu went also to Whakamaru, to Maroa, to Tuata, to Tutuka, to Tuaropaki, to Hauhungaroa, to Hurakia, and to Horohoro, the districts which lie between Lakes Taupo and Roto-rua, and between Roto-rua and the head of the Waikato River, to snare birds for themselves, and followed their sport for many a day, until they had hunted for several months; but their little brother Hatupatu was all this time thinking to himself that they never gave him any of the rare dainties or nice things that they got, so that they might all feast together, but at each meal he received nothing but lean tough birds; so when the poor little fellow went and sat down by the side of the fire to his food, he every day used to keep on crying and eating, crying and eating, during his meals. At last, saucy, mischievous thoughts rose up in his young heart. So one day, whilst his brothers were out snaring birds, and he, on this as on every other day, was left at their resting-place to take care of the things, the little rogue crept into the storehouse, where the birds, preserved in their own fat, were kept in calabashes, and he stole some, and set resolutely to work to eat them, with some tender fern-root, nicely beaten and dressed, for a relish; so that to look at him you could not help thinking of the proverb: 'Bravo, that throat of yours can swallow anything.'

He finished all the calabashes of preserved birds, and then attacked those that were kept in casks, and when he had quite filled himself he crept out of the storehouse again, and there he went trampling over the pathway that led to their resting-place, running about this side, and that side, and all round it, that his brothers might be induced to think a war party had come, and had eaten up the food in their absence. Then he came back, and ran a spear into himself in two or three places, where he could not do himself much harm, and gave himself a good bruise or two upon his bead, and laid down on the ground near their hut.

When his brothers came back they found him lying there in appearance very badly wounded; they next ran to the storehouse, and found their preserved birds all gone: so they asked him who had done all this, and he replied: 'A war party.' Then they went to the pathways and saw the foot-marks, and said: 'It is too true.' They melted some fat, and poured warm oil on his wounds, and he revived; and they all ate as they used to do in former days, the brothers enjoying all the good things, whilst Hatupatu kept eating and crying, and he went and sat on the smoky side of the fire, so that his cruel brothers might laugh at him, saying: 'Oh, never mind him; those are not real tears, they are only his eyes watering from the smoke.'

Next day Hatupatu stopped at home, and off went his brothers to snare birds, and he began to steal the preserved birds again, and thus he did every day, every day, and of course at last his brothers suspected him, and one day they laid in wait for him, when he not foreseeing this, again crouched into the storehouse and began eating, "Ha, ha, ha, we've caught you now then; your thievish tricks are found out, are they, you little rogue?' His brothers killed him at once, and buried him in the large heap of feathers they had pulled out from the snared birds; after this they went back to Roto-rua, and when they arrived their parents asked them: 'Where is Hatupatu? What's become of your little brother? And they answered: 'We don't know; we have not seen him.' And their parents said: 'You've killed him.' And they replied: 'We have not'; and they disputed and disputed together, and at last their parents said: 'It is too true that you must have killed him, for he went away with you, and he is missing now when you return to us.'

At length Hatupatu's father and mother thought they would send a spirit to search for him; so they sent one, and the spirit went. Its form was that of a flag, and its name was Tamumu-ki-te-rangi, or He-that-buzzes-in-the-skies, and it departed and arrived at the place where Hatupatu was buried, and found him and performed enchantments, and Hatupatu came to life again, and went upon his way, and met a woman who was spearing birds for herself, and her spear was nothing but her own lips: and Hatupatu had a real wooden spear. The woman speared at a bird with her lips, but Hatupatu had at the same moment thrown his spear at the same bird, and it stuck into her lips: and when he saw this he ran off with all his speed, but he was soon caught by the woman, not being able to go so fast as she could, for her feet bore her along, and wings were upon her arms, like those of a bird, and she brought him to her house, and they slept there.

Hatupatu found that this woman never ate anything but raw food, and she gave the birds to Hatupatu to eat without their being in any way dressed, but he only pretended to eat them, lifting them up to his mouth, and letting them fall slily. At dawn the woman prepared to go and spear birds, but Hatupatu always remained at home, and when she had departed, he began to cook food for himself, and to look at all the things in the cave of rocks that the woman lived in--at her two-handed wooden sword, at her beautiful cloak made of red feathers torn from under the wing of the Kaka, at her red cloak of thick dog's fur, at her ornamented cloak woven from flax; and he kept thinking how he could run off with them all: and then he looked at the various tame lizards she had, and at her tame little birds, and at all her many curiosities, and thus he went on day after day, until at last one day he said to her: 'Now, you'd better go a long distance to-day; to the first mountain range, to the second range, the tenth range, the hundredth range, the thousandth mountain range, and when you get there, then begin to catch birds for us two.' To this she consented, and went. He remained behind roasting birds for himself, and thinking: 'I wonder how far she's got now'; and when he thought she had reached the place he had spoken of, then be began to gather up her cloak of red feathers, and her cloak of dogs' skins, and her cloak of ornamented flax, and her carved two-handed sword; and the young fellow said: 'How well I shall look when all the fine feathers on these cloaks are rustled by the wind.' And he brandished the two-handed sword, and made cuts at the lizards, and at all the tame animals, and they were soon killed. Then he struck at the perch on which the little pet birds sat, and he killed them all but one, which escaped, and it flew away to fetch back the woman they all belonged to. Her name was Kurangaituku. And as the little bird flew along, these are the words he kept singing: 'Oh, Kurangaituku, our home is ruined, our things are all destroyed'; and so it kept singing until it had flown a very long way. At last Kurangaituku heard it, and said: 'By whom is all this done? And the little bird answered: 'By Hatupatu--everything is gone.' Then Kurangaituku made haste to get home again, and as she went along she kept calling out: 'Step out, stretch along; step out, stretch along. There you are, O Hatupatu, not far from me. Step out, stretch along; step out, stretch along. There you are, O Hatupatu, not far from me now.'

She only made three strides before she had reached her cave, and when she looked about, she could see nothing in it; but the little bird still guided her on, as she kept saying: 'Step out, stretch along; step out, stretch along; I'll catch you there now, Hatupatu; I'll catch you there now, Hatupatu'; and she almost caught Hatupatu; and he thought, I'm done for now. So he repeated his charm: 'O rock, open for me, open.' Then the rock opened, and he hid himself in it, and the woman looked and could not find him; and she went on to a distance, and kept calling out: 'I'll catch you there, Hatupatu'; and when her voice had died away at a great distance, Hatupatu came up out of the rock and made off; and thus they went on, and thus they went on, the whole way, until they came to Roto-rua; and when they arrived at the sulphur-springs (called Te Whaka-rewa-rewa), Hatupatu jumped over these; but Ku-rangaituku thinking they were cold, tried to wade through, but sank through the crust, and was burnt to death.

Hatupatu proceeded on and sat on the shore of the lake, and when the evening came, he dived into the water, and rose up at the island of Mokoia, and sat in the warm-bath there; just at this time his father and mother want-ed some water to drink, and sent their slave to fetch some for them, and he came to the place where he found Hatupatu lying in the warm-bath; Hatupa-tu laid hold of him, and asked him: 'Whom are you fetching that water for at this time of night? and he answered, 'For so and so.' Then Hatupatu asked him: 'Where is the house of Ha-nui and of Ha-roa?'--and the slave answered: 'They live in a house by themselves; but what can your name be?'--and be answered him: 'I am Hatupatu.' So the old slave said: 'O Hatupatu, are you still alive?'--and he replied: 'Yes, indeed.' And the old slave said to him: 'Oh, I'll tell you; I and your father and mother live together in a house by our-selves; and they sent me down here to fetch water for them'; and Hatupatu said: 'Let us go to them together'; and they went: and on coming to them, the old people began to weep with a loud voice; and Hatupatu said: 'Nay, nay; let us cry with a gentle voice, lest my brethren who slew me should hear; and I, moreover, will not sleep here with you, my parents, it is better for me to go and remain in the cave you have dug to keep your sweet potatoes in, that I may overhear each day what they say, and I'll take all my meals there.' So he went, and he said: 'Let my father sleep with me in the cave in the night, and in the daytime let him stop in the house'; and his father consented, and thus they did every day and every night, and his brothers noticed that there was a change in their food, that they did not get so much or such good food as whilst their brother had been away (for his mother kept the best of every-thing for him); they had worse food now; so they beat their mother and their slaves, and this they did continually.

At last, they heard the people all calling out: 'Oh, oh, Hatupatu's here'; and one of them said: 'Oh, no, that can't be; why, Hatupatu is dead'; but when they saw it was really he, one of them caught hold of his two-handed wooden sword, and so did the others; and Hatupatu also caught hold of his two-handed wooden sword; he had decorated his head in the night, and had stuck it full of the beautiful feathers befitting a chief; and he had placed a bunch of the soft white down from the breast of the albatross in each ear; and when his brothers and the multitude of their followers dared him to come forth from the storehouse and fight them, he caught hold of his girdle and of his apron of red feathers, and girding on his apron he repeated an incantation suited for the occasion. When this was finished his head appeared rising up out of the storehouse, and he repeated another incantation, and afterwards a third over his sword.

Hatupatu now came out of the storehouse, and as his brothers gazed on him, they saw his looks were most noble; glared forth on them the eyes of the young man, and glittered forth the mother-of-pearl eyes of the carved face on the handle of his sword, and when the many thousands of their tribe who had gathered round saw the youth, they too were quite astonished at his nobleness; they had no strength left, they could do nothing but admire him: he was only a little boy when they bad seen him before, and now, when they met him again, he was like a noble chief, and they now looked upon his brothers with very different eyes from those with which they looked at him.

His three brothers sprang at him; three wooden swords were at the same time levelled at Hatupatu to slay him; be held the blade of his sword pointed to the ground, till the swords of his brothers almost touched him, when he rapidly warded off the blows, and whirling round his wooden sword, two of the three were felled by the blade of it, and one by a blow from the handle; then they sprang up, and rushed at him once more; over they go again, two felled by the blade of his sword, and one by the handle; it was enough-they gave in. Then their father said to them: 'Oh! my sons, I would that you were as strong in peace as you are in attacking one another; in seeking revenge for your ancestral canoe, Te Arawa, which was consumed in a fire by the chief Raumati. Long have you been seeking to revenge yourselves upon him, but you have not succeeded, you have gained no advantage; perhaps you are only strong and bold when you attack your young brother, my last-born child.'

When his sons Ha-nui, Ha-roa, and Karika heard these words of their father, they and their many followers felt their hearts grow sad; they began to prepare for a war party, by beating flat pieces of prepared fern-root; and they cooked sweet potatoes in ovens, and mashed them, and packed them up in baskets of flax, and again put them in the ovens, that the food might keep for a long time; and they cooked shell-fish in baskets, and thus collected food for an expedition to Maketu. Whilst his brothers were making all these preparations for the expedition, their father was secretly teaching Hatupatu the tattoo marks and appearance of Raumati, so that he might easily recognize that chief; and when the canoes started with the warriors, he did not embark with them, but remained behind; the canoes had reached the middle of the lake, when Hatupatu rose up, and taking thirty cloaks of red feathers with him, went off to the war; he proceeded by diving under the water--that was the path he chose; and when he reached the deepest part of the lake, he stopped to eat a meal of mussels in the water, and then rose up from the bottom and came out. He had got as far as Ngaukawakawa, when his brothers and the warriors in the canoes arrived there, and found him spreading out the cloaks he had brought with him to dry; and as soon as their canoes reached the shore they asked him: 'Where is your canoe, that you managed to get here so fast?'--and he answered: 'Never mind, I have a canoe of my own.'

Hatupatu. threw off here the wreath of leaves he wore round his brow, and it took root, and became a pohutukawa-tree, which bears such beautiful red flowers. His brothers' canoes had by this time got out into Roto-iti; then he again dived after them, and rose to the surface, and came out of the water at Kuha-rua, where he threw off his wreath of totara-leaves, and it took root and grew, and it is still growing there at this day; when his brothers and the warriors arrived at Kuha-rua, they found him sitting there, and they were astonished at his doings; they landed at Otaramarae, and marching overland, encamped for the night at Kakaroa-a-Tauhu, and the next day they reached Maketu; and when the evening came they ranged their warriors in divisions; three hundred and forty warriors were told off for each of the divisions, under the command of each of Hatupatu's three brothers; but no division was placed under his command.

Hatupatu knew that the jealousy of his brothers, on account of their former quarrels, was the reason they had not told off any men for him; so he said: 'Oh, my brothers, I did not refuse to hearken to you, when you asked me to come with you; but I came, upon that occasion when you killed me, and here I am now left in a very bad position; so I pray you, let some of the warriors be placed under my command, let there be fifty of them.' But they said to him: 'Pooh, pooh; come now, you be off home again. What can you do? The only thing you are fit to destroy is food.' He, the young man, said no more; but at once left his brothers, and on the same night he sought out a rough thicket as his resting-place; and when he saw how convenient for his purpose was the place he had selected, he turned to and began to tie together in bundles the roots of the creeping plants, and of the bushes, and dressed them up with the cloaks he had with him; and when he had finished, the war band of these figures, which the young man had made, looked just like a band of real warriors. The day had hardly dawned, when the inhabitants of the place they had come to attack saw their enemies, and sent off messengers to tell the warriors, on this side and that side, that they should come and fight with them against the common enemy.

In the meantime, all the warriors of the columns of Hatupatu's brothers were exhorting their men, and encouraging them by warlike speeches; first one chief stood up to speak, and then another, and when they had all ended, Hatupatu himself got up, to encourage his mock party. He had been sitting down, and as he gracefully arose, it was beautiful to see his plumes and ornaments of feathers fluttering in the breeze; the long hair of the young man was tied up in four knots, or clubs, in each of which was stuck a bunch of feathers; you would have thought he had just come from the gannet island of Karewa (in the Bay of Plenty), where birds' feathers abound; and when he had done speaking to one party of his column, he unloosened his hair, leaving but one clump of it over the centre of his forehead, and now he wore a cloak of red feathers; then he made another speech, encouraging his men to be brave; then after sitting down again, he ran to the rear, and took all the feathers and knots from his hair, and he this time wore a cloak of flax with a broidered border; again he addressed his men, and this being finished, he was seen again in the centre of the body, standing up to speak, naked, and stripped for the fight. Once more he appeared at the head of the column; this time he had the hair at the back of his head tied up in a knot and ornamented with feathers, he wore a cloak made of the skins of dogs, and the long wooden war-axe was the weapon he had in his hands. Having concluded this speech, he appeared again in a different place, with his hair tied in five bunches, each ornamented with feathers, whilst a large rough dog-skin formed his cloak; and the weapon in his hand was a *mere* [1] made of white whalebone: thus he ended his speeches to his party. When the people of the place they had come to attack saw how numerous were the chiefs in the column of Hatupatu, and what clothes and weapons they had, they dreaded his division much more than those of his brothers.

His brothers' divisions had many warriors in them, although the number of chiefs was only equal in number to the divisions; thus there were three divisions, and also three chiefs; whilst, although Hatupatu had only one division, it appeared to be commanded by a multitude of chiefs, who had superb dresses; thence the enemy burnt with fear of that division, which they accounted to be composed of men; but no; it was only formed of clumps of grass dressed up.

Now the people of the place they were attacking drew out to the battle, and as they pressed nearer and nearer, they pushed forth long heavy spears, and sent forth volleys of light spears made of the branches of manuka-trees, at the column of Ha-nui. Alas! it is broken; they retreat, they fly, they fall back on the division of Ha-roa; they are here rallied, and ordered to charge; but they do not--they only poke forward their heads, as if intending to go; the enemy has reached them, and is on them again; they are again broken and disordered; they run in now upon the third line, that of Karika; they are rallied, and again ordered to charge; but they only press forward the upper part of their bodies, as if intending to advance, when the enemy is already upon them in full charge. It is over; all the divisions of Hatupatu's brothers are broken and flying in confusion; what did it matter whether they were many or few, they were all cowards.

[paragraph continues] Their enemies saw no brave men's faces, only the black backs of heads running away.

All this time the division of Hatupatu appears to be sitting quietly upon the ground, and when the men in full retreat came running in upon it, Hatupatu rose up to order them to charge again. He cried out: 'Turn on them again, turn on them again'; for a long time the enemy and Hatupatu. were hidden from each other's view; at last they saw him. Then rushes forward Hatupatu from one party, and a chief of the enemy, named also Karika (like his brother), from the other, and the latter aims a fierce blow at Hatupatu with a short spear; he parries it, and strikes down Karika with his two-handed sword, who dies without a struggle; motionless, as food hidden in a bag, he draws forth his whalebone *mere*, cuts off Karika's head, and grasps it by the hair. It is enough--the enemy break--fall back--fly; then his brothers and their warriors turn again on the foes, and slay them; many thousands of them fall. Whilst his brothers are thus slaying the enemy, he is eagerly seeking for Raumati; he is found; Hatupatu catches him, his head is cut off; it is concealed. The slaughter being ended, they return to their encampment; they cook the bodies of their enemies; they devour them; they smoke and carefully preserve their heads: and when all is done, each makes speeches boasting of his deeds; and one after the other, vaunting to have slain the great chief Raumati. But Hatupatu said not a word of his having Raumati's head.

They return to Roto-rua; this time he goes in the canoe with them; they draw near to the island of Mokoia, and his brothers, as they are in the canoe, chant songs of triumph to the gods of war; they cease; their father inquires from the shore: 'Which of you has the head of Raumati?'--and one, holding up the head he had taken, said: 'I have'; and another said: 'I have'; at last, their father calls out: 'Alas, alas! Raumati has escaped.'

Then Hatupatu stands up in the canoe, and chants a prayer to the god of war over a basket heaped up with heads, whilst holding up in his hand the head of Karika.

Then his hand grasps the head of Raumati, which he had kept hid under his cloak, and he cries: 'There, there; I have the head of Raumati.' All rejoice. Their father strips off his cloak, rushes into the lake, and repeats a thanksgiving to the gods.

When he had ended this, he promoted in honour his last-born child, and debased in rank his eldest sons.

Thus at last was revenge obtained for the burning of the Arawa, and the descendants of Tama-te-kapua emigrated, and came and dwelt in Pakotore, and Rangitihi was born there, and his children, and one of them came to Rangiwhakakapua, or Rotorua, and dwelt there; and afterwards one of his daughters went to the Whakatohea tribe, at Apotiki. After that Rangitihi and all his sons went to Ahuriri, to revenge the death of the husband of Rongo-mai-papa, and she was given up to them as a reward; then grew up to manhood Uenukuko-pako, and began to visit all the people subject to him at Whakamaru, at Maroa, at Tutukau, at Tuata, and he went and afterwards returned to Pakotore, and whilst going backwards and forwards, he lost his dog, named Potaka-tawhiti, at Mokoia; it was killed by Mata-aho and Kawa-arero.

He came back from Whakamaru to look for it, and when he found it had been killed, a great war was commenced against Roto-rua, and some were slain of each party. After this, Rangi-te-aorere, the son of Rangi-whakaekeau, grew up to man's estate; in his time they stormed and took the island of Mo-koia, and Roto-rua was conquered by the son of Rangitihi, who kept it still and still, until the multitude of men there increased very greatly, and spread themselves in all parts; and the descendants of Ngatoro-i-rangi also multiplied there, and some of them still remain at Roto-rua. Tumakoha begat Ta-rawhai, and Te Rangi-takaroro, was one of his sons; his second son was Tarewa, and his third was Taporahitaua.

[1] A sharp instrument of war made of stone.

Legend of the Emigration of Turi

(The Progenitor of the Whanganui Tribes)

THE following narrative shows the cause which led Turi, the ancestor of the Whanganui tribes, to emigrate to New Zealand, and the manner in which he reached these islands.

Hoimatua, a near relation of Turi, had a little boy named Potikiroroa; this young fellow was sent one day with a message to Uenuku, who was an *ariki*, or chief high-priest, to let him know that a burnt-offering had been made to the gods, of which Uenuku, as *ariki*, was to eat part, and the little fellow accidentally tripped and fell down in the very doorway of Wharekura, the house of Uenuku, and this being a most unlucky omen, Uenuku was dreadfully irritated, and he laid hold of the little fellow, and ate him up, without even having the body cooked, and so the poor boy perished.

Turi was determined to have revenge for this barbarous act, and to slay some person as a payment for little Potikiroroa, and, after casting about in his thoughts for some time as to the most effectual mode of doing this, he saw that his best way of revenging himself would be to seize Hawepotiki, the little son of Uenuku, and kill him.

One day Turi, in order to entice the boy to his house, ordered the children of all the people who dwelt there with him to begin playing together, in a place where Hawepotiki could see them; so they began whipping their tops, and whirling their whiz-gigs, but it was of no use; the little fellow could not be tempted to come and play with them, and that plan failed.

At last summer came with its heats, scorching men's skins; and Turi, one very hot day, ordered all the little children to run and bathe in the river Waimatuhirangi; so they all ran to the river and began sporting and playing in the water. When little Hawepotiki saw all the other lads swimming and playing in the river, he was thrown off his guard and ran there too, and Turi waylaid him, and killed him in a moment, and thus revenged the death of Potikiroroa.

After killing the poor boy, Turi cut the heart out of his body, which was eaten by himself and his friends; but when, shortly afterwards, a chieftainess, named Hotukura, sent up a present of baskets of food to their sacred prince, to Uenuku, carried in the usual way by a long procession of people, some of Turi's friends pushed into the basket of baked sweet potatoes prepared for

Uenuku the heart of Hawepotiki, cut up and baked too, and so it was carried up to Uenuku in the basket, and laid before him, that he might eat it.

Uenuku, who had missed his little boy, being still unable to ascertain what had become of him, could not help sighing when he saw such an excellent feast, and said: 'Poor little Hawepotiki, how he would have liked this, but he now no longer comes running to sit by my side at mealtime'; and then he himself ate the food that was laid before him. He had hardly, however, ended his meal, when one of his friends, who had found what had been done, came and told him, saying: 'They have made you eat a part of Hawepotiki.' And he answered: 'Very well, let it be; he lies in the belly of Toi-te-huatahi'; meaning by this proverb that he would have a fearful revenge; but he showed no other signs of feeling, that he might not gratify his enemies by manifesting his sorrow, or alarm them by loud threats of revenge.

At this time Turi was living in a house, the name of which was Rangiatea, and there were born two of his children, Turangaimua and Taneroroa. One evening, shortly after the death of Hawepotiki, Rongo-rongo, Turi's wife, went out of the house to suckle her little girl, Taneroroa, and she heard Uenuku in his house, named Wharekura, chanting a poem, of which this was the burden:

'Oh! let the tribes be summoned from the south,
Oh! let the tribes be summoned from the north;
Let Ngati-Ruanui come in force;
Let Ngati-Rongotea's warriors too be there,
That we may all our foes destroy,
And sweep them utterly away.
Oh, they ate one far nobler than themselves.'

When Rongo-rongo heard what Uenuku was chanting, she went back to her house, and said to her husband: 'Turi, I have just heard them chanting this poem in Wharekura.' And Turi answered: 'What poem do you say, it was? Then she hummed it gently over to her husband, and Turi at once divined the meaning of it, [1] and said to his wife: 'That poem is meant for me'; and he knew this well, because, as he had killed the child of Uenuku, he guessed that they meant to slay him as a payment for the boy, and that the lament his wife had heard evinced that they were secretly laying their plans of revenge.

He, therefore, at once started off to his father-in-law, Toto, to get a canoe from him, in which he might escape from his enemies; and Toto gave him one, the name of which was Aotea; the tree from which it had been made grew upon the banks of the Lake Waiharakeke. Toto had first hewn down the tree, and then split it, breaking it lengthways into two parts; out of one part of the tree he made a canoe, which he named Matahorua, and out of the other part he made a canoe which he named Aotea. He gave the canoe which he had named Matahorua to Kuramarotini; and the canoe which he had named

Aotea he made a present of to Rongo-rongo; thus giving a canoe to each of his two daughters. Matahorua was the canoe in which a large part of the world was explored, and Reti was the name of the man who navigated it.

One day Kupe and Hoturapa went out upon the sea to fish together, and when they had anchored the canoe at a convenient place, Kupe let down his line into the sea; and he said to his cousin, Hoturapa: 'Hotu', my line is foul of something; do you, like a good young fellow, dive down and release it for me'; but Hoturapa said: 'Just give me your line, and let me see if I cannot pull it up for you.' But Kupe answered: 'It's of no use, you cannot do it; you had better give a plunge in at once, and pull it up.' This was a mere stratagem upon the part of Kupe, that he might obtain possession of Kuramarotini, who was Hoturapa's wife; however, Hoturapa not suspecting this, good-naturedly dived down at once to bring up Kupe's line; and as soon as he had made his plunge, Kupe at once cut the rope which was attached to the anchor, and paddled off for the shore as fast as he could go, to carry off Hoturapa's wife, Kuramarotini. When Hoturapa came up to the surface of the water, the canoe was already a long distance from him, and he cried out to Kupe: 'Oh, Kupe, bring the canoe back here to take me in.' But Kupe would not listen to him, he brought not back the canoe, and so Hoturapa perished. Kupe then made haste, and carried off Kuramarotini, and to escape from the vengeance of the relations of Hoturapa, he fled away with her, on the ocean, in her canoe Matahorua, and discovered the islands of New Zealand, and coasted entirely round them, without finding any inhabitants.

As Kupe was proceeding down the cast coast of New Zealand, and had reached Castle Point, a great cuttle-fish, alarmed at the sight of a canoe with men in it, fled away from a large cavern which exists in the south headland of the cove there; it fled before Kupe, in the direction of Raukawa, or Cook's Straits; when Kupe arrived at those straits, he crossed them in his canoe, to examine the middle islands; seeing the entrance of Awa-iti (now called Tory Channel), running deep up into the land, he turned his canoe in there to explore it; he found a very strong current coming out from between the lands, and named the entrance Kura-te-au; strong as the current was, Kupe stemmed it in his canoe, and ascended it, until he was just surmounting the crown of the rapid. The great cuttle-fish or dragon, that had fled from Castle Point, which Kupe named Te Wheke-a-Muturangi, or the cuttle-fish of Muturangi, had fled to Tory Channel, and was lying hid in this part of the current. The monster heard the canoe of Kupe approaching as they were pulling up the current, and raised its arms above the waters to catch and devour the canoe, men and all. As it thus floated upon the water, Kupe saw it, and pondered how he might destroy the terrible monster. At last he thought of a plan for doing this; he had already found that, although he kept on chopping off portions of its gigantic arms, furnished with suckers, as it tried to fold them about the canoe, in order to pull it down, the monster was too fierce to care for this; so Kupe seized an immense hollow calabash he had on board to carry his water in, and threw it overboard; hardly had it touched the water ere the monster flew at it, thinking that it was the canoe of Kupe, and that he would destroy it; so it reared its whole body out of the water, to press down the huge calabash under it, and Kupe, as he stood in his canoe, being in a most excellent position to cut it with his axe, seized the opportunity, and, striking it a tremendous blow, he severed it in two, and killed it. [2]

The labours of Kupe consisted in this, that he discovered these islands, and examined the different openings which he found running up into the country. He only found two inhabitants in the country, a bird which he named the Kokako, and another bird which he named the Tiwaiwaka; he, however, did not ultimately remain in these islands, but returned to his own house, leaving the openings he had examined in the country as signs that he had been here.

Thus he left his marks here, but he himself returned to his own country, where he found Turi and all his people still dwelling; although it was now the fourth year from that one in which he had slain little Hawepotiki; but Turi was then on the point of flying to escape from the vengeance of Uenuku, and as he heard of the discoveries Kupe had made, he determined to come to these islands. So he bad his canoe, the Aotea, dragged down to the shore in the night, and Kupe, who happened to be near the place, and heard the bottom of the canoe grating upon the beach as they hauled it along, went to see what was going on; and when he found what Turi was about to do, he said to him: 'Now, mind, Turi, keep ever steering to the eastward, where the sun rises; keep the bow of your canoe ever steadily directed towards that point of the sky.' Turi answered him: 'You had better accompany me, Kupe. Come, let us go together.' And when Kupe heard this, he said to Turi: 'Do you think that Kupe will ever return there again?'--and he then continued: 'When you arrive at the islands, you had better go at once and examine the river that I discovered [said to be the Patea]; its mouth opens direct to the westward; you will find but two inhabitants there [meaning the Kokako and Tiwaiwaka]; one of them carries its tail erect and sticking out; now do not mistake the voice of one of them for that of a man, for it calls out just like one; and if you stand on one side of the river, and call out to them, you will hear their cries answering you from the other. That will be the very spot that I mentioned to you.' [3]

Turi's brother-in-law, Tuau, now called out to him: , why, Turi, the paddles you are taking with you are good for nothing, for they are made from the huhoe-tree'; Turi replied: 'Wherever can I get other paddles now?'--and Tuau answered: 'Just wait a little, until I run for the paddles of Taiparaeroa'; and he brought back, and put on board the canoe, two paddles, the names of which were Rangihorona and Kautu-ki-te-rangi, and two bailers, the names of which were Tipuahoronuku and Rangi-ka-wheriko. Then Turi said: 'Tuau, come out a little way to sea with me, and then return again, when you have seen me fairly started upon my long voyage.' To this Tuau cheerfully consented, and got into the canoe, which was already afloat; then were carried on board all the articles which the voyagers were to take; and their friends put on board for them seed, sweet potatoes, of the species called Te Kakau, and dried stones of the berries of the Karaka-tree; and some five edible rats in boxes, and some tame green parrots; and added some pet Pukeko, or large water-hens; and many other valuable things were put on board the canoe, whence the proverb: 'Aotea of the valuable cargo.'

At last away floated the canoe, whilst it was yet night, and Tuau sat at the stem, gently paddling as they dropped out from the harbour; but when they got to its mouth, Turi called out to his brother-in-law: 'Tuau, you come and sit for a little at the house amidships, on the floor of the double canoe, and let me take the paddle and pull till I warm myself.' So Tuau came amidships, and sat down with the people there, whilst Turi went astern and took his paddle. Then Turi and his people pulled as hard as they could, and were soon far outside the harbour, in the wide sea, Tuau, who had intended to land at the heads, at last turned to see what distance they had got. Alas! alas! they were far out at sea; then he called out to Turi: 'Oh, Turi, Turi, pray turn back the canoe and land me.' But not the least attention did Turi pay to him; he persisted in carrying off his brother-in-law with him, although there was Tuau weeping and grieving when he thought of his children and wife, and lamenting as he exclaimed: 'How shall I ever get back to my dear wife and children from the place where you are going to!' But what does Turi care for that; he still thinks fit to carry him off with him, and Tuau cannot now help himself. They were now so far out at sea that he could not gain the shore, for he could scarcely have seen where the land was whilst swimming in the water, as it was during the night-time that they started.

Lo! the dawn breaks; but hardly had the daylight of the first morning of their voyage appeared, than one of the party, named Tapo, became insolent and disobedient to Turi. His chief was therefore very wroth with him, and hove him overboard into the sea; and when Tapo found himself in the water, and saw the canoe shooting ahead, he called out to Turi quite cheerfully and jocosely: 'I say, old fellow, come now, let me live in the world a little longer'; and when they heard him call out in this manner, they knew he must be under the protection of the god Maru, and said: 'Here is Maru, here is Maru.' So they hauled him into the canoe again, and saved his life.

At last the seams of Turi's canoe opened in holes in many places, and the water streamed into it, and they rapidly dipped the bailers into the water and dashed it out over the sides; Turi, in the meanwhile, reciting aloud an incantation, which was efficacious in preventing a canoe from being swamped; they succeeded at length, by these means, in reaching a small island which lies in mid-ocean, which they named Rangitahua; there they landed, and ripped all the old lashings out of the seams of the canoe, and relashed the top sides on to it, and thoroughly refitted it.

Amongst the chiefs who landed there with them was one named Potoru, whose canoe was called Te Ririno. They were carrying some dogs with them, as these would be very valuable in the islands they were going to, for supplying by their increase a good article of food, and skins for warm cloaks; on this island, they, however, killed two of them, the names of which were Whaka-papa-tuakura and Tanga-kakariki; the first of these they cooked and shared amongst them, but the second they cut up raw as an offering for the gods, and laid it cut open in every part before them, and built a sacred place, and set up pillars for the spirits, that they might entirely consume the sacrifice; and they took the enchanted apron of the spirits, and spread it open before them, and wearied the spirits by calling on them for some omen, saying: 'Come, manifest yourselves to us, O gods; make haste and declare the future to us. It may be now, that we shall not succeed in passing to the other side of the ocean; but if you manifest yourselves to us, and are present with us, we shall pass there in safety.' Then they rose up from prayer, and roasted with fire the dog which they were offering as a sacrifice, and holding the sacrifice aloft, called over the names of the spirits to whom the offering was made; and having thus appeased the wrath of the offended spirits, they again stuck up posts for them, saying as they did so:

'Tis the post which stands above there;
'Tis the post which stands in the heavens,
Near Atutahimarehua.'

Thus they removed all ill-luck from the canoes, by repeating over them prayers called Keuenga, Takanga, Whakamumumanga, etc., etc.

When all these ceremonies were ended, a very angry discussion arose between Potoru and Turi, as to the direction they should now sail in; Turi persisted in wishing to pursue an easterly course, saying: 'Nay, nay, let us still sail towards the quarter where the sun first flares up'; but Potoru answered him: 'But I say nay, nay, let us proceed towards that quarter of the heavens in which the sun sets.' Turi replied: 'Why, did not Kupe, who had visited these islands, particularly tell us? Now mind, let nothing induce you to turn the prow of the canoe away from that quarter of the heavens in which the sun rises.' However, Potoru still persisted in his opinion, and at last Turi gave up the point, and let him have his own way; so they embarked and left the island of Rangitahua, and sailed on a westerly course.

After they had pursued this course for some time, the canoe Ririno getting into the surf, near some rocks, was lost on a reef which they named Taputapuatea, being swept away by a strong current, a rapid current, by a swift-running current, swiftly running on to the realms of death; and the Ririno was dashed to pieces: hence to the present day is preserved this proverb: 'You are as obstinate as Potoru, who persisted in rushing on to his own destruction.'

When the Ririno had thus been lost, Turi, in the Aotea, pursued his course towards the quarter of the rising sun, and whilst they were yet in mid-ocean, a child, whom he named Tutawa, was born to Turi; they had then but nine sweet potatoes left, and Turi took one of these, leaving now but eight, and he offered the one he took as a sacrifice to the spirits, and touched with it the palate of little Tutawa, born in mid-ocean, at the same time repeating the fitting prayers. When they drew near the shore of these islands, one of the crew, named Tuanui-a-te-ra, was very disobedient and insolent to Turi, who, getting exceedingly provoked with him, threw him overboard into the sea. When they had got near enough to the shore to see distinctly, they foolishly threw the red plumes they wore on their heads into the sea, these being old, dirty, and faded, from length of wear, for they thought, although wrongly, the red things they saw in such abundance on the shore were similar ornaments.

At length the Aotea is run up on the beach of these islands, and the wearied voyagers spring out of her on to the sands, and the first thing they remark are the footprints of a man; they run to examine them , and find them to be those of Tuanui-a-te-ra, whom Turi had shortly before thrown overboard; there can be no doubt of this, because some of the footprints are crooked, exactly suiting a deformed foot which he had.

Turi having rested after his voyage, determined to start and seek for the river Patea, which Kupe had described to him, and he left his canoe Aotea in the harbour, which he named after it. He travelled along the coast-line from Aotea to Patea, having sent one party before him, under Pungarehu, ordering them to plant the stones of the berries of the Karaka-tree, which they had brought with them, all along their route, in order that so valuable an article of food might be introduced into these islands. Turi, who followed with another party after Pungarehu, gave names to all the places as they came along; when he reached the harbour of Kawhia, he gave it that name or the *awhinga* of Turi; then he came to Marokopa, or the place that Turi wound round to another spot; the river Waitara he named from the *taranga*, or wide steps which he took in fording it at its mouth; Mokau, or Moekau, he named from his sleeping there; at Manga-ti, they opened and spread out an enchanted garment named Hunakiko, and as all the people gazed at it, Turi named the place Mataki-taki; at another place (near the lake at the Gray institution at Taranaki), Turi took up a handful of earth to smell it, that he might guess whether the soil was good enough, and he named that place Hongihongi; another place, six miles to the south of Taranaki, he named Tapuwae, or the footsteps of Turi; another place he named Oakura, from the bright redness of the enchanted cloak Hunakiko; another place Katikara, twelve miles south of Taranaki; another river he named Raoa, from a piece of food he was eating nearly choking him there; another spot he named Kaupoko-nui (a river thirty-four miles north-west of Patea), or the head of Turi; when they arrived there, the enchanted cloak Hunakiko was twice opened and spread out, so he called the spot Marae-kura; a place that they encamped at he named Kapuni (a river at Waimate), or the encampment of Turi; another place he called Waingongoro, or the place at which Turi snored; another spot he named Tangahoe, after his paddle; Ohingahape, he named after the crooked foot of Tuanui-a-te-ra; a headland where there was a natural bridge running over a cave, he named Whitikau, from the long time he was fording in the water to turn the headland, because he did not like to cross the bridge (this is five miles north of Patea).

At length he reached the river which Kupe had described to him; there he built a *pa*, or fortress, which he named Rangitaawhi, and there he erected a post which he named Whakatopea, and he built a house which he named Matangirie, and he laid down a door-sill, or threshold, which he named Paepaehakehake; and he built a small elevated storehouse to hold his food, and he named it Paeahua; the river itself he named Patea; and he dug a well which he named Parara-ki-te-uru. The farm he cultivated there he named Hekeheke-i-papa; the wooden spade he made he called Tipu-i-ahuma: then he had his farm dug up, and the chant they sang to encourage themselves, and to keep time as they dug, was:

'Break up our goddess mother,
Break up the ancient goddess earth;
We speak of you, oh, earth! but do not disturb
The plants we have brought hither from Hawaiki the noble;
It was Maui who scraped the earth in heaps round the sides,
In Kuratau.'

There they planted the farm; they had but eight seed potatoes, but they divided these into small pieces, which they put separately into the ground; and when the shoots sprang up, Turi made the place sacred with prayers and incantations, lest any one should venture there and hurt the plants; the name of the incantation he used was Ahuroa; then harvest-time came, they gathered in the crop of sweet potatoes, and found that they had eight hundred baskets of them. The deeds above related were those which our ancestor Turi performed; Rongo-rongo was the name of his principal Wife, and they had several children, from whom sprang the tribes of Whanganui and the Ngati-Ruanui tribe.

[1] The discovery of a plot by guessing the meaning of a song which persons were overhead singing was a common circumstance with all the races and throughout all the islands of the Pacific; for instance, in Pitcairn's Island, when first occupied by part of the crew of *The Bounty* and some Tahitian men and women, we find:
'Brown and Christian were very intimate, and their two wives overhead one night Williams's second wife sing a song. *Why should the Tahitian men sharpen their axes to cut off the Englishmen's heads?* The wives of Brown and Christian told their husbands what Williams's second wife had p. 152 been singing; when Christian heard of it, he went by himself with his gun to the house where all the Tahitian men were assembled; he pointed his gun at them, but it missed fire. Two of the natives ran away into the bush.'-- *Pitcairn's island and the Islander.*
[2] They show several spots upon the east coast where Kupe touched with his canoes; but I have not yet had time to arrange and transcribe the various traditions connected with his landing at those places.--G. G.

[3] It will be seen that they did not follow Kupe's directions, thinking that he was deceiving them, he being probably friendly to Uenuku.

Legend of the Emigration of Manaia

(The Progenitor of the Ngati-awa Tribe)

THE cause which led Manaia to come here from Hawaiki, was his being very badly treated by a large party of his friends and neighbours, whom, according to the usual custom when a chief has any heavy work to be done, he had collected to make his spears for him, for they violently ravished his wife Rongotiki.

It chanced thus: One day Manaia determined to have his neighbours all warned to come to a great gathering of people for the purpose of making spears for him, so he sent round a messenger to collect them, and the messenger arrived at the place of Tupenu, who listened to his message, and he being chief of the tribe who lived at that place, encouraged his people to go in obedience to the message of Manaia; they went and set to work, and after some time it happened that Manaia felt a wish to go and catch some fish for his workmen; so he went off in his canoe with several of his people. After he had been gone for some time the workmen proposed amongst themselves to assault Rongotiki, the wife of Manaia; and they carried their intentions into execution without any one knowing what they were doing; all this time Manaia, suspecting nothing, was paddling in his canoe out to sea, and when he reached the fishing-ground, they lay on their paddles. Manaia's people soon caught plenty of fish, but he had not even a single bite, until at last, as they were on the point of returning, he felt a fish nibbling at his hook, so he gave a jerk to his line to pull it up; and when he got the fish up to the side of the canoe, to his surprise he saw that the hook was not in the mouth of the fish, but fast in its tail; and as this had long been esteemed as a sign that your wife was being insulted by somebody he at once knew how his had been treated by his workmen; without waiting, therefore, a moment longer, he said to his crew: 'Heave up the anchor, we will return to the shore'; so they hove up the anchor, and shaped a course for the landing-place on the main; whilst they were pulling into the shore, Manaia took the fish he had caught, and with the hook still fast in its tail, tied it on to one of the thwarts of the canoe, and left it there, in order that when Rongotiki saw it she might know without his telling her, that he was aware that she had been badly treated by his workmen.

At length his canoe reached the shore, and the crew jumping out, hauled it up on the sandy beach, and Manaia leaving it there, walked home towards his village; when he had got near home, his wife seeing him approach, arose and made the fire ready to roast some fern-root for her husband, who she thought would come back hungry; and when he reached home the fire was lighted, and she was sitting by the side of it roasting the fern-root, and she made signs to him by which he might know what had happened; but he knew it already from the manner in which his hook had caught in the tail of the fish; then he sent his wife to fetch the fish, saying: 'Mother, go and fetch the fish I have caught from my canoe'; so she went, and when she got there, she found that there were no fish but the single one, hanging to the thwart of the canoe, with a hook fast in its tail; then she took that fish and carried it home with her, and when she got there, Manaia said: 'That is the fish I meant you to bring, lest you should have said that I did not know what had taken place until you told me.'

Manaia then turned over in his mind various plans for revenging himself upon the people who had acted in so brutal a manner towards his wife, and he consulted with his own tribe how they might destroy those who had thus injured him; when the tribe of Manaia heard what had taken place, they all arose to seek revenge; but before the fighting which arose from this affair broke out, Manaia went to the people who had wronged his wife, and told them that he hoped they would make the spears large and strong, and not put him off with weak things, but rather make them stout and strong; this was a mere piece of deceit on his part, in order that when he attacked them, their weapons might be too heavy readily to parry their enemies' blows with them.

All these preparations having been made, Manaia lay in ambush with some of his people, and when the opportunity of rushing on their enemies presented itself, Manaia nudged with his elbow his son, Tu-ure-nui, who was lying by his side, to encourage him to distinguish himself by rushing in, and killing the first man of the enemy; but being afraid to go he did not move, and whilst Manaia was encouraging him in vain, another young man, the name of whose father had never been told by his mother, rushed forward and slew the first of the enemy, and as with his weapon he struck him down, he cried out: 'The first slain of the enemy belongs to me, to Kahu-kaka-nui, the son of Manaia'; then for the first time Manaia knew that this young man was his son, his last born son; he had before thought that Tu-ure-nui had been his only son; but when the other young man called out his name, he knew that he also was his son, and, pleased with his courage, he loved him very much.

The people lying in ambush, all followed the youth when he rushed on their enemies, and slaughtered them; but their chief Tupenu fled by the way of the beach of Pikopikoi-wheti, and Manaia pursued him closely, but was not fleet enough of foot to catch him; then he called out to his wife, Rongotiki, to utter incantations to weaken his enemy; and she did so, repeating an incantation termed Tapuwae, and when she had finished that, by her enchantments she rendered the flying warrior faint and feeble, so that Manaia rapidly gained on him, caught him, and slew him.

Thus perished Tupenu and the party of people whom he had taken with him to work for Manaia; the report of what had occurred soon spread throughout the country, and at last reached the tribe of Tupenu; and when they heard it, they said: 'Your relatives have perished.' Their army collected and started to avenge themselves on Manaia and his tribe, and to destroy them; they slew many of them, and continued from time to time to attack them, so that their numbers dwindled away, till at length Manaia began to reflect within. himself saying: Ah, ah, my warriors are wasting away, and by and by, perhaps, I also shall be slain; rather than let this state of things continue, I had better abandon this country, and, removing to a great distance, seek a new one for myself and my people.'

Having made up his mind to act in this way, he began to repair a canoe and to fit it for sea; the name of the canoe was Tokomaru, it belonged to his brother-in-law. when it was fit for sea, he asked his brother-in-law: 'Will you not consent to accompany me on this voyage?'--and the latter asked in reply: 'Where do you want me to accompany you to? Manaia said: 'I wish you to bear me company on this voyage which I am about to undertake, to search for a new and distant country for both of us'; but his brother-in-law when he understood what Manaia was pressing him to do, replied: 'No, I will not go with you'; Manaia answered: 'That is right, do you remain here.'

When the canoe was quite fit for sea, they dragged it down to the water, and hauled it into the sea until it floated; then they brought down the cargo and stowed it away, and Manaia embarked in it with his wife, his children, and his dependants, and then he said to some of his warriors: 'Let my brother-in-law now be slain as an offering for the gods, that they may prove propitious to this canoe of ours.'

So he called to his brother-in-law, who was standing on the shore, bidding him farewell: 'I say, wade out to me for one minute, that I may tell you something, and take my last farewell, for I am going to part for ever from you, leaving you here behind me.'

When Manaia's brother-in-law heard this, he began to wade out to him; at first the water hardly covered his ankles, next it touches his knees, at last it came up above his loins, and when it had reached so high he said: 'Shove the canoe in a little nearer the shore, I shall be under water directly'; but Manaia answered him: 'Wade away, there is no depth of water'; and to deceive him better, he kept on pretending to touch the bottom with a stick; and the poor fellow having no suspicion, believed what Manaia said, that the water was not deep; but Manaia had spoken before to his people, saying: 'Let him come on, out into the deep water, until his feet cannot touch the bottom, then seize him by the head and slay him.' At length his feet could no longer touch the bottom, and he found himself swimming close to the canoe; then Manaia seized him by the head, with one blow of his stone battle-axe he clave it, and his brother-in-law perished.

Having thus slain his victim, he caught up his dog which had swum out with its master, and lifting it into the canoe, he sailed away, to search for a new country for himself.

He sailed on and on, and had proceeded very far from the land they had quitted, when one day the dog Manaia had taken into the canoe scented land,

102

and howled loudly, struggling to get loose and jump overboard into the water; the people in the canoe were much surprised at this, and said: 'Why, what can be the matter with the dog? And some of them said: 'We'd better let him go if he wishes it, and see what comes of it'; so they let the dog loose, and he jumped overboard, and swam on ahead of the canoe, howling loudly as he went, and this he continued to do, till at last night fell on them: the canoe still followed for a long time the low faint howling of the dog, which they could only indistinctly hear; at last he had got so far off they could no longer distinguish it, but the dog, after swimming for a long time, finally reached land.

In the meantime the canoe came following straight on the track which the dog had taken and when at length the night ended, and the day began to break, they again heard the howling of the dog, which had landed close to the stranded carcass of a whale; they pulled eagerly to the shore, and as soon as they reached it, there they saw the whale lying stranded, and the dog by its side; and there they landed on this island--on Aotea.

They were rejoiced, indeed, when they ascertained this was the country for which they had been seeking; first, they allotted out equally amongst them the whale they had found; but first Manaia addressed his men, saying: 'We must now build a house to shelter us, and then we will cut up the whale.' His people at once obeyed their chief's directions; some of them began to collect materials for building a shelter, and others to clear spots of ground, and to prepare them for planting.

Some few of them called out: 'Here is the best place for our village'; whilst others, on the contrary, cried out: 'No, no, this is the best place for it'; and others still, who had got a little farther along the beach, cried out: 'Here is still a better place'; and others, yet further ahead, said: 'Here, here, this is the best place we have yet seen'; thus all were led to leave their proper work, and to wander a long way along the shore, exploring the new country, and seeking for a site for their future home; at last they found that little by little they had been drawn a long way from the spot where they had landed, and from the whale which they had found.

Now there were some other canoes coming close after the canoe, Tokomaru, which presently made the land, too, and reached the shore just at the point where the Tokomaru had been drawn up upon the beach, and they saw the marks of the Tokomaru upon the sand, and the sheds that had been put up, and the bits of land that had been cleared; and they, without delay, began to claim each one as his own, the sheds, the cleared ground, and the whale, which all belonged to the people of the canoe which had first landed.

Then they went to search for the people who had come in that canoe, and when they had found them, each party saluted the other, and when their mutual greetings were over, those who had come in the first canoe asked those who had come in the second: 'When did you arrive here? And they answered them by saying: 'When did you arrive here? Those of the first canoe answered: 'A long time ago.' Then the people of the second canoe answered: 'And we also arrived a long time ago.' Those who had come in the first canoe now replied: 'Nay, nay, we arrived here before you.' Then those of the second canoe answered: 'Nay, nay, but we arrived here before you'; and they continued disputing, arguing each party with the other.

At last Manaia asked them: 'What are the proofs you give to show when you arrived here? And they answered: 'That is all very well; but what proofs have you to show when you arrived here? But Manaia replied: 'The proof I have to show when I arrived here is a whale of mine which I found upon the beach.' Then the people who had come in the second canoe answered: I No, indeed, that whale belongs to us.' But Manaia answered quite angrily: 'No, I say that whale belongs to me; just look you, you will find my sheds standing there, and my temporary encampment, and the pieces of land which my people have cleared.' But the others answered him: 'Nay, indeed those are our sheds, and our pieces of cleared land; and as for the whale, it is our whale; now let us go and examine them.'

So the whole party returned together, until they came to the place where they had landed, and when they saw all these things there, Manaia said: 'Look you, that whale belongs to me; as well as those sheds and the cleared pieces of land.' But the others laughed at him and said: 'Why, you must have gone mad, all these houses belong to us, and the clearings, and that whale too.' And Manaia, who was now quite provoked, replied: 'I say no; the clearings are mine, the sheds are mine, as well as the whale.' The others, however, answered him: 'Very well, then, if that is the case, where is your sacred place? But Manaia replied: 'Where is your sacred place also then? And they answered: 'Come along, and see it.' And they all went together to see the sacred place of these newly-arrived people, and when they saw it, Manaia believed them.

Although he gave credit to the fact of their having arrived first, Manaia was sorely perplexed and troubled, and he abandoned altogether the part of the country he had first reached, and started again to seek for another for himself, for his relations, and his people; they coasted right along the shores of the island from Whanga-Paraoa, and doubled the North Cape, and from thence made a direct course to Taranaki, and made the land at Tongaporutu, between Pariwinihi and Mokau, and they landed there, and remained for some time, and left the god they worshipped there; the name of their god was Rakeiora.

They then turned to journey back towards Mokau; some of them went by land along the coast line, and others in their canoe, the two parties keeping in sight of one another as they examined the coast; and when they reached the river Mokau those in the canoe landed, and they left there the stone anchor of their canoe; it is still lying near the mouth of the river, on its north side, and the present name of the rock is the Punga-o-Matori. Then they pulled back in the Tokomaru, to Tongaporutu, and leaving the canoe there, explored the country unto Pukearuhe, thence they went on as far as Papatiki, and there descended to the shore to the beach of Kukuriki, and travelling along it, they reached the river of Onaero, forded it, and passed the plain of Motu-nui, and Kaweka, and Urenui; that river had a name before Manaia and his people reached it; but when Manaia arrived there with his son, Tu-ure-nui, he changed its name, and called it after his son, Tu-ure-nui; and they forded the river, and travelled on until they reached Rohutu, at the mouth of the river Waitara, and they dwelt there, and there they found people living, the native inhabitants of these islands; but Manaia and his party slew them, and destroyed them, so that the country was left for himself and for his descendants, and for his tribe and their descendants, and Manaia and his followers destroyed the original occupants of the country, in order to obtain possession of it.

Manaia was the ancestor of the Ngati-Awa tribe; he fought two great battles in Hawaiki, the names of which were Kirikiriwawa and Rotorua; the fame *of his weapons* resounded there--their names were Kihia and Rakea; and there also was known the fame of his son, of Kahu-kaka-nui-a-Manaia, of the youth who was baptized with the baptism of children whose fathers are not known.

The Story of Hine-Moa

(The Maiden of Rotorua)

AND the man said to him, 'Now, O governor, just look round you, and listen to me, for there is something worth seeing here; that very spot that you are sitting upon, is the place on which sat our great ancestress Hine-Moa, when she swam over here from the main. But I'll tell you the whole story.

'Look you now, Rangi-Uru was the name of the mother of a chief called Tutanekai; she was, properly, the wife of Whakaue-Kaipapa (the great ancestor of the Ngatiwhakaue tribe); but she at one time ran away with a chief named Tuwharetoa (the great ancestor of the Te Heuheu and the Ngatituwharetoa tribe); before this she had three sons by Whakaue, their names were Tawakeheimoa, Ngararanui, and Tuteaiti. It was after the birth of this third son, that Rangi-Uru eloped with Tuwharetoa, who had come to Rotorua as a stranger on a visit. From this affair sprang Tutanekai, who was an illegitimate child; but finally, Whakaue and Rangi-Uru were united again, and she had another son whose name was Kopako; and then she had a daughter whom they named Tupa; she was the last child of Whakaue.

'They all resided here on the island of Mokoia. Whakaue was very kind indeed to Tutanekai, treating him as if he was his own son; so they grew up here, Tutanekai and his elder brothers, until they attained to manhood.

'Now there reached them here a great report of Hine-Moa, that she was a maiden of rare beauty, as well as of high rank, for Umukaria (the great ancestor of the Ngati Umu-karia-hapu, or sub-tribe) was her father; her mother's name was Hine-Maru. When such fame attended her beauty and rank, Tutanekai and each of his elder brothers desired to have her as a wife.

'About this time Tutanekai built an elevated balcony, on the slope of that hill just above you there, which is called Kaiweka. He had contracted a great friendship for a young man named Tiki; they were both fond of music: Tutanekai played on the horn, and Tiki on the pipe; and they used to go up into the balcony and play on their instruments in the night; and in calm evenings the sound of their music was wafted by the gentle land--breezes across the lake to the village at Owhata, where dwelt the beautiful young Hine-Moa, the young sister of Wahiao.

'Hine-Moa could then hear the sweet sounding music of the instruments of Tutanekai and of his dear friend Tiki, which gladdened her heart Within her-- every night the two friends played on their instruments in this manner--and Hine-Moa then ever said to herself: "Ah! that is the music of Tutanekai which I hear."

'For although Hine-Moa was so prized by her family, that they would not betroth her to any chief; nevertheless, she and Tutanekai had met each other on those occasions when all the people of Rotorua come together.

'In those great assemblies of the people Hine-Moa had seen Tutanekai, and as they often glanced each at the other, to the heart of each of them the other appeared pleasing, and worthy of love, so that in the breast of each there grew up a secret passion for the other. Nevertheless, Tutanekai could not tell whether he might venture to approach Hine-Moa to take her hand, to see would she press his in return, because, said he: "Perhaps I may be by no means agreeable to her"; on the other hand, Hine-Moa's heart said to her: "If you send one of your female friends to tell him of your love, perchance he will not be pleased with you."

'However, after they had thus met for many, many days, and had long fondly glanced each at the other, Tutanekai sent a messenger to Hine-Moa, to tell of his love; and when Hine-Moa had seen the messenger, she said: "Eh-hu! have we then each loved alike?"

'Some time after this, and when they had often met, Tutanekai and his family returned to their own village; and being together one evening, in the large warm house of general assembly, the elder brothers of Tutanekai said: 'Which of us has by signs, or by pressure of the hand, received proofs of the love of Hine-Moa?" And one said: "It is I who have"; and another said: "No, but it is I." Then they also questioned Tutanekai, and he said: "I have pressed the hand of Hine-Moa, and she pressed mine in return"; but his elder brother said: "No such thing; do you think she would take any notice of such a low-born fellow as you are?" He then told his reputed father, Whakaue, to remember what he would then say to him, because he really had received proofs of Hine-Moa's love; they had even actually arranged a good while before the time at which Hine-Moa should run away to him; and, when the maiden asked: "What shall be the sign by which I shall know that I should then run to you?" he said to her: "A trumpet will be heard sounding every

106

night, it will be I who sound it, beloved--paddle then your canoe to that place." So Whakaue kept in his mind this confession which Tutanekai had made to him.

'Now always about the middle of the night Tutanekai, and his friend Tiki, went up into their balcony and played, the one upon his trumpet, the other upon his flute, and Hine-Moa heard them, and desired vastly to paddle in her canoe to Tutanekai; but her friends suspecting something, had been careful with the canoes, to leave none afloat, but had hauled then all up upon the shore of the lake; and thus her friends had always done for many days and for many nights.

'At last she reflected in her heart, saying: "How can I then contrive to cross the lake to the island of Mokoia; it can plainly be seen that my friends suspect what I am going to do." So she sat down upon the ground to rest; and then soft measures reached her from the horn of Tutanekai, and the young and beautiful chieftainess felt as if an earthquake shook her to make her go to the beloved of her heart; but then arose the recollection, that there was no canoe. At last she thought, perhaps I might be able to swim across. So she took six large dry empty gourds, as floats, lest she should sink in the water, three of them for each side, and she went out upon a rock, which is named Iri-iri-kapua, and from thence to the edge of the water, to the spot called Wairere-wai, and there she threw off her clothes and cast herself into the water, and she reached the stump of a sunken tree which used to stand in the lake, and was called Hinewhata, and she clung to it with her hands, and rested to take breath, and when she had a little eased the weariness of her shoulders, she swam on again, and whenever she was exhausted she floated with the current of the lake, supported by the gourds, and after recovering strength she swam on again; but she could not distinguish in which direction she should proceed, from the darkness of the night; her only guide was, however, the soft measure from the instrument of Tutanekai; that was the mark by which she swam straight to Waikimihia, for just above that hot-spring was the village of Tutanekai, and swimming, at last she reached the island of Mokoia.

'At the place where she landed on the island, there is a hot-spring separated from the lake only by a narrow ledge of rocks; this is it--it is called, as I just said, Waikimihia. Hine-Moa got into this to warm herself, for she was trembling all over, partly from the cold, after swimming in the night across the wide lake of Rotorua, and partly also, perhaps, from modesty, at the thoughts of meeting Tutanekai.

'Whilst the maiden was thus warming herself in the hot-spring, Tutanekai happened to feel thirsty, and said to his servant: "Bring me a little water"; so his servant went to fetch water for him, and drew it from the lake in a calabash, close to the spot where Hine-Moa was sitting; the maiden, who was frightened, called out to him in a gruff voice like that of a man: "Whom is that water for?" He replied: "It's for Tutanekai." "Give it there, then", said Hine-Moa. And he gave her the water, and she drank, and having finished drinking, purposely threw down the calabash, and broke it. Then the servant asked her: "What business had you to break the calabash of Tutanekai?" But Hine-Moa did not say a word in answer. The servant then went back, and Tutanekai said to him: "Where is the water I told you to bring me?" So he answered: "Your calabash was broken." And his master asked him: "Who broke it?"--and he answered: "The man who is in the bath." And Tutanekai said to him: "Go back again then, and fetch me some water."

'He, therefore, took a second calabash, and went back, and drew water in the calabash from the lake; and Hine-Moa again said to him: "Whom is that water for?"--so the slave answered as before: "For Tutanekai." And the maiden again said: "Give it to me, for I am thirsty"; and the slave gave it to her, and she drank, and purposely threw down the calabash and broke it; and these occurrences took place repeatedly between those two persons.

'At last the slave went again to Tutanekai, who said to him: "Where is the water for me?"-and his servant answered: "It is all gone--your calabashes have been broken." "By whom?" said his master. "Didn't I tell you that there is a man in the bath?" answered the servant. "Who is the fellow?" said Tutanekai. "How can I tell?" replied the slave; "why, he's a stranger." "Didn't he know the water was for me?" said Tutanekai; "how did the rascal dare to break my calabashes? Why, I shall die from rage."

'Then Tutanekai threw on some clothes, and caught hold of his dub, and away he went, and came to the bath, and called out: "Where's that fellow who broke my calabashes?" And Hine-Moa knew the voice, that the sound of it was that of the beloved of her heart; and she hid herself under the overhanging rocks of the hot-spring; but her hiding was hardly a real hiding, but rather a bashful concealing of herself from Tutanekai, that he might not find her at once, but only after trouble and careful searching for her; so he went feeling about along the banks of the hot-spring, searching everywhere, whilst she lay coyly hid under the ledges of the rock, peeping out, wondering when she would be found. At last he caught hold of a hand, and cried out: "Hollo, who's this?" And Hine-Moa answered: "It's I, Tutanekai." And he said: "But who are you?--who's I?" Then she spoke louder, and said: "It's I, 'tis Hine-Moa." And he said: "Ho! ho! ho! can such in very truth be the case? Let us two go then to my house." And she answered: "Yes"; and she rose up in the water as beautiful as the white heron, and stepped upon the edge of the bath as graceful as the shy white crane; and he threw garments over her and took her, and they proceeded to his house, and reposed there; and thenceforth, according to the ancient laws of the Maori, they were man and wife.

'When the morning dawned, all the people of the village went forth from their houses to cook their breakfasts, and they all ate; but Tutanekai tarried in his house. So Whakaue said: "This is the first morning that Tutanekai has slept in this way, perhaps the lad is ill--bring him here--rouse him up." Then the man who was to fetch him went, and drew back the sliding wooden window of the house, and peeping in, saw four feet. Oh! he was greatly amazed, and said to himself: "Who can this companion of his be?" However, he had seen quite enough, and turning about, hurried back as fast as he could to

Whakaue, and said to him: "Why, there are four feet, I saw them myself in the house." Whakaue answered: "Who is his companion then? hasten back and see." So back he went to the house, and peeped in at them again, and then for the first time he saw it was Hine-Moa. Then he shouted out in his amazement: "Oh! here's Hine-Moa, here's Hine-Moa, in the house of Tutanekai"; and all the village heard him, and there arose cries on every side, "Oh! here's Hine-Moa, here's Hine-Moa with Tutanekai." And his elder brothers heard the shouting, and they said: "It is not true!"--for they were very jealous indeed. Tutanekai then appeared coming from his house, and Hine-Moa following him, and his elder brothers saw that it was indeed Hine-Moa; and they said: "It is true! It is a fact!"

'After these things, Tiki thought within himself: "Tutanekai has married Hine-Moa, she whom he loved; but as for me, alas! I have no wife"; and he became sorrowful, and returned to his own village. And Tutanekai was grieved for Tiki; and he said to Whakaue: "I am quite ill from grief for my friend Tiki"; and Whakaue said: "What do you mean?" And Tutanekai replied: "I refer to my young sister Tupa; let her be given as a wife to my beloved friend, to Tiki"; and his reputed father Whakaue consented to this; so his young sister Tupa was given to Tiki, and she became his wife.

'The descendants of Hine-Moa and of Tutanekai are at this very day dwelling on the lake of Rotorua, and never yet have the lips of the offspring of Hine-Moa forgotten to repeat tales of the great beauty of their renowned ancestress Hine-Moa, and of her swimming over here; and this too is the burden of a song still current.'

The Story of Maru-tuahu, the Son of Hotunui, and of Kahurare-moa, the daughter of Paka

HOTU-NUI was one of those chiefs who arrived in New Zealand from a land beyond the ocean. The Tainui was the canoe in which he arrived in these islands. He left Kawhia, where he first settled, and came overland to Hauraki, and finally took up his residence in a village called Whakatiwai. He had, at Kawhia, a son called Maru-tuahu, but Hotunui was not there when this child was born.

The cause which made him come from Kawhia to Hauraki was a false accusation that was brought against him regarding a store-house of sweet potatoes belonging to another chief, a friend of his. The accusation arose in this way. Hotunui went out of his house one night, almost at the same moment that a thief had gone out to rob this store-house; it was very unfortunate that they should both have gone out nearly at the same moment, just about midnight. When day dawned, Hotunui came out of his house, and people in the morning had seen his footsteps, right along the path by which the thief had gone, and there were the sweet potatoes dropped all along the path, and as the soles of Hotunui's feet were very large, his foot-prints had quite erased those of the thief; so presently they brought an accusation against Hotunui, that he had stolen the sweet potatoes. At this time Hotunui's wife had just conceived Maru-tuahu, but he was so overcome by shame at the accusation brought against him, that the thought came into his mind to run away from wife and all and go to Hauraki to seek another residence for himself. His seed was ready, and he had dug his land, and prepared the ground for planting it, but had not yet put in the seed, when he went to his wife and said: 'Now, re-member, when the child is born, if it is a boy call it Maru-tuahu, and if it is a girl, call it Pare-tuahu [either name meaning the field made ready for plant-ing], in remembrance of that cultivation of mine, prepared for planting to no purpose.' Then Hotunui went off to Hauraki, and resided at Whakatiwai, and became the chief of the people of that country, and he took another wife, the young sister of a chief named Te Whatu, and she bore him a child named Pa-ka.

When Maru-tuahu came to man's estate, he took up his club, and asked his mother, saying: 'Mother, show me the mountain range that is near my fa-ther's abode'; and the mother said: 'Look my child towards the place of sun-rise.' And her son said: 'What, there?'--and he was answered by his mother: 'Yes, that is it--Hauraki'; and Maru-tuahu answered: "Tis well; I understand.'

Then Maru-tuahu started with his slave, and travelled towards Hauraki, and they carried with them a spear for killing birds; this they took as a means of procuring food on the journey, as they came by way of the wooded moun-tains where birds are plentiful; they were a whole month before they arrived at Kohukohunui, and reached the outskirts of the forests there early one morning, at the same time that two young girls, the daughters of Te Whatu, the chief of Hauraki, were coming along the same path from the opposite di-rection. Maru-tuahu was up in a forest tree, spearing Tui birds, at the mo-ment when the two girls saw the slave sitting under the tree in which Maru-tuahu was killing birds, and his master's cloak lying on the ground by him. The two girls came merrily along the path; the youngest sister was very beautiful, but the eldest was plain; and when they saw the slave of Maru-tuahu, the youngest one, who had seen him first, called out playfully: 'Ah! there's a man will make a nice slave for me.' 'Where? said the eldest sister, 'where is he?'--and the youngest replied: 'There, there, cannot you see him sitting at the root of that tree? Then up they ran towards him, sportively con-testing with one another whose slave he should be; and the youngest got there first, and therefore claimed him as her slave.

All this time Maru-tuahu was peeping down at the two girls from the top of the tree; and they asked the slave, saying: 'Where is your master? he an-swered; 'I have no master but him.' Then the girls looked about, and there was the cloak lying on the ground, and a heap of dead birds; and they kept on asking: 'Where is he?'--but it was not long before a flock of Tuis settled on the tree where Maru-tuahu was sitting; he speared at them, and struck a Tui, which made the tree ring with its cries; the girls heard it, and looking up, the youngest saw the young chief sitting in the top boughs of the tree; and she at once called up to him: 'Ah! you shall be my husband'; but the eldest sister exclaimed: 'You shall be mine', and they began jesting and disputing between themselves which should have him for a husband, for he was a very handsome young man.

Then the two girls called up to him to come down from the tree, and down he came, and dropped upon the ground, and pressed his nose against the nose of each of the young girls. They then asked him to come to their village with them; to which he consented, but said: 'You two go on ahead, and leave me and my slave, and we will follow you presently'; and the girls said: 'Very well, do you come after us.' Maru-tuahu then told his slave to make a present to the girls of the food they had collected, and he gave them two bark baskets of pigeons, preserved in their own fat, and they went off to their village with these. Maru-tuahu stopped behind with his slave, and as soon as the girls had gone, he went to a stream, and washed his hair in the water, and then came back, and combed it very carefully, and after combing it, he tied it up in a knot, and stuck fifty red Kaka feathers in his head, and amongst them he placed the plume of a white heron, and the tail of a huia, as ornaments; he thus looked extremely handsome, and said to his slave: 'Now, let us go.'

It was not very long before the two young girls came back from the village to meet their so-called husband, that they might all go in together; and when they came up to him, there he was seated on the ground, looking quite different from what he did before, for he now appeared as handsome as the large crested cormorant; he had on outside, a Pueru cloak, within that, a cloak called the Kahakaha, and under that again, a garment called the Kopu (this in ancient times made up the dress of a great chief); the two young girls felt deeply in love with him when they saw him and they said to Maru': 'Come along to our father's village with us'; and he again consented, and told his slave to keep with them, and as they all went along, Maru' stopped a little until he was some way behind, for he thought that the girls had not found out who he was: as they proceeded, seeing that Maru' did not follow them fast, they asked his slave, who kept along with them: 'What is the name of your master!'--and the slave answered: 'Is there no chief of the west coast of the island whose fame has reached this place!'--and the young girls said: 'Yes, the fame of one man has reached this place, the fame of Maru-tuahu, the son of Hotunui';--and the slave answered: 'This is he': and the girls replied: 'Dear, dear, we had not the least idea that it was he.' By this time Maru' was coming up again to join them, for he guessed the girls had asked his slave who he was, and that they had been told, but the girls ran off together to Hotunui, and their father Te Whatu, to inform them who was coming, as they had previously left the old men waiting for their return: but presently the two girls changed their plan, and arranged between themselves, that the youngest should run quickly to tell Hotunui that his son was coming, and that the eldest sister should be left to lead Maru-tuahu to the village: and in this way

111

they proceeded, those who were going slowly to the village loitering along, whilst the younger sister was far ahead, running as fast as she could, and crying out as she came near the village: 'Are you there, O Hotunui! here's your son coming--here is Maru-tuahu.' Then Hotunui called out with a loud voice: 'Where is he!'--and she replied: 'Here he comes, he is coming along close behind me: make haste and have the floor of the house covered with fine mats for him, so that he may have a fitting reception.'

Maru-tuahu soon came in sight, and as he was seen approaching, he looked as handsome as the beautiful crested cormorant. The people got upon the defences of the village, and ran outside the gates, to look at him: and the young girls all waved the corners of their cloaks, crying out: 'Welcome, welcome, welcome, welcome, make haste, make haste': and he stepped boldly out, and reached the village. As soon as he had arrived there, they all wept over him: and when they had done weeping, they sat down, and formed a semicircle, with Maru-tuahu at the open part: and Hotunui stood up to make a speech of welcome to his son, and he spoke thus: 'Welcome, welcome, oh, my child, welcome to Hauraki, welcome. You are very welcome. You have suddenly appeared here, urged by your own affections. You are very welcome.' Having said this, Hotunui sat down again; then Maru-tuahu jumped up to make a speech in reply, and he said: 'That is right, that is right, oh, my father, call out to your child: "You are welcome." Here I am arrived at Hauraki, here I am seeking out my father's village in Hauraki, but I, who am the mere slave of my father, can say nothing in answer to his welcome; here I am arrived at your village, it is for you to speak; a young man just arrived from the forests has no fitting word to say in your presence.'

Thus he ended his speech, and a feast was spread out, and they all fell to eating, for they had killed ten dogs for the feast, and the chiefs all ate, and the two young girls; but, although no one knew it, the two sisters were all the time quarrelling with each other as to which of them should have Maru-tuahu for a husband: the heart of one of them whispered to her, he shall be mine; but the heart of the other young girl said just the same thing to her.

The feast being ended, they left the common part of the pa where food was eaten, and moved on one side, to the sacred precincts. When the evening came on a fire was kindled in the house, and the eldest girl. not seeing her younger sister, went to her father to ask for her, and was told that she had been given as a wife to Maru-tuahu. At this she was exceedingly vexed, and provoked with her sister; for although she was plain, she thought to herself, I am very pretty, and I am sure, there's not the least reason why Maru-tuahu should be frightened at me; and she went off to quarrel with her younger sister; but Maru-tuahu did not like her upon account of her plainness, and her pretty sister kept him as her husband.

Te Paka, the son of Hotunui, the nephew of Te Whatu, and the younger brother of Maru-tuahu, had grown up to be a young man, so they gave him the elder daughter of Te Whatu to be his wife; thus the elder sister was married, as well as the young one, who was given to Maru-tuahu for his wife; and

Te Paka's wife bore him a daughter, whom they called Te Kahureremoa.

The youngest daughter of Te Whatu, whom Maru-tuahu married, bore him three children, Tama-te-po, Tama-te-ra, and Whanaunga; from Tama-te-po sprang the Ngati-Rongou tribe; from Tama-te-ra sprang the tribe of Ngati-Tama-te-ra and from Whanaunga sprang the Ngati-Whanaunga tribe.

Whilst Maru-tuahu was living at Hauraki, his father Hotunui told him how very badly some of the people of that place had treated him; these were the facts of the case, as the old chief related them to him: 'One day, when the canoes of the tribe came in full of fish, after hauling their nets, he sent down one of his servants from his house to the canoe to bring back some fish for him, and when the servant ran down for this purpose, the man who owned the nets said to him: "Well, what brings you here?"--upon which his servant answered: "Hotunui sent me down, to bring up some fish for him, he quite longs to taste them." Upon which the owner of the nets cursed Hotunui in the most violent and offensive manner, saying: "Is his head the flax that grows in the swamp at Otoi?--or is his topknot flax, that the old fellow cannot go there to get some flax to make a net for himself with, instead of troubling me?" When Hotunui's servant heard this, he returned at once to the house, and his master not seeing the fish, said: "Well, tell me what is the matter"; so he replied: "I went as you told me, and I asked the man who had been hauling the net for some fish; and he only looked up at me. Again I asked him for some fish; and then he said, Who sent you here to fetch fish, pray?" Then I told him, "Hotunui sent me down to bring up some fish for him, be quite longs to taste them"; then the man cursed you, saying to me, "Is Hotunui's head the flax that grows in the swamp at Otoi; or is his topknot flax, that the old fellow cannot go there, to get some flax to make a net with for himself?"

When Hotunui had told this story to Maru-tuahu, he said: 'Now, oh, my son, this tribe is a very bad one, they seem bent upon lowering the authority of their chiefs.'

The heart of Maru-tuahu felt very gloomy when he heard his father had been treated thus, and Hotunui said to him: 'You may well look sad, my son, at hearing what I have just said; this tribe is composed of very bad people.' And Maru-tuahu replied: 'Leave them alone, they shall find out what such conduct leads to.'

Then Maru-tuahu began to catch and dry great quantities of fish for a feast, and he worked away with his men at making fishing-nets, until he had collected a very great number; it was in the winter that he began to make these nets, and the winter, spring, summer, and part of autumn passed, before they were finished; then he sent a messenger to the tribe who had cursed his father, to ask them to come to a feast, and to help him to stretch these nets; and when the messenger came back, Maru-tuahu asked him: 'Where are they?'--and the messenger answered: 'The day after to-morrow they will arrive here.' Then Maru-tuahu gave orders, saying: 'To-morrow let the feast be ranged in rows, so that when they arrive here they may find it all ready for them.' Upon this they all retired to rest, and when the dawn appeared they arranged the food to be given to the strangers in rows: the outside of the rows was composed of fish piled up; but under these was placed nothing but rotten wood and filth, although the exterior made a very goodly show. He intended this feast to be a feast at which those who came as guests should be slaughtered, in revenge for the curse against Hotunui, which had exceedingly pained his heart.

Soon after daybreak the next morning the guests came, and seeing the piles of provisions which were laid out for them, they were exceedingly rejoiced, and longed for the time of their distribution, and when they might touch this food, little thinking how dearly they were to pay for it. The guests had all arrived and taken their seats upon the grass, when Maru-tuahu and his people came together;--they were only one hundred and forty.

As they were to stretch the great net made up of all the small ones upon the next morning, on that evening they put all the nets and ropes into the water to soak them, in order to soften the flax of which they were made, so that they might be more easily stretched; and when the morning dawned those who had come for the purpose began to draw out the net, stretching the rope and the bottom of the net along the ground, and pegging it tight down from comer to comer, and thus whilst Maru-tuahu's people were preparing food for them to eat, the others worked away at stretching the net taut, and pegging it fast to the ground to hold it; it was not long before they had finished this and had put on the weights to sink it.

Maru-tuahu sent a man to see whether they had finished stretching the net, and when the man came back, he said: 'Have they done stretching the net?'-- and the man answered: 'Yes, they have finished.' Then Maru-tuahu said: 'Let us go and lift the upper end of the net from the ground; they have finished the lower end of it.' Then the one hundred and forty men went with him, each one carrying a weapon, carefully concealed under his garments, lest their guests should see them; and when they reached the place where the net was, they found the guests, nearly a thousand in number, had finished stretching the lower end of the net. Then the priest of Maru-tuahu who was to consecrate the net said: 'Let the upper end of the net be raised, so that the net may be stretched straight out'; and Maru-tuahu said: 'Yes, let it be done at once, it is getting late in the day.' Then the one hundred and forty men began to lift up the net, with the left hand they seized the ropes to raise it, but with the right hand each firmly grasped his weapon, and Maru-tuahu shouted out: 'Lift away, lift away, lift it well up'; when they had raised it high in the air, they walked on with it; holding it up as if they were spreading it out, until they got it well over the strangers, who were either pegging the lower end down, or were seated on the ground looking on; then Maru-tuahu shouted out: 'Let it fall'; and they let it fall, and caught in it their guests, nearly a thousand in number; they caught every one of them in the net, so that they could not move to make any effectual resistance, and whilst some of the one hundred and forty men of Maru-tuahu held the net down, the rest slew with their weapons the whole thousand, not one escaped, whilst they lost not a single man themselves. Hence 'The feast of rotten wood' is a proverb amongst the descendants of Maru-tuahu to this day. This feast of rotten wood was given at a place which was then named Pukeahau, but which was afterwards called Karihitangata (or, men were the weights which were attached to the net to sink it), upon account of the thousand people who were there slain by treachery in the net of Maru-tuahu; for men were the weights that were attached to that net to sink it. After the death of all these people, the country they inhabited became the property of Maru-tuahu, and his heirs dwell there to the present day.

About the time that Te Kahureremoa, Paka's daughter, became marriageable, a large party of visitors arrived at Whare-kawa, the village of Te Paka; they came from Aotea, or the Great Barrier Island; at their head was the principal chief of Aotea, and he brought in his canoes a present of two hundred and sixty baskets of mackerel for Te Paka, and they became such good friends that they thought they would like to be connected; so it was arranged that Te Paka's daughter, Te Kahureremoa, should be given as a wife to the son of that chief; part of Te Paka's plan was to get possession of Aotea for his family, for he thought when his daughter had children, and they were grown up, that it was possible they would secure the island for their grandfather, or for their mother's family.

When the party of visitors was about to return to Aotea, having formed this connection with Te Paka's tribe through the girl, her father gave her up to them to take to Aotea to her husband, and he told his daughter to go on board the canoe, and to accompany them to Aotea; but he told her to no purpose, for she did not obey him; in short, Te Kahureremoa refused to go. So the old chief to whom the canoes belonged said: 'Never mind, never mind, leave her alone, we shall not be long away, we shall soon return, we shall not be long before we are back'; and they left Te Kahureremoa with her father, and paddled off in their canoes.

In one month's time they came back again, and brought with them a present of thirty baskets of mackerel, and as soon as they arrived they distributed these amongst their friends; and down ran Te Kahureremoa from the village to the landing-place to take a basket of mackerel for herself. As soon as Paka saw this, he gave his daughter a sound scolding for going and taking the fish; this is what Paka said to his daughter: 'Put that down, you shall not have it; I wanted you to go and become the wife of the young chief of the place where these good fish abound, and you refused to go, therefore you shall not now have any.'

This was quite enough; poor little Te Kahureremoa felt entirely overcome with shame, she left the basket of fish, dropping it just where she was, and ran back into the house, and began to sob and cry; then her thoughts suggested to her, that after this, it would be better that she should be no more seen by the eyes of her father, and that her father's face should be no more seen by her, and her heart kept on urging her to run away to Takakopiri, and to take him for her lord; she had seen him, and liked him well; he was a great

115

chief, and had abundance of food of the best kind on his estates; plenty of potted birds of all kinds; and *kiwis*, and *kiores* and *wekas*, and eels, and mackerel, and crayfish; in short, he had abundance of all kinds of food, and was rich in every sort of property.

As she thought of all this, the chief's young daughter continued weeping and sobbing in the house, quite overcome with shame, and when evening came she was still crying, but at night, she said to herself: 'Now I'll be off, whilst all the men are fast asleep'; so she got up and ran away, accompanied by her female slave. The next morning when the sun rose they found she was gone, and she had fled so far, that those who were sent to seek her came to the footprints of herself and her slave; their edges had so sunk down that the pursuers could not tell how long it was since she had passed.

Waipuna was the village from which Te Kahureremoa started, and they had left Pukorokoro behind them, and by the time it was full daybreak they had reached Waitakaruru, and as the full rays of the sun shone on the earth, they were passing above Pouarua; then for a little time they travelled very fast and reached Riwaki, at the mouth of the river Piako; this they crossed and pushed on for Opani, and thence those in pursuit of them returned, they could follow them no farther; the tide also was flowing, which stopped the pursuit.

Just then some of the canoes of the up-river country were returning from Ruawehea, and when the people in the canoes saw her, they raised loud cries of 'Ho, ho! here's Te Kahureremoa, here's the daughter of Paka'; she stepped into one of the canoes with them, and the people kept crying out the whole way from the mouth of the river up its course as they ascended it: 'Here's Te Kahureremoa'; and they rowed very fast, feeling alarmed at having so great a chieftainess on board, and so confused were they at her presence, that throughout the whole day they kept on bending their heads down to their very paddles, as they pulled. They stopped at Raupa, where the Awa-iti branches off to Tauranga, and there they spent one night; and the next day they went over the range towards Kati-kati: the people of Raupa urged her to stop there for a little; she, however, would not, but driven by the fond thoughts of her heart, she pressed onwards, and reached the summit of the ridge of Hikurangi, and looked down upon Kati-kati, and saw also Tauranga; then the young girl turned, and looked round at the mountain at Otawa, and although she knew what it was, she liking to hear his name, and of his greatness, spoke to the people of the country, who, out of respect were accompanying her, and asking, said: 'What is the name of yonder mountain?'--and they answered her: 'That is Otawa.' And the young girl asked again: 'Is the country of that mountain rich in food?'--and they replied: 'Oh, there are found *kiores*, and *kiwis*, and *wekas*, and pigeons, and *tuis*; why that mountain is famed for the variety and number of birds that inhabit it.' Then the young girl took courage, and asked once more: 'Whom does all that fruitful country belong to?'--and they told her: 'The Waitaha is the name of the tribe that inhabit that country, and Takakopiri is the chief of it. He is the owner of that

116

mountain, and he is the great chief of the Waitaha: and when the people of that tribe collect food from the mountains, they bear everything to him; the food of all those districts, whatever it may be, belongs to that great lord alone.' When the young girl heard all this, she said to the people: 'I and my female slave are going there, to Otawa.' And the people said to her: 'No; is that really the case?'--and she said: 'Yes, we are going there. Paka sent us there, that we should ask Takakopiri to pay him a visit at Whare-kawa.' She said this to deceive the people, and prevent them from stopping her; and immediately started again upon her journey, and came down upon the sea-shore at Kati-kati. The Waitaha, the tribe of Takakopiri, inhabited that village; and as soon as they saw the young girl coming, there arose joyful cries of 'Here is Kahureremoa! Oh, here is the daughter of Paka!'--and the people collected in crowds to gaze at the young chieftainess; she rested at the village, and they immediately began to prepare food, and when it was cooked, they brought it to her, and she partook of it, and when she had done it was night-time; then they brought plenty of firewood into the house, and made up a clear fire, so that the house might be quite light, and they all stood up to dance, that she might pass a cheerful evening.

After they had all danced, they continued soliciting Te Kahureremoa to stand up and dance also, whilst they sat looking on to see how gracefully and beautifully she moved. Upon which she coyly said: 'Ah, yes, that's all very well; do you want me to dance indeed? At last, however, the young girl sprang up, and she had hardly stretched forth her lovely arms in the attitude of the dance before the people all cried out with surprise and pleasure at her beauty and grace; her arms moved with an easy and rapid action like that of swimming; her nimble lissom fingers were reverted till their tips seemed to touch the backs of the palms of her hands; and all her motions were so light, that she appeared to float in the air; then might be seen, indeed, the difference between the dancing of a nobly-born girl and a slave; the latter being too often a mere throwing about of the body and of the arms. Thus she danced before them; and when she had finished, all the young men in the place were quite charmed with her, and could think of nothing but of Te Kahureremoa.

When night came on, and the people had dispersed to their houses, the chief of the village came to make love to her, and said, that upon account of her great beauty he wished her to become his wife; but she at once started up with her female slave, and notwithstanding the darkness, they plunged straight into the river, forded it, and proceeded upon their journey, leaving the chief overwhelmed with shame and confusion, at the manner in which Te Kahureremoa had departed: however, away she went, without any fearful thought, on her road to Tauranga, and by daybreak they had reached the Wairoa. When the people of the village saw her coming along in the dawn, they raised joyful cries of 'Here is Te Kahureremoa'; and some of Takakopiri's people, who were there, would detain the young girl for a time: so she rested, and ate, and was refreshed; thence she proceeded along the base of

117

the mountains of Otawa, and at night slept at its foot; and when morning broke, she and her slave continued their journey.

There, just at the same time, was Takakopiri coming along the path, to sport in his forests at Otawa; his sport was spearing birds, and right in the pathway there stood a tall forest tree covered with berries, upon which large green pigeons had settled in flocks to feed. The two girls came toiling along, with their upper cloaks thrown round their shoulders like plaids, for the convenience of travelling, the slave-girl carrying a basket of food on her back for her mistress. As the girls drew near the forest they heard the loud flapping of the wings of a pigeon, for the young chief had struck one with his spear; so they stopped at once, and Te Kahureremoa said to her slave: 'Somebody is there, just listen how that bird flaps its wings'; and her slave answered: 'Yes, I hear it.' And Te Kahureremoa said: 'That was the flapping of the wings of a bird which somebody has speared'; and her slave replied: 'Yes, we had better go and see who it is.' And they had not gone far before they heard a louder flap, as the bird was thrown upon the ground; they at once approached the spot, and seeing a heap of pigeons which had been killed lying at the root of a tree, they sat down by them. Takakopiri had observed them coming along, and as he watched the girls from the tree, he said to himself: 'These girls are travelling, and they come from a long distance, for their cloaks are rolled over their shoulders like plaids; they are not from near here; had they come from the neighbourhood they would have worn their cloaks hanging down in the usual way.'

Then the young chief came down from the tree, leaving his spear swinging to a bough: as he was descending the girls saw him, and the slave knew him at once at a distance, and said: 'Oh, my young mistress, that is Takakopiri'; and Te Kahureremoa said: 'No, no, it is not indeed'; but the slave said: 'Yes, it is he, I saw him when he came to Hauraki'; and the young girl said: 'You are right, it is Takakopiri'; and her slave said: 'Yes, yes, this is the young chief who has caused us to come all this distance.' By this time he had reached the ground, and he and the girls cried out at the same time to each other: 'Welcome, welcome'; and the young man came up to them, and stooped down, and pressed his nose to the nose of each of them. Te Kahureremoa felt and knew whose face touched hers, but Takakopiri did not know whose nose he had pressed.

Then he said to them: 'We had better go to my village, which is on the other side of the forest'; and he pressed them to go, and the girls consented to go to the village with him; as they went along the path, he kept urging them to make haste, and Te Kahureremoa thought that he might still not know who she was, or he would never speak so impatiently, and tell her to make haste, so she made an excuse to arrange her dress, and stopped behind on one side of the path, in order that the young chief might have an opportunity of asking her slave who she was: as soon as he saw she had left the path, he went on with her slave a little distance until they had got over a rising ground, and then he asked her, saying: 'Who is your mistress?'--and the slave answered:

'Is it my young mistress that you are asking about?'--and the young chief said: 'Yes, it is one nobly-born person asking after another'; and the slave said: 'Well, if it is my mistress you arc asking about, the young lady's name is Te Kahureremoa'; and he answered her: 'What! Is this Te Kahureremoa, the daughter of Paka?'--and the slave replied: 'Yes, do you think there are more Pakas than one, or more Te Kahureremoas than one?--this is really she'; and the young chief said: 'Well, who would ever have suspected that this was she, or that a young girl from so distant a place could have reached this country? Let us sit down here at once, and wait until she comes up.' In a very little time she appeared coming along to them, and the young chief called out to her: 'You had really better make haste, or you'll suffer from want of food, for it is still a long distance from this place to my village'; and when she had reached them he said: 'Do you follow me, and pray do not lose time.' Then away he ran, and as soon as he got in sight of his own fortress, he began to call loudly to his people as he ran: 'Te Kahureremoa has arrived; the daughter of Paka is come.' 'Why', said some of them, 'our master is in love with that girl, and has lost his senses, and thinks she is really here'; but he kept calling out as he ran: 'Here comes Te Kahureremoa, here comes the daughter of Paka.' Then some of them said: 'Why, after all, it must be true, or he would not continue calling it out in that way'; and others said; 'But who could ever believe that a young girl could have travelled to such a distance? the place is strange to her, and we are all strangers to her, perhaps, after all, it is only the wind wafting up from afar this name which we hear called out in our ears.' However, they all either climbed up on the defences, or went outside to see who was coming; and as soon as they saw the young girl approaching, they began to wave their garments, and to sing, in songs of welcome:

Welcome, welcome, thou who comest
From afar, from beyond the far horizon;
Our dearest child hath brought thee thence;
Welcome, oh, welcome here.'

And each of the many hundreds of persons who had come out to welcome her, as she passed his residence, prayed her to stop there; but Takakopiri continued to say to her: 'Press on, follow close, quite close, after me'; and so he led her through the throng of people, each of whom felt so moved towards the young girl, that, although they were in the very presence of their young lord, they could not help soliciting her to stop at each house as she came by. At length she arrived at Takakopiri's dwelling, and there for the first time she stopped and sat down, and the people came thronging in crowds to gaze upon her; and they spread before the two young girls food in abundance, the birds which the young chief had taken upon the mountains; and a feast was made for the crowd that surrounded them; thus they remained feasting, and admiring that young girl, and when the sun sank below the horizon, they were still sitting there gazing upon her; the youths of the village thought they could never be weary of looking at her, but none dare to utter one word of love for fear of Takakopiri. Before a month had passed she was married to the young chief, and she bore him a daughter, named Tuparahaki, from whom in eleven generations, or in about 275 years have sprung all the principal chiefs of the Ngatipaoa tribe who are now alive (in 1853).

The Two Sorcerers

(Ko Te Matenga O Kiki)

KIKI was a celebrated sorcerer, and skilled in magical arts; he lived upon the river Waikato. The inhabitants of that river still have this proverb: 'The offspring of Kiki wither shrubs'. This proverb had its origin in the circumstance of Kiki being such a magician, that he could not go abroad in the sunshine; for if his shadow fell upon any place not protected from his magic, it at once became *tapu*, and all the plants there withered.

This Kiki was thoroughly skilled in the practice of sorcery. If any parties coming up the river called at his village in their canoes as they paddled by, he still remained quietly at home, and never troubled himself to come out, but just drew back the sliding door of his house, so that it might stand open, and the strangers stiffened and died; or even as canoes came paddling down from the upper parts of the river, he drew back the sliding wooden shutter to the window of his house, and the crews on board of them were sure to die.

At length, the fame of this sorcerer spread exceedingly, and resounded through every tribe, until Tamure, a chief who dwelt at Kawhia, heard with others, reports of the magical powers of Kiki, for his fame extended over the whole country. At length Tamure thought he would go and contend in the arts of sorcery with Kiki, that it might be seen which of them was most skilled in magic; and he arranged in his own mind a fortunate season for his visit.

When this time came, he selected two of his people as his companions, and he took his young daughter with him also; and they all crossed over the mountain range from Kawhia, and came down upon the river Waipa, which runs into the Waikato, and embarking there in a canoe, paddled down the river towards the village of Kiki; and they managed so well, that before they were seen by anybody, they had arrived at the landing-place. Tamure was not only skilled in magic, but he was also a very cautious man; so whilst they were still afloat upon the river, he repeated an incantation of the kind called 'Mata-tawhito', to preserve him safe from all arts of sorcery; and he repeated other incantations, to ward off spells, to protect him from magic, to collect good genii round him, to keep off evil spirits, and to shield him from demons; when these preparations were all finished, they landed, and drew up their canoe on the beach, at the landing-place of Kiki.

120

As soon as they had landed, the old sorcerer called out to them that they were welcome to his village, and invited them to come up to it: so they went up to the village: and when they reached the square in the centre, they seated themselves upon the ground; and some of Kiki's people kindled fire in an enchanted oven, and began to cook food in it for the strangers. Kiki sat in this house, and Tamure on the ground just outside the entrance to it, and he there availed himself of this opportunity to repeat incantations over the threshold of the house, so that Kiki might be enchanted as he stepped over it to come out. When the food in the enchanted oven was cooked, they pulled off the coverings, and spread it out upon clean mats. The old sorcerer now made his appearance out of his house and he invited Tamure to come and eat food with him; but the food was all enchanted, and his object in asking Tamure to eat with him was, that the enchanted food might kill him; therefore Tamure said that his young daughter was very hungry, and would eat of the food offered to them; he in the meantime kept on repeating incantations of the kind called Mata-tawhito, Whakangungu, and Parepare, protections against enchanted food, and as she ate she also continued to repeat them; even when she stretched out her hand to take a sweet potato, or any other food, she dropped the greater part of it at her feet, and hid it under her clothes, and then only ate a little bit. After she had done, the old sorcerer, Kiki, kept waiting for Tamure to begin to eat also of the enchanted food, that he might soon die. Kiki having gone into his house again, Tamure still sat on the ground outside the door, and as he had enchanted the threshold of the house, he now repeated incantations which might render the door enchanted also, so that Kiki might be certain not to escape when he passed out of it. By this time Tamure's daughter had quite finished her meal, but neither her father nor either of his people had partaken of the enchanted food.

Tamure now ordered his people to launch his canoe, and they paddled away, and a little time after they had left the village, Kiki became unwell; in the meanwhile, Tamure and his people were paddling homewards in all haste, and as they passed a village where there were a good many people on the river's bank, Tamure stopped, and said to them: 'If you should see any canoe pulling after us, and the people in the canoe ask you, have you seen a canoe pass up the river, would you be good enough to say: "Yes, a canoe has passed by here"?--and then, if they ask you: "How far has it got?" would you be good enough to say: "Oh, by this time it has got very far up the river"?'--and having thus said to the people of that village, Tamure paddled away again in his canoe with all haste.

Some time after Tamure's party had left the village of Kiki, the old sorcerer became very ill indeed, and his people then knew that this had been brought about by the magical arts of Tamure, and they sprang into a canoe to follow after him, and puffed up the river as hard as they could; and when they reached the village where the people were on the river's bank, they called out and asked them: 'How far has the canoe reached, which passed up the river?'--and the villagers answered: 'Oh, that canoe must got very far up the river by this time.' The people in the canoe that was pursuing Tamure, upon hearing this, returned again to their own village, and Kiki died from the incantations of Tamure.

Some of Kiki's descendants are still living--one of them, named Mokahi, recently died at Tau-ranga-a-Ruru, but Te Maioha is still living on die river Waipa. Yes, some of the descendants of Kiki, whose shadow withered trees, are still living. He was indeed a great sorcerer: he overcame every other sorcerer until he met Tamure, but be was vanquished by him, and had to bend the knee before him.

Tamure has also some descendants living, amongst whom are Mahu and Kiake of the Ngati-Mariu tribe; these men arc also skilled in magic: if a father skilled in magic died, he left his incantation to his children; so that if a man was skilled in sorcery, it was known that his children would have a good knowledge of the same arts, as they were certain to have derived it from their parent.

The Magical Wooden Head

(Kon Ga Puhi a Puarata Raua Ko Tautohito)

THIS head bewitched all persons who approached the hill where the fortress in which it was kept was situated, so that, from fear of it, no human being dared to approach the place, which was thence named the Sacred Mount.

Upon that mount dwelt Puarata and Tautohito with their carved head, and its fame went through all the country, to the river Tamaki, and to Kaipara, and to the tribes of Nga-Puhi, to Akau, to Waikato, to Kawhia, to Mokau, to Hauraki, and to Tauranga; the exceeding great fame of the powers of that carved head spread to every part of Aotea-roa, or the northern island of New Zealand; everywhere reports were heard , that so great were its magical powers, none could escape alive from them; and although many warriors and armies went to the Sacred Mount to try to destroy the sorcerers to whom the head belonged, and to carry it off as a genius for their own district, that its magical powers might be subservient to them, they all perished in the attempt. In short, no mortal could approach the fortress, and live; even parties of people who were travelling along the forest track, to the northwards towards Muri-whenua, all died by the magical powers of that head; whether they went in large armed bodies, or simply as quiet travellers, their fate was alike--they all perished from its magical influence, somewhere about the place where the beaten track passes over Waimatuku.

The deaths of so many persons created a great sensation in the country, and, at last, the report of these things reached a very powerful sorcerer named Hakawau, who, confiding in his magical arts, said he was resolved to go and see this magic head, and the sorcerers who owned it. So, without delay, he called upon all the genii who were subservient to him, in order that he might be thrown into an enchanted sleep, and see what his fate in this undertaking would be; and in his slumber he saw that his genius would triumph in the encounter, for it was so lofty and mighty, that in his dream its head reached the heavens, whilst its feet remained upon earth.

Having by his spells ascertained this, he at once started on his journey, and the district through which he travelled was that of Akau; and, confiding in his own enchantments, he went fearlessly to try whether his arts of sorcery would not prevail over the magic head, and enable him to destroy the old sorcerer Puarata.

He took with him one friend, and went along the sea-coast towards the Sacred Mount, and passed through Whanga-roa, and followed the sea-shore to Rangikahu and Kahuwera, and came out upon the coast again at Karoroumanui, and arrived at Maraetai; there was a fortified village, the people of which endeavoured to detain Hakawau and his friend until they rested themselves and partook of a little food; but he said: 'We ate food on the road, a short distance behind us; we are not at all hungry or weary.' So they would not remain at Maraetai, but went straight on until they reached Putataka, and they crossed the river there, and proceeded along the beach to Rukuwai; neither did they stop there, but on they went, and at last reached Waitara.

When they got to Waitara, the friend who accompanied Hakawau began to get alarmed, and said: 'Now we shall perish here, I fear'; but they went safely on, and reached Te Weta; there the heart of Hakawau's friend began to beat again, and he said: 'I feel sure that we shall perish here'; however they passed by that place too in safety, and on they went, and at length they reached the most fatal place of all--Waimatuku. Here they smelt the stench of the carcasses of the numbers who had been previously destroyed; indeed the stench was so bad that it was quite suffocating, and they both now said: 'This is a fearful place; we fear we shall perish here.' However, Hakawau kept on unceasingly working at his enchantments, and repeating incantations, which might ward off the attacks of evil genii, and which might collect good genii about them, to protect them from the malignant spirits of Puarata, lest these should injure them: thus they passed over Waimatuku, looking with horror at the many corpses strewed about the beach, and in the dense fern and bushes which bordered the path; and as they pursued their onward journey, they expected death every moment.

Nevertheless they died not on the dreadful road, but went straight along the path till they came to the place where it passes over some low hills, from whence they could see the fortress which stood upon Puke-tapu. Here they sat down and rested, for the first time since they had commenced their journey. They had not yet been seen by the watchmen of the fortress. Then Hakawau, with his incantations, sent forth many genii, to attack the spirits who kept watch over the fortress and magic head of Puarata. Some of his good genii were sent by Hakawau in advance, whilst he charged others to follow at some distance. The incantations by the power of which these genii were sent forth by Hakawau was a Whangai. The genii he sent in front were ordered immediately to begin the assault. As soon as the spirits who guarded the fortress of Puarata saw the others, they all issued out to attack them; the good genii then feigned a retreat the evil ones following them, and whilst they were thus engaged in the pursuit some of the thousands of good genii, who had last been sent forth by Hakawau, stormed the fortress now left without defenders; when the evil spirits, who had been led away in the pursuit, turned to protect the fortress, they found that the genii of Hakawau had already got quite close to it, and the good genii of Hakawau without trouble caught them one after the other, and thus all the spirits of the old sorcerer Puarata were utterly destroyed.

When all the evil spirits who had been subject to the old sorcerer had been thus destroyed, Hakawau walked straight up towards the fortress of this fellow, in whom spirits had dwelt as thick as men stow themselves in a canoe, and whom they had used in like manner to carry them about. When the watchmen of the fortress, to their great surprise, saw strangers coming, Puarata hurried to his magic head, to call upon it; his supplication was after this mariner: 'Strangers come here! strangers come here! Two strangers come! two strangers come!' But it uttered only a low wailing sound; for since the good genii of Hakawau had destroyed the spirits who served Puarata, the old sorcerer addressed in vain his supplications to the magic head, it could no longer raise aloud its powerful voice as in former times, but uttered only low moans and wails. Could it have cried out with a loud voice, straightway Hakawau and his friend would both have perished; for thus it was, when armies and travellers had in other times passed the fortress, Puarata addressed supplications to his magic head, and when it cried out with a mighty voice, the strangers all perished as they heard it.

Hakawau and his friend had, in the meantime, continued to walk straight to the fortress. When they drew near it, Hakawau said to his friend: 'You go directly along the path that leads by the gateway into the fortress; as for me, I will show my power over the old sorcerer, by climbing right over the parapet and palisades': and when they reached the defences of the place, Hakawau began to climb over the palisades of the gateway. When the people of the place saw this, they were much exasperated, and desired him, in an angry manner, to pass underneath the gateway, along the pathway which was common to all, and not to dare to climb over the gateway of Puarata and of Tautohito; but Hakawau went quietly on over the gateway, without paying the least attention to the angry words of those who were calling out to him, for he felt quite sure that the two old sorcerers were not so skilful in magical arts as he was; so Hakawau persisted in going direct to all the most holy places of the fortress, where no person who had not been made sacred might enter.

After Hakawau and his friend had been for a short time in the fortress, and had rested themselves a little, the people of the place began to cook food for them; they still continued to sit resting themselves in the fortress for a long time, and at length Hakawau said to his friend: 'Let us depart.' Directly his servant heard what his master said to him, he jumped up at once and was ready enough to be off. Then the people of the place called out to them not to go immediately, but to take some food first; but Hakawau answered: 'Oh, we ate only a little while ago; not far from here we took some food.' So Hakawau would not remain longer in the fortress, but departed, and as he started, he smote his hands on the threshold of the house in which they had rested, and they had hardly got well outside of the fortress before every soul in it was dead--not a single one of them was left alive.

The Art of Netting Learned by Kahukura from the Fairies

Ko Te Korero Mo Nga Patupaiarehe

ONCE upon a time, a man of the name of Kahukura wished to pay a visit to Rangiaowhia, a place lying far to the northward, near the country of the tribe called Te Rarawa. Whilst he lived at his own village, he was continually haunted by a desire to visit that place. At length he started on his journey, and reached Rangiaowhia, and as he was on his road, be passed a place where some people had been cleaning mackerel, and he saw the inside of the fish lying all about the sand on the sea-shore: surprised at this, he looked about at the marks, and said to himself: 'Oh, this must have been done by some of the people of the district.' But when he came to look a little more narrowly at the footmarks, he saw that the people who had been fishing had made them in the night-time, not that morning, nor in the day; and he said to himself: 'These are no mortals who have been fishing here--spirits must have done this; had they been men, some of the reeds and grass which they sat on in their canoe would have been lying about.' He felt quite sure from several circumstances, that spirits or fairies had been there; and after observing everything well, he returned to the house where he was stopping. He, however, held fast in his heart what he had seen, as something very striking to tell all his friends in every direction, and as likely to be the means of gaining knowledge which might enable him to find out something new.

So that night he returned to the place where he had observed all these things, and just as he reached the spot, back had come the fairies too, to haul their net for mackerel; and some of them were shouting out: 'The net here! the net here!' Then a canoe paddled off to fetch the other in which the net was laid, and as they dropped the net into the water, they began to cry out: 'Drop the net in the sea at Rangiaowhia, and haul it at Mamaku.' These words were sung out by the fairies, as an encouragement in their work and from the joy of their hearts at their sport in fishing.

As the fairies were dragging the net to the shore, Kahukura managed to mix amongst them, and hauled away at the rope; he happened to be a very fair man, so that his skin was almost as white as that of these fairies, and from that cause he was not observed by them. As the net came close in to the shore, the fairies began to cheer and shout: 'Go out into the sea some of you, in front of the rocks, lest the nets should be entangled at Tawatawauia by Teweteweuia', for that was the name of a rugged rock standing out from the sandy shore; the main body of the fairies kept hauling at the net, and Kahukura pulled away in the midst of them.

When the first fish reached the shore, thrown up in the ripple driven before the net as they hauled it in, the fairies had not yet remarked Kahukura, for he was almost as fair as they were. It was just at the very first peep of dawn that the fish were all landed, and the fairies ran hastily to pick them up from the sand, and to haul the net up on the beach. They did not act with their fish as men do, dividing them into separate loads for each, but every one took up what fish he liked, and ran a twig through their gills, and as they strung the fish, they continued calling out: 'Make haste, run here, all of you, and finish the work before the sun rises.'

Kahukura kept on stringing his fish with the rest of them. He had only a very short string, and, making a slip-knot at the end of it, when he had covered the string with fish, he lifted them up, but had hardly raised them from the ground when the slip-knot gave way from the weight of the fish, and off they fell; then some of the fairies ran good-naturedly to help him to string his fish again, and one of them tied the knot at the end of the string for him, but the fairy had hardly gone after knotting it, before Kahukura had unfastened it, and again tied a slip-knot at the end; then he began stringing his fish again, and when he had got a great many on, up he lifted them, and off they slipped as before. This trick he repeated several times, and delayed the fairies in their work by getting them to knot his string for him, and put his fish on it. At last full daylight broke, so that there was light enough to distinguish a man's face, and the fairies saw that Kahukura was a man; then they dispersed in confusion, leaving their fish and their net, and abandoning their canoes, which were nothing but stems of the flax. In a moment the fairies started for their own abodes; in their hurry, as has just been said, they abandoned their net, which was made of rushes; and off the good people fled as fast as they could go. Now was first discovered the stitch for netting a net, for they left theirs with Kahukura, and it became a pattern for him. He thus taught his children to make nets, and by them the Maori race were made acquainted with that art, which they have now known from very remote times.

Te Kanawa's Adventure with a Troop of Fairies

TE KANAWA, a chief of Waikato, was the man who fell in with a troop of fairies upon the top of Puke-more, a high hill in the Waikato district.

This chief happened one day to go out to catch kiwi with his dogs, and when night came on he found himself right at the top of Puke-more. So his party made a fire to give them light, for it was very dark. They had chosen a tree to sleep under--a very large tree, the only one fit for their purpose that they could find; in fact, it was a very convenient sleeping-place, for the tree had immense roots, sticking up high above the ground: they slept between these roots, and made the fire beyond them.

As soon as it was dark they heard loud voices, like the voices of people coming that way; there were the voices of men, of women, and of children, as if a very large party of people were coming along. They looked for a long time, but could see nothing; till at last Te Kanawa knew that noise must proceed from fairies. His people were all dreadfully frightened, and would have run away if they could; but where could they run to? They were in the midst of a forest, on the top of a lonely mountain, and it was dark night.

For long time the voices grew louder and more distinct as the fairies drew nearer and nearer, until they came quite close to the fire; Te Kanawa and his party were half dead with fright. At last the fairies approached to look at Te Kanawa, who was a very handsome fellow. To do this, they kept peeping slily over the large roots of the tree under which the hunters were lying, and kept constantly looking at Te Kanawa, whilst his companions were quite insensible from fear. Whenever the fire blazed up brightly, off went the fairies and hid themselves, peeping out from behind stumps and trees; and when it burnt low, back they came close to it, merrily singing as they moved:

'Here you come climbing over Mount Tirangi
To visit the handsome chief of Ngapuhi,
Whom we have done with.' [1]

A sudden thought struck Te Kanawa that he might induce them to go away if he gave them all the jewels he had about him; so he took off a beautiful little figure, carved in green jasper, which he wore as a neck ornament, and a precious carved jasper ear-drop from his ear. Ah, Te Kanawa was only trying to amuse and please them to save his life, but all the time he was nearly frightened to death. However, the fairies did not rush on the men to attack them, but only came quite close to look at them. As soon as Te Kanawa had taken off his neck ornament, and pulled out his jasper pendant, and his other ornament, made of a tooth of the tiger-shark, he spread them out before the fairies, and offered them to the multitude who were sitting all round about the place; and thinking it better the fairies should not touch him, he took a stick, and fixing it into the ground, hung his neck ornament and ear-rings upon it.

As soon as the fairies had ended their song, they took the shadows of the pendants, and handed them about from one to the other, until they had passed through the whole party, which then suddenly disappeared, and nothing more was seen of them.

The fairies carried off with them the shadows of all the jewels of Te Kanawa, but they left behind them his jasper neck ornament and his pendants, so that he took them back again, the hearts of the fairies being quite contented at getting the shadows alone; they saw, also, that Te Kanawa was an honest, well-dispositioned fellow. However, the next morning, as soon as it was light, he got down the mountain as fast as he could without stopping to hunt longer for kiwis.

The fairies are a very numerous people; merry, cheerful, and always singing, like the cricket. Their appearance is that of human beings, nearly resembling a European's; their hair being very fair, and so is their skin. They are very different from the Maoris, and do not resemble them at all.

Te Kanawa had died before any Europeans arrived in New Zealand.

[1] Te Wherowhero did not remember the whole song, but that this was the concluding verse; it was probably in allusion to their coming to peep at Te Kanawa.

The Loves of Takarangi and Rau-mahora

THERE was, several generations since, a chief of the Taranaki tribe, named Rangirarunga. His pa was called Whakarewa; it was a large pa, renowned for the strength of it fortifications. This chief had a very beautiful daughter, whose name was Rau-mahora; she was so celebrated for her beauty that the fame of it had reached all parts of these islands, and had, therefore, come to the ears of Te Rangi-apitirua, a chief of the Ngati-Awa tribes, to whom belonged the pa of Puke-ariki, on the hill where the Governor's house stood in New Plymouth. This chief had a son named Takarangi; he was the hero of his tribe. He, too, naturally heard of the beauty of Rau-mahora; and it may be that his heart sometimes dwelt long on the thoughts of such great loveliness.

Now in those days long past, there arose a war between the tribes of Te Rangi-apitirua and of the father of Rau-mahora; and the army of the Ngati-Awa tribes marched to Taranaki, to attack the pa of Rangirarunga, and the army invested that fortress, and sat before it night and day, yet they could not take it; they continued nevertheless constantly to make assaults upon it, and to attack the garrison of the fortress, so that its inhabitants became worn out from want of provisions and water, and many of them were near dying.

At last the old chief of the pa, Rangirarunga, overcome by thirst, stood on the top of the defences of the pa, and cried out to the men of the enemy's army: 'I pray you to give me one drop of water.' Some of his enemies, pitying the aged man, said: 'Yes'; and one ran with a calabash to give him water. But the majority being more hard-hearted were angry at this, and broke the calabash in his hands, so that not a drop of water reached the poor old man; and this was done several times, whilst his enemies continued disputing amongst themselves.

The old chief still stood on the top of the earthen wall of the fortress, and he saw the leader of the hostile force, with the symbols of his rank fastened on his head: he wore a long white comb, made from the bone of a whale, and a plume of the long downy feathers of the white heron, the emblems of his chieftainship. Then was heard by all, the voice of the aged man as he shouted to him from the top of the wall: 'Who art thou? And the other cried out to him: 'Lo, he who stands here before you is Takarangi.' And the aged chief of the pa called down to him: 'Young warrior, art thou able to still the wrathful surge which foams on the hidden rocks of the shoal of O-rongo-mai-ta-kupe?' meaning: 'Hast thou, although a chief, power to calm the wrath of these fierce men?' Then proudly replied to him the young chief: 'The wrathful surge shall be stilled; this arm of mine is one which no dog dares to bite', meaning that no plebeian hand dared touch his arm, made sacred by his deed and rank, or to dispute his will. But what Takarangi was really thinking in his heart was: 'That dying old man is the father of Rau-mahora, of that so lovely maid. Ah, how I should grieve if one so young and innocent should die tormented with the want of water.' Then he arose, and slowly went to bring water for that aged man, and for his youthful daughter; and he filled a calabash, dipping it up from the cool spring which gushes up from the earth, and is named Oringi. No word was spoken, or movement made, by the crowd of fierce and angry men, but all, resting upon their arms, looked on in wonder and in silence. Calm lay the sea, that was before so troubled, all timid and respectful in the lowly hero's presence; and the water was taken by Takarangi, and by him was held up to the aged chief; then was heard by all, the voice of Takarangi, as he cried aloud to him, 'There; said I not to you: "No dog would dare to bite this hand of mine?" Behold the water for you--for you and for that young girl.' Then they drank, both of them, and Takarangi gazed eagerly at the young girl, and she too looked eagerly at Takarangi; long time gazed they, each one at the other; and as the warriors of the army of Takarangi looked on, lo, he had climbed up and was sitting at the young maiden's side; and they said amongst themselves: 'O comrades, our lord Takarangi loves war, but one would think he likes Rau-mahora almost as well.'

At last a sudden thought struck the heart of the aged chief, of the father of Rau-mahora; so he said to his daughter: 'O my child, would it be pleasing to you to have this young chief for a husband?'--and the young girl said: 'I like him.' Then the old man consented that his daughter should be given as a bride to Takarangi, and he took her as his wife. Thence was that war brought to an end, and the army of Takarangi dispersed, and they returned each man to his own village, and they came back no more to make war against the tribes of Taranaki--for ever were ended their wars against them.

And the descendants of Rau-mahora dwell here in Wellington. They are Te Puni, and all his children, and his relatives. For Takarangi and Rau-mahora had a daughter named Rongouaroa, who was married to Te Whiti; and they had a son named Aniwaniwa, who married Tawhirikura; and they had a son named Rerewha-i-te-rangi, and he married Puku, who was the mother of Te Puni.

Stratagem of Puhihuia's Elopement with Te Ponga

THERE was formerly a large fortified town upon Mount Eden; its defences were massive and strong, and a great number of persons inhabited the town. In the days of olden time a war was commenced by the tribes of Awhitu and of Waikato, against the people who inhabited the town at Mount Eden or Maunga-whau.

There they engaged in a fierce war: one side first persisted in their efforts for victory, until they were successful in beating the other party; then the other side in their turn succeeded in resisting their enemies, and gained a victory in their turn; thus the tribes of Waikato did not succeed in destroying their enemies as they desired.

After this the people of Waikato thought, for a long time: 'Well, what had we better do now to destroy these enemies of ours? And seeing no way to accomplish this, they determined to make peace with them; so, at last, they arranged a peace, and it appeared to be a sure one.

When this peace had been made, Te Ponga, a chief from Awhitu, and one of the fiercest enemies of the people of that town, went, attended by a large company, to Maunga-whau, and whilst he was yet a long way off, he and his party were seen coming along by the people of the fortified town, and they ran to the gates of the fortress, calling out: 'Welcome, oh, welcome, strangers from afar!'--and they waved their garments to them; and the strangers, encouraged by these cries, came straight on to the town until they reached it, and then walked direct to the large court-yard in front of the house of the chief of the town, and there they all seated themselves.

The inhabitants being all now assembled in the town as well as the strangers, the chiefs of each party stood up and made speeches, and when they had concluded this part of the ceremony, the women lighted fires to cook food for the strangers, and when the ovens were heated, they put the food in and covered them up. In a very short time the food was all cooked, when they opened the ovens, placed the food in baskets, and ranged it in a long pile before the visitors; then, separating it into shares, one of their chiefs called aloud the name of each of the visitors to whom a share was intended, and when this allotment was completed they fell to at the feast.

The strangers, however, ate very slowly, knowing they had better take but little food, in order not to surfeit themselves, and so that their waists might be slim when they stood up in the ranks of the dancers, and that they might look as slight as if their waists were almost severed in two; and as the strangers sat they kept on thinking: 'When will night come and the dance begin?' and the thoughts of the others were of the same kind.

As soon as it began to get dark, the inhabitants of the village rapidly assembled, and when they had all collected in the courtyard of the house, which was occupied by the strangers, they stood up for the dance, and rank after rank of dancers was duly ranged in order, until at length all was in readiness.

Then the dancers began, and whilst they sprang nimbly about, Puhihuia, the young daughter of the chief of the village stood watching a good opportunity to bound forward before the assembly, and made the gestures usual with dancers, since she knew that she could not dance so well, or so becomingly, if she pressed on before the measure was completed, but that when the beating time by the assembly With their feet and hands, and the deep voices of the men, were all in exact unison, was the fitting moment for her to bound forward into the dance, with the becoming gestures.

Then, just as they were all beating time together, Puhihuia perceived the proper moment had come, and forth she sprang before the assembled dancers; first she bends her head with many gestures towards the people upon the one side, and then towards those upon the other, as she performed her part beautifully; her full orbed eyes seemed clear and brilliant as the full moon rising in the horizon, and whilst the strangers looked at the young girl, they all were quite overpowered with her beauty; and Te Ponga, their young chief, felt his heart grow wild with emotion, when he saw so much loveliness before him. In the meanwhile the people of the village went on dancing, until all the evolutions of the dance were duly completed, when they paused.

Then up sprang the strangers to dance in their turn, and they duly ranged themselves in order, rank behind rank of the dancers, and began with their hands to beat time, and whilst they thus gave the time of the measure, the young chief, Te Ponga, stood peeping over them and waiting a good opportunity for him to spring forward, and in his turn make gestures; at last forth he bounded; then he, too, bent his head with many gestures, first upon the one side and then upon the other; indeed, he performed beautifully! The people of the village were so surprised at his agility and grace, that they could do nothing but admire him, and as for the young girl Puhihuia, her heart conceived a warm passion for Te Ponga.

At length the dance concluded, and all dispersed, each to the place where he was to rest; then, overcome with weariness, they all reclined in slumber, except Te Ponga, who lay tossing from side to side, unable to sleep, from his great love for the maiden, and devising scheme after scheme by which he might have an opportunity of conversing alone with her. At last he formed a project, or rather it originated in the suggestions of his slave, who said to his master: 'Sir, I have found out a plan by which you may accomplish your wishes; listen to me whilst I detail it to you. To-morrow evening, just at night-fall, as you sit in the court-yard of the chief of the village, feign to be very thirsty, and call to me to bring you a draught of water; on my part, I will take care to be at a distance from the place, but do you continue to shout loudly and angrily to me: "Sirrah, I want water, fetch me some"; call loudly, so that the father of the young girl may hear; then he will probably say to his daughter: "My child, my child, why do you let our guest call in that way for water, without running to fetch some for him?" Then, when the young girl, in obedience to her father's orders, runs down the hill to fetch water from the fountain for you, do you follow her to the spring; there you can uninterrupt-edly converse together; but when you rise to follow the young girl, in order to prevent them from suspecting your intentions, do you pretend to be in a great passion with me, and speak thus: "Where's that deaf slave of mine? I'll go and find the fellow. Ah! you will not hear when you do not like, but I'll break your head for you, my fine fellow."'

Thus the slave advised his master, and they arranged fully the plan of their proceedings; the next day Te Ponga went to visit the chief of the village, and sat in his house watching the young girl, and before long evening closed in, and they retired to rest, and some time afterwards Te Ponga, pretending to be thirsty, called out loudly to his slave: 'Holloa! sir, fetch me some water'; but not a word did the slave answer him; and Te Ponga continued to call out to him louder and louder, until at last he seemed to become weary of shout-ing. When the chief of the village heard him calling out in this way for water, he at length said to his young daughter: 'My child, run and fetch some water for our guest; why do you allow him to ao on calling for water in that way, Without fetching some for him? Then the maiden arose, and, taking a cala-bash went off to fetch water; and no sooner did Te Ponga see her starting off than he too arose, and went out of the house, feigning by his voice and words to be very angry with his slave, so that all might think he was going to give him a beating; but as soon as be was out of the house, he went straight off after the young girl; he did not, indeed, well know the path which led to the fountain, but led by the voice of the maiden, who tripped along the path sing-ing blithely and merrily as she went, Te Ponga followed the guidance of her tones.

When the maiden arrived at the brink of the fountain and was about to dip her calabash into it, she heard someone behind her, and, turning suddenly round, ah! there stood a man close behind her; yes, there was Te Ponga him-self. She stood quite astonished for some time, and at length asked: 'What can have brought you here? He answered, 'I came here for a draught of water.' But the girl replied: 'Ha, indeed! Did not I come here to draw water for you? Why, then, did you come? Could not you have remained at my father's house until I brought the water for you? Then Te Ponga answered: 'You are the water that I thirsted for.' And as the maiden listened to his words, she thought within herself: 'He, then, has fallen in love with me'; and she sat down, and he placed himself by her side, and they conversed together, and to each of them the words of the other seemed most pleasant and engaging. Why need more be said? Before they separated they arranged a time when they might escape together, and then each of them returned to the village to wait for the occasion they had agreed upon.

When the appointed time had arrived, he desired some chosen men of his followers to go to the landing-place on Manuka harbour, where the canoes were all hauled on shore, there to wait for him; and Puhihuia and he directed them when they got there to prepare one canoe in which he and all his followers might escape; he desired that this canoe should be launched and kept afloat in the water with every paddle in its place, so that the moment they embarked it might put off from the shore; he further directed them to go round every one of the other canoes, to cut the lashings which made the top sides fast to the hulls, and to pull out all the plugs, so that those following them might be checked and thrown into confusion at finding they had no canoes in which to continue the pursuit. Those of his people to whom Te Ponga gave these orders immediately departed, and did exactly as their chief had directed diem.

The next morning Te Ponga having told his host that he must return to his own country, all the people of the place assembled to bid him farewell; and when they had all collected, the chief of the fortress stood up, and, after a suitable speech, presented his jade *mere* to Te Ponga as a parting gift, which might establish and make sure the peace which they had concluded. Te Ponga in his turn presented with the same ceremonies his jade *mere* to the chief of the fortress; and when all the rites observed at a formal parting were completed, Te Ponga and his followers arose, and went upon their way: then the people of the place all arose too, and accompanied them to the gates of the fortress to bid them farewell; and as the strangers quitted the gates, the people of the place cried aloud after them: 'Depart in peace! Depart in peace! May you return in safety to your homes!'

Just before the strangers had started, Puhihuia and some of the young girls of the village stole a little way along the road, so as to accompany the strangers some way on their path; and when they joined them, the girls stepped proudly along by the side of the band of strange warriors, laughing and joking with them; at last they got some distance from the village, and Puhihuia's father, the chief of the place, seeing his daughter was going so far, called out: 'Children, children, come back here!' Then the other girls stopped and began to return towards the village, but as to Puhihuia, her heart beat but to the one thought of escaping with her beloved Te Ponga. So she began to run. She drew near to some large scoria rocks, and glided behind them, and, when thus hidden from the view of those in the village, she redoubled her speed; well done, well done, young girl! She runs so fast that her body bends low as she speeds forward. When Te Ponga saw Puhihuia running in this hurried manner, he called aloud to his men: 'What is the meaning of this? Let us be off as fast as we can too.' Then began a swift flight, indeed, of Te Ponga, and his followers, and of the young girl; rapidly they flew, like a feather drifting before the gale, or as runs the waka which has broken loose from a fowler's snare.

When the people of the village saw that their young chieftainess was gone, there was a wild rushing to and fro in the village for weapons, and whilst they thus lost their time, Te Ponga and his followers, and the young girl, went unmolestedly upon their way; and when the people of the fortress at last came out ready for the pursuit, Te Ponga and his followers, and Puhihuia, had got far enough away, and before their pursuers had gained any distance from the fortress, Te Ponga and his people had almost reached the landing-place at Manuka harbour, and by the time the pursuing party had arrived near the landing-place, they had embarked in their canoe, had grasped their paddles, and being all ready, they dashed their paddles into the water, and shot away, swift as a dart from a string, whilst they felt the sides of the canoe shake from the force with which they drove it through the water.

When the pursuers saw that the canoe had dashed off into Manuka harbour, they laid hold of another canoe, and began to haul it down towards the water, but as the lashings of the top sides were cut, what was the use of their trying to haul it to the sea? they dragged nothing but the top sides-there lay the bottom of the canoe unmoved. Pursuit was impossible; the party that had come to make peace escaped, and returned uninjured and joyful to their own country, and went cheerfully upon their way, carrying off with them the young chieftainess from their enemies, who could only stand like fools upon the shore, stamping with rage and threatening them in vain.

The Story of Te Huhuti

[1]

NOW this woman, Te Huhuti, was just like Hine-Moa. As Hine-Moa swam Lake Rotorua, so Te Huhuti swam Lake Roto-a-Tara. She belonged to the Ngati-Kahu-ngunu tribe and from her Te Hapuku is descended. The reason why she swam the lake is that she had fallen in love with Te Whatuiapiti, attracted by his handsome appearance.

She did not stop to consider the difficulty or the danger. No; all she thought was, 'Although the lake is wide and deep, what does it matter? Only let me try it and if I should sink, never mind, but if I should succeed, all the better.' (Now, my friend, just realize what this young girl had in her mind. She had no hesitation because for a long time she had longed to see this handsome young man--the darling of her heart.)

And so she swam and reached Te Whatuiapiti's home. As she was swimming she was seen by his mother and the old lady was greatly surprised.

Then she looked at Te Huhuti as she stepped out of the water on to the shore. What a lovely skin, gleaming like a white cliff! The girl slowly approached the old woman, who could now see how lovely she was, like a sunbeam lingering in the western sky.

As she came nearer the old woman said to Te Huhuti, 'You look lovelier than ever, like the rocky cliffs or like a ray of the setting sun.' The maiden kept silent. Then the old woman said, 'My dear, where are you going? And still there was no reply. Again the question was asked, and again without success. Then the old woman cried out, 'What nonsense! Why do you not answer me?' Then the maiden opened her lips and said to the old woman, 'Where is the house of Te Whatuiapiti? The old woman said, 'This is where we live, come along with me.' She took the girl by the hand and they went on to Te Whatuiapiti's house. He heard them coming and at once arose. He looked at her and greeted her warmly, as might be expected. He was glad at seeing the delight of his heart, and the maiden--well, she was happy at having reached Te Whatuiapiti with whom she had long been deeply in love.

And so they were married, and here are their descendants, and right up to the present time they keep in memory the feat of their ancestress Te Huhuti in swimming lake Roto-a-Tara, and we celebrate it in song--'Te Huhuti swam hither', etc.

You see that her descendants do not forget the part played by their ancestress. Te Huhuti was drawn to Te Whatuiapiti because of his personal attraction, but there were two other advantages possessed by him-one we might personify as Tahu and the other as Tu. Hence her reason for undertaking the journey across the lake, as she thought that by marrying Te Whatuiapiti she would share in these two, Tahu (the husband) for the harmony of peaceful days, and Tu (the warrior) for the bold face needed outside the home. Hence she was so keen to acquire Te Whatuiapiti as her husband.

[1] This legend was not given in the original English 1855 version of the text, but was included in the 1854 Maori edition. The translation is by W.W. Bird.

Appendix - On the Native Songs of New Zealand

AND A COMPARISON OF THE INTERVALS DISCERNIBLE IN THEM WITH THE INTERVALS STATED TO HAVE BEEN PERFORMED BY THE ANCIENT GREEKS IN SOME OF THEIR DIVISIONS OF THE MUSICAL SCALE, CALLED γένοσ ἐναρμονικὸν {Greek *génos enarmonikòn*}, on BY OTHERS ἁρμονία {Greek *armonía*}.

A_{LL} nations, perhaps, without excepting any, have some method of expressing the more energetic emotions beyond mere speaking or acting; a sense of joy or pain, naturally calling forth ejaculations and vociferations exceeding in limit the tone of voice used in ordinary discourse. The cry of war, the encouraging to battle, the shout of victory, or the lament of the vanquished, the wailing over a deceased friend, grief at the departure of a lover, each in its turn has prompted or suggested some modification of sound beyond the ordinary range of mere tame every-day discourse; and this modification of voice we may call, in a wide sense, *natural music*.

But as the highest art is to conceal the art, [1] and to imitate nature, that mighty nation, the Greeks, with an art almost peculiarly their own, having observed these expressions of sentiment, thence deduced certain laws [2] of interval, by which, while they kept within the limits of art, they took care not to transgress those of nature, but judiciously to adopt, and as nearly as possible to define, with mathematical exactness, those intervals which the uncultured only approach by the irregular modulation of natural impulses; so their art was the schooling of nature by the more exact observance of her laws, and by training nature by perfect art, they made art like nature, and corrected nature by art, as the sculptor or painter gives the classic embodiment or personification, not the commonplace, and often defective representation of an object.

This I opine to have been the real nature of the enharmonic scale of the Greeks; and hence I conceive the reason of the remnant of that scale being found among most of those nations who have been left to the impulses of a 'nature-taught' song rather than been cramped by the trammels of a conventional system--the result of education and civilisation.

It may not he amiss, before going farther into this analogy of nature, and of an art reciprocally reflecting back that nature, to endeavour to give the uninitiated an idea of what is meant by the 'enharmonic: genus' of the Greeks.

I must first remark that while we have, properly speaking, only one scale of musical notes and two genera, the Greeks had three scales and five genera.

For we have only the diatonic scale, but by a certain introduction of one or more semitones, we make what is called the chromatic.

Whereas, the Greeks had three scales, comprising five genera, or, according to some, nine [3], all differing not only, as ours do, in the position of intervals, but in the intervals themselves; this difference of interval (rather than position of interval) gave rise to the expression 'genera of a system', and depended on the distribution of two intermediate sounds in the tetrachord or 4th.

The principal scales and genera were three; the diatonic, the chromatic, and the enharmonic. The *diatonic* (genus) consisted of a limma or minor half tone, a major tone, and a major tone ascending, this had another modification, by which, while it retained the same semitone, it contracted the next tone, and extended the last; the latter was called soft diatonic.

The *chromatic*, which consisted of semitone, semitone, one tone and a half interval, or nearly our minor third, was called tonaæon, and had two modifications, one called hemiolion, and the other malakon; these shades or modifications seem of later invention, and soon to have fallen into disuse.

The enharmonic consisted of a quarter tone, a quarter tone and an interval of two tones, an interval somewhat greater than our third major.

Wallis says that we have no idea of these intervals at the present day, as in any way connected with a scale, since they amount to little more than an imperfect elevation or depression of the voice within the limits of what we call a sound or harmonic note; though a certain use is made of the term enharmonic, and the existence of the interval is admitted in the higher researches on music, and said to be apparent in the so-called tierce wolf of the organ, in untempered instruments, and in the systems of equal temperament.

Writers of the present day, greatly differ as to the existence or use of these χρόαι {Greek *xróai*}, or shades of distinction, some wishing to modify them by a modern application of the term, amounting to those shades, 'nuances' or slurs, which the best vocalists or performers are sometimes heard to introduce [4]; others again [5] declaring them to be in practice nimpossible; and all for the most part alleging that, whatever might have been the case in former times, no such modifications do exist in practice at the present day.

Now, with regard to the existence of them in ancient times, innumerable authorities might be quoted; but, not to exceed a reasonable limit, I shall only cite one or two testimonies, and shall confine myself to those referring to the enharmonic.

Vitruvius (lib. v, c. 5) says: '*Diatonic vero quod naturalis est facilior est intervallorum distantia*'; of the enharmonic he says: '*Est autem harmonia, modulatio ab arte concepta et ea re cantio ejus maxime gravem et egregiam habet auctoritatem.*' The graveness and seriousness are given as the striking characteristics of this genus.

We may here incidentally remark that. though he says 'ab arte concepta', it does not prove that it might not have been art imitating nature; and more, it is not impossible that these, at present so-called uncivilised and savage nations, might have retained this character of song from a period of the highest state of civilisation, at an epoch of great antiquity.

Plutarch (Περὶ Μουσικῆσ {Greek *Perì Mousikh's*) remarks, that the most beautiful of the musical genera is the enharmonic, on account of its grave and solemn character, and that it was formerly most in esteem.

Aristides Quintilian tells us it was the most difficult of all, and required a most excellent ear.

Aristoxenus observes that it was so difficult, that no one could sing more than two dieses consecutively, and yet the perceptions of a Greek audience wore fully awake to, and their judgment could appreciate, a want of exactness in execution; for Dionysius of Halicarnassus says, he himself has been in the most crowded theatre, where, if a singer or citharoedist mistook the smallest interval (presumed to be the enharmonic diesis), he was hissed off the stage.

Isaac Vossius [6], from a multitude of authorities, has established, that transitions were made by ancient singers and performers, from the diatonic to the chromatic and enharmonic, with the greatest facility; and he adds: '*which, because the moderns cannot do, they even positively and seriously assert that the ancients could not sing the enharmonic.*' Whereas, continues he: '*not only did they sing it, but accompanied it with instruments.*'

So *Plutarch* (Περὶ Μουσικῆσ {Greek *Perì Mousikh^s*}), who adds a remark, the purport of which is, such persons (who affirm that the ancients could not accompany the enharmonic) forget that if they can accompany greater intervals which were composed of less, there can be no reason why the scale of an instrument might not be so adjusted as to accompany the less intervals which compose those greater.

The doubt of the possibility of using the enharmonic as a scale is not confined to our own day, for Plutarch, as we have seen (and in other places also), speaks of the decline of it; and Athenæus speaks of certain Greeks who, from time to time, retired by themselves to keep up the recollection of the good old music, since the art had become so corrupted.

In *Plutarch's* time (*De Musica*) he bitterly complains that certain people '*affirmed the enharmonic diesis to be absolutely undistinguishable,*' and that, therefore, it had no place in the scales of nature, and that those who attempted to prove it were mere triflers (pefluarhkénai) [7]

He then makes the remark about the possibility of accompanying the enharmonic intervals with instruments, and adds: 'and these very people who talk about the enharmonic having no foundation in nature, have an extraordinary attachment to dissonances and irrational intervals' (περιττά · · · ἤ ἄλογα {Greek *perittá . . . h^áloga*}), which have no existence in the real science of the proportions of natural intervals, and may be compared to certain irregular tenuities or awkward excrescences on what should be a beautiful tree or other object. For whatever reason, it appears it was wholly laid aside in Plutarch's time, which he attributes to the dulness of the ears of those of his day.

Wallis supposes the genera of the chromatic and enharmonic to have fallen into disuse for many ages; Scaliger, not till Domitian: the enharmonic, because of the extreme difficulty; the chromatic, on account of its softness and effeminacy. Dr Wallis adds: 'modern music never affected to appreciate such subtilty and delicate nicety, for neither voice could execute, nor ear easily distinguish so minute differences, at least so we suppose now-a-days.'

Dr Burney, in his *History of Music* (i. 433), from various authorities, concludes, that this genus (the *close* enharmonic) was almost exclusively in use before Aristoxenus (about the time of Alexander the Great), and we gather from Aristoxenus that there were exercises in it for practice, and this observation is corroborated in the Notices of *Extraits des MSS.*, t. xvi., in a most elaborate and clever paper, by Mr Vincent, from certain MSS. in the King of France's library.

Dr Burney, in common with most other modern writers on the subject, says. 'intervals of the close enharmonic tetrachord appear wholly strange and unmanageable', and hence it has been concluded that the enharmonic was impossible in practice.

Dr Burney, however, one day received a letter from his friend Dr Russell, regarding the ' state of music in Arabia, and to the Doctor's utter astonishment, he learnt from that letter that the Arabian scale of music was divided into quarter tones; and that an octave, which, upon our keyed instruments is only divided into 12 semitones, *in the Arabian scale* contained 24, *for all of which they had particular denominations.*

This latter observation would seem to tally very well with what Mr Lane [8] says of the canoon (κάνων {Greek *kánwn*}) of the present Arabs, which, he says, has 24 treble notes. Only, that he adds, each note has *three* strings to it, which (later, as we shall see) he affirms to have been *thirds of tones*. If so, the system is a shade of the chromatic; and if Mr Lane is right (and he gives a drawing of the instrument), Dr Russell must err, or speak of another instrument. I should be inclined to give preference to Lane, because of the great pains he has taken in describing the instrument.

Mr Lay Tradescant [9], speaking of the Chinese intervals, says that 'it is impossible to obtain the intervals of their scale on our keyed instruments, but they may be perfectly effected on the violin.'

Mr Vincent [10] gives a most scientific description of an elaborate instrument made at Paris, exhibited at the Institut, on which the quarter tones were most correctly illustrated, and observes, that a much less interval than the quarter-tone, perhaps eight or ten times less, is discernible, as proved by a M. Delezenne [11], 1827; and our own ears attest that universally in the modulations of the voice of the so-called savage tribes, and in the refined and anomalously-studied Chinese, there are intervals which do not correspond to any notes on our keyed instruments, and which to an untrained ear appear almost monotonous.

There is another matter with which incidentally we have to do, namely, an apparent difference of opinion between ancient authors themselves about the enharmonic. Plutarch [12] says that Aristoxenus (in a book not now extant) informs us that Olympus was the inventor of an enharmonic, but of a kind consisting of a scale in which certain notes, the 'lichani' or 'indicatrices', were omitted, and that the airs of Olympus were so simple and beautiful, that there was nothing like them.

This Scale would approximate to the Scotch, or rather to that given as Chinese by Dr Russell. [13] But there is nothing repugnant in this, to the division of the intermediate half-note between this saltus; and, as here, it is the division of the halfnote interval with which we have to do; the discussion as to the variety or difference introduced by Olympus--(as to whether he made use of this design or not)--is not of any importance to our subject, our object being merely to show that the smaller interval, called a quarter tone, has its representative in modern times.

Suffice it to say, that many Chinese airs, of which I have two, show the diesic modulations and the saltus combined; but the majority of the New Zealand airs which I have heard are softer and more 'ligate', and have a great predominance of the diesic element.

It may not be amiss to define in what sense we wish 'diesis' to be understood, for sometimes, by modern writers especially, it is used for the simple minor half-tone of 24/25 in contradistinction to the major of 15/16. In Dr Smith's Harmonies it is the limma of equal temperament. Sometimes the moderns use the term for the *double sharp*. It was Rameau's these major; Henfling's Harmonia; Boyce's quarter-note; the Earl of Stamford's tierce wolf; observed in the tuning of an organ. Dr Maxwell makes 2025/2048 the maj. diesis, and 32768/32805 the min. But the sense in which I shall use it is that of the ancient quarter-tone, being an approach to the quarter of a tone major, or rather the division of the limma 243/256 into two unequal parts; this is called the Aristoxenian *diesis* quadrantalis; which is represented nearly by 120 being the lowest note; then 116.60: 113.39.

I shall not trouble the reader with chronological or scholastic differences; the diesis of Archytas; that of being given by Vincent as 115 5/7: 112½, Eratosthenes as 117: 114, for keen indeed must be the ear that could discern between 15/16 and 24/25 (except in harmony); much more difficult still would it be to discover a difference between 116.60. 113.39 and 115 5/7 / 112 ½ or 117/114.

If any wish to examine this matter more closely, they can consult the Treatises on Harmonies. Mr Vincent has calculated these differences by logarithms to the 60 root of 2.

My point is, to prove that the ancients did possess and practise a modulation which contained much less intervals than ours, and that such, or an approach to such, modulation (though probably but imperfect) is still retained among some people, and that the principles on which the Greeks founded their enharmonic genus, still survive in natural song, though I will not be bold enough to assert that sometimes these songs may not change into one of the chromatic Χρόαι {Greek *Xróai*}, which, for want of practice, I might not be able to decide. One thing, however, is certain, that, as Aristoxenus tells us, no perfect ear could modulate more than *two* dieses at a time (and then there was a '*saltus*' or interval of two tones), and as the New Zealand songs frequently exhibit more than *two* close intervals together, it is more than probable that many of these songs are a chromatic, represented by 120, 114 or 108, or 120, 112½, 108; but it will not be worth while for the present purpose to discuss this nicety, as all we want is a practical approximation.

In proof that a system, of modulation like the above still survives, I shall produce, as nearly as my ear could discern, the modulation of some of the New Zealand melodies; and shall show a still nearer approach to the system of the real Greek enharmonic, in a Chinese air which I heard and noted.

A few remarks on the *system* itself, the *intervals*, and the *notation*.

System

First, that an enharmonic modulation might; exist is admitted by many modern writers. Mr Donkin, for instance, author of the able article on Ancient Music in Dr W. Smith's *Dictionary of Greek and Roman Antiquities*, observes (under the title of Music) of the different genera less frequently named, [14] 'that it would be wrong to conclude hastily, that the others would he *impossible* in practice, or *necessarily* unpleasing'; and of the enharmonic he says: 'but it is impossible to form a judgment of its merits without a much greater knowledge of the rules of composition than seems now attainable.'

Mr Lay Tradescant having shown the differences of interval of the Chinese instruments from the intervals generally in use in Europe, adds: 'It will therefore very readily appear from the respective rules, that the character of the music, or, if you please, the mood (he should have said genus), must be very different from our own, and that none of our instruments (he should have said keyed or bored) are capable of doing justice to any air that is played on the kin' (or scholar's lute). He subjoins: 'In my travels I sometimes *wrote down* the airs that I had heard among the natives, but though I took much pains to learn them accurately, I always found they had lost something of their peculiarity when played upon the violin.

'The reason of this defect seems to have been that the *intervals* of the Indian music did not agree with those of Europe.' [15]

Mr Tradescant might have added, that there will always be some difference in an air played on the guitar and on the violin, though the intervals used axe esteemed the same; and, again, perhaps the learned traveller did not take care to divide the scale of his violin mathematically, like that of the kin, before he tried the effect,; he might also riot have noted the right interval. He concludes: 'There is, however, a connection between the Chinese and old Scotch music, so that when any highly-admired airs of Scotland happen to fall within the compass of the kin, they seem at home when played upon this instrument.'

Mr Lane says the 'canoon' of the Arabians had twenty-four notes. Dr Russell to Burney says that the Arab scale of *twenty-four* notes was equal to one octave. But Mr Lane adds that 'the most remarkable peculiarity in the Arab system of music is the division of tones into *thirds*.' Hence, from the system of thirds of tones, I have heard the Egyptian musicians urge against the European systems of music that they are deficient in the *number of sounds*.

The same remark was made to me by Selim Agar, a Nubian, when singing some Amharic songs: 'Your instrument' (piano), said he, 'is very much out of tune, and *jumps very much*.'

Mr Lane adds: 'These small and delicate gradations of sound give a peculiar softness to the performances of the Arab musicians, which are generally of a *plaintive character*; but they are difficult to discriminate with exactness, and therefore seldom observed in the vocal and instrumental music of those persons who have not made a regular study of the art.'

Had Mr Lane been describing the character and difficulties of the ancient Greek enharmonic or chromatic, he could not have used other terms; they are almost the words of Aristoxenus, Vitruvius, Plutarch, and other ancient writers on these genera; and yet, he adds: 'he took great delight in the more refined kind of music', and found 'the more he became habituated to the style the more he was pleased with it.' He continues: 'He was perfectly charmed with the performance of some female singers, and that the natives are so fascinated as to lavish considerable sums on them.'

Precisely so the Greeks of old.

Intervals

We must not suppose that the Greek enharmonic was a consecutive gamut of quarter-tones--no; we are told distinctly by all authors (except, perhaps, Salinas), that there was a quarter-tone, then another quarter-tone, then a great interval completing the fourth; or reversely, a great interval of two major tones, or about our third major, the quarter-tone, mother quarter-tone, thus completing the *fourth*.

So with these nations, and especially in the Chinese airs I have heard, there is either the two quarter-tones, then an interval of about a third, or, the interval of the third, and then the two dieses or quarter-tones, or it is a mixed genus, and adds a tone or half-tone at either extreme.

I here beg to state that, though with great care and the assistance of a graduated monochord, and an instrument divided like the intervals of the Chinese kin, I have endeavoured to give an idea of those airs of New Zealand which I heard, yet so difficult is it to discover the exact interval, that I will not vouch for the *mathematical* exactness: neither will I pledge myself not to have written a chromatic for an enharmonic interval, or *vice versa*.

I must also, in justice to myself, add, that the singer did not always repeat the musical phrase with precisely the same modulation, though, without a very severe test, this would not have been discernible, nor then to many ears; the general effect being to an European ear very monotonous.

But I may say that, when I sang them from my notation, they were recognised and approved of by competent judges; and that the New Zealander himself said he should 'soon make a singer of me'.

I may also add that I have studied the subject for more than twenty years, and have read something out of almost every book of note that has been written on it; but yet I only offer these airs as an approximation, and if any-one shall be found who may do more justice to them, I shall be delighted to hear of the result.

Notation

The notation that I have adopted is, for the enharmonic diesis, the St Andrew's cross or saltier ✕, quarter tone or half sharp; the usual ♯ for the sharp; and for ♯ three-quarter sharp. In like manner, the ♭ for quarter tone or half flat; ♭ for the flat; and ♭ (or I might have said: ♭) for the three-quarter flat.

In the Arab ternal division I should use-one third sharp, ♯ ; two-third sharp, ♯ ; one-third flat, ♭ ; two-third flat, ♭ .

In my notation, also, it must be observed, that a sign ♯ or ♭ never conveys its influence beyond the note to which it is attached; thus...

143

would read E half-flat, E natural, E half-sharp, E natural; and is a delicate expression of the chromatic

or of the diatonic

I now give the airs as best I can.

One word as to *time*. Though I have timed the airs I have given, I am free to confess there was neither metre nor rhythm of any marked character discernible in them; and even in the divisions of the lines or verses, the singer seemed to stop indifferently now at one, now at another word. I have, however, followed in my divisions those given in the book, taking it for granted that the learned author, who has given himself so much pains about the matter, will have chosen the most authentic.

James A. DAVIES [16]
Formerly of Trin. Coll., Camb.
Late Private See. to H.R.H. Prince Leopold,
Count of Syracuse, Naples.
17, Great Ormond Street, Queen Square,
September, 1854.

Mr McGregor gives the following specimens of Arabian Music (see his *Eastern Music*)

O   Mo - ha - med   Al   -   lah.

Which I represent thus:

144

or thus, perhaps clearer:

The run at the end is also met with in the New Zealand songs. The cadence is mixed, *i.e.* enharmonic and diatonic.

The Chinese Air sung under my window in London:

The Waiata Aroha: Or, The Bride's Complaint

Reduced by James Davies. Page 30 [17]

Te - ra - te   pu-ko-hu   mau to - nu

mai   Pu - ke - hi - na;

Ko-te-ar-a   to-nu-i-a   i - ha - e - re

ar - ta - ku   to - re - re.

Ta-hu-ri-mai   ki-mu-ri-ra   ki-a-rin-gia

a - tu - he - wai   ke - i - a - ku - ka-mo

V.S.

Marks or signs : ¼ sharp ×, sharp ♯ or ♮ above
note, ¾ sharp ♯.
¼ flat, flat or ♮ below, ¾ flat.

This last bar would perhaps be better written:

but I have avoided as much as possible ♯ or ♭ as being so very unusual, and it is evident to the musician that D three-quarters sharp is equal to E quarter flat, at least sufficiently near in practice.

No. 2

A LAMENTATION

Largo

Page 28

Ra-te - ha - e-ta ta - ki - na - (mai*)

i - to - ri - pa Te - ta - ra - ki

ta - ha - ra Ko - ta - ku

ho - a - pe - a te - ne - i - ka - ko - ki mai

a - ve ka - u a - tu - a - wa

a - u - i - te a - o

* The Singer omitted this word every time he sang the air.

Whakarongo

No. 4

Child's Song, To Teach Singing

E paw-a ko-ia ki-wi-te

hau-wu-tonga e - we

pu-pu-hi-wi mai-ner-wi

ki-ta-ku-wu ki-ri-no.

[1] Cicero.

[2] Cicero, *Orat.*

[3] Ptolomæus the Magian, Mr. Vincent's paper in *Notices et Extraits des MSS.*, tom. xvi, Paris.

[4] Smith.

[5] Burney.

[6] *De Poematum Cantu.*

[7] That the enharmonic has no foundation in nature is false, for what tree tapers 'per saltum?'--'what river flows in heaps?--this gradation is p. 232 nature's life-stream; the other scales may be compared to the proportional parts, the enharmonic to the continuous procession.

[8] Lane's *Modern Egypt.*

[9] Lay Tradescant's *Chinese as they Are.*

[10] *Notices et Extraits des MSS.*, tom. xvi.

[11] Memoire de la Societe Royale de Lille.

[12] Περὶ Μουσικῆσ {Greek *Perì Mousikh^s*}.

[13] Burney, vol. i.

[14] As the soft diatonic, the hemi-olion chromatic, the soft chromatic.

[15] Lay Tradescant's *Chinese as they Are.*

[16] Author of the Papers on the Rhythm of the p. 242 Ancient Greek Orators of the Psalms, Selah, the Evil Eye, read before the Royal Society Of Literature; and of Papers on Accent and Quantity, discovering their true and real difference, from authentic sources. See *English Journal of education*, February, March, April, June, July, and August; G. Bell, 186, Fleet Street.

[17] The pages refer to Sir George Grey's collection of New Zealand Songs, Mau Konga moteatea, me nga Haki rara.